LEGENDS III

Stories in Honour of
David Gemmell

LEGENDS III

Stories in Honour of
David Gemmell

Edited by Ian Whates

NEWCON
PRESS

NewCon Press
England

First edition, published in the UK May 2019
by NewCon Press
41 Wheatsheaf Road, Alconbury Weston, Cambs, PE28 4LF

NCP 194 (hardback)
NCP 195 (softback)
10 9 8 7 6 5 4 3 2 1

ISBN: 978-1-912950-19-5 (hardback)
978-1-912950-20-1 (softback)

Cover art © 2013 by Dominic Harman
Cover layout and design by Ian Whates
Text layout by Storm Constantine

Contents

Remembering David Gemmell

An Introduction by Stan Nicholls

Wearing my journalist's hat I first met David Gemmell in 1991, in the run-up to the publication of the first of his two novels about Alexander the Great, *Lion of Macedon*. My friend Deborah Beale (now Mrs Tad Williams), who was Gemmell's editor at the time, invited me to interview him, and assured me he'd make an ideal subject. That was no lie.

I knew Gemmell's name but confess that I hadn't read any of his books, although he'd had eight or nine published at that point. So I applied the due diligence all interviewers should carry out and set to reading them, starting with his 1984 debut, *Legend*. I loved it. It had a few flaws common to a maiden novel but they were nothing compared to its raw power and compelling narrative.

As I worked my way through his subsequent titles – *The King Beyond the Gate*, *Waylander*, *Quest For Lost Heroes* and the rest – I witnessed an author displaying increasing confidence and a powerful talent for storytelling. His characters were a cut above most in the fantasy genre at that time – heroes and villains alike were neither all good nor totally bad. They were imperfect, like real people. He put this down to the fact that in many cases his characters actually *were* drawn from real people, based on the thousands he interviewed as a reporter. Gemmell also had an enviable skill in using minimum words to achieve maximum emotional impact, in a clean, accessible style. This, too, he attributed to his years in journalism, which demands clarity and pace.

Stuffed with research I arrived at his Hastings home for the interview, which was scheduled to last for 90 minutes. By the time I was poured into a taxi to catch the last train back, some seven hours later, we'd got through four packs of cigarettes (I was almost as dedicated a smoker as he was at that time), a bottle of brandy and a bottle of champagne (quite something for me as I drink so little I could officially be classed teetotal).

We spoke a great deal about his books and writing generally, as you'd expect, but the conversation ranged much wider than that. I think one reason we got on, apart from our mutual association with journalism and authorship, and a passion for fantasy, was because we shared similar backgrounds. We both grew up in humble circumstances in London – he West, me North – without benefit of a father; though that changed for Dave when his stepfather, Bill Woodford, the inspiration for *Legend's* Druss the Axeman, came on the scene. When my interview with Dave was published he liked it and was good enough to get in touch and say he thought I'd represented him well. (A somewhat expanded version of the piece was subsequently included in my book *Wordsmiths Of Wonder: Fifty Interviews With Writers Of The Fantastic;* Orbit, 1993.)

Dave Gemmell was a poser. That isn't my word; he used it about himself. He put something of that aspect of his personality into Rek, one of the principal characters in *Legend*, who despite being a bit of a show-off ended up doing what was right. In a way, Dave couldn't help making an impact physically, being very tall and fairly muscular; and he often dressed flamboyantly, sporting his trademark leather cowboy hat. He was a big man with a personality to match. Couple that with the fact that he was as much of a raconteur in person as he was on the page and you have a clue as to why his personal appearances and public talks were so entertaining.

But don't run away with the wrong idea. He had a sharp sense of humour, and many of his anecdotes were self-depreciating. One example that comes to mind was an occasion when he gave a talk to a packed bookshop. The organisers had placed a trestle table on the stage, stacked high with his books. He sauntered on, struck a pose, and made to lean casually with one hand on the table. Which promptly collapsed, taking him with it. Covered in books, he had the presence of mind to call out, "Can you hear me at the back?"

In early 1992 Dave agreed to having *Legend* turned into a graphic novel, and I was delighted, and a little taken aback when he asked me to handle the adaptation. The artwork was by Chris (Fangorn) Baker, who did a fantastic job, with lettering by comicbook veteran Elitta

Fell, all of us under the editorship of John Jarrold. The really nice thing about the project was that Dave gave us an almost entirely free hand. Given how important the book was to him, that was very generous, and trusting, on his part. The graphic novel was published the following year. By which time our team had embarked on a second graphic novel adaptation, of Gemmell's *Wolf In Shadow*, which came out in 1994.

When we were touring to promote the *Legend* graphic novel, Dave did something for which I'll be eternally grateful. He introduced me to science fiction author Anne Gay, who later became my wife. I was never entirely sure if that had been his plan all along. I suspect it was, even if Dave was an unlikely Cupid. So when we came to marry, in the spring of 1997, it was only natural that I should ask him to be my best man. He attended with his first wife, Val.

We decided that we'd like a couple of readings from Kahlil Gibran's *The Prophet* during the ceremony and Dave, who knew and favoured the book himself, offered to do it. Now, neither of us were really suit people – one of the great things about being a freelance is that you get to dress casually – and as we sat there in our ill-fitting outfits waiting for the future Anne Nicholls to arrive, Dave began patting his unfamiliar pockets. What he wasn't keen on letting most people know – the poser again – was that he occasionally needed reading glasses, particularly on this occasion as the text from *The Prophet* was in quite a small typeface, and he'd forgotten to bring them. When the time came for him to go to the lectern we feared disaster. But he recited the passages, one quite long, *from memory*. We thought that was really impressive. He explained later that he'd always had a good memory and learned to discipline it further when working as a journalist. I asked him if he'd acquired any other skills. He said that in order to get through lengthy signing sessions he'd taught himself to be ambidextrous. I told him I was amazed that he could breathe underwater.

I last spoke to Dave, on the phone, a few days before we lost him. He'd been in Alaska with his second wife, Stella, when he was taken ill. Rushed back to the UK, he was diagnosed with a serious heart problem (probably exacerbated, it has to be said, by nicotine addiction). He underwent major surgery at London's Wellington Hospital, coincidentally situated just a couple of streets away from where I was born and brought up. Our final conversation took place when he was back home convalescing. We spoke about mortality. I remember telling him I was sure he'd still be telling stories when he was 90, that he'd outlive all of us.

David Gemmell died on the morning of 28th July 2006. He was found sitting at his desk in his study. The PC was on, and he'd been working on the final volume of his *Troy* trilogy. He was 57 years old.

I won't try to describe the effect his passing had on his family and friends, and indeed his many readers. The sense of shock, of loss. The unfairness of it.

When things settled down there was a general feeling that Dave's life and work should be commemorated in some way. I think one of the first people to publically articulate the idea of an award in his name was the author David Lee Stone. Others supported the notion.

Dave acted as a mentor to a lot of people, and there are quite a few writers out there, not only in the fantasy genre, who are indebted to him for the help and breaks he gave them. This wasn't something he shouted about. He saw giving aspiring writers a leg up as something he could do and no need to boast about it. He had a similar attitude to charity. For example, I'd known him for years before I found out, quite by chance, that he'd been financially supporting a local women's refuge.

One protégé was Deborah Miller (published as Miller Lau) who was especially keen to repay Dave's kindness by honouring his name. Deborah became the driving force behind establishing an award. She charmed, cajoled, enticed and bulldozed a bunch of us into forming a committee and getting on with it. I was made an offer which in all conscience I couldn't refuse and accepted the role of Chair. Deborah was so focused on the job that the awards might well have not happened without her single-minded determination. Even so, it took over two years of discussion and organising to get the thing off the ground. Finally, with the approval and support of Stella Gemmell, and Dave's children, Kate and Luke, we got it into shape.

Adopting what became something of a mantra for us – "What would Dave have wanted?" – we decided that the recipient of our proposed award should be arrived at by an open vote. We felt, as we were sure he would, that readers were a vital part of the process, and if they were good enough to buy books they were good enough to vote. Once we'd got all the publishers to submit relevant titles (which we characterised as "in the spirit of David Gemmell") and weeded out the ineligible science fiction, horror and even crime novels we'd been sent, we posted the longlist online for the first round of voting. It ran to almost a hundred titles.

There have been very few attempts to game or otherwise nobble the awards. But the most blatant was in that first year. Someone used a program that generated over 100,000 votes for one particular author! As if we wouldn't notice. Fortunately we had very robust security. We were able to trace the origin of the bogus votes, which were of course removed, and block the source. Genuine votes in that first year amounted to well over 30,000, which we regarded as a great start.

We had just one category that first year – the Legend Award for best heroic/epic fantasy. Simon Fearnhamm of Raven Armoury, who had been another of Dave's friends, very generously donated the specially made trophy: a beautifully fashioned scaled down reproduction of Snaga the Sender, Druss's butterfly axe. Generous indeed, as it was priced at around £3,500. We believe it was one of the most valuable literary prize trophies in any genre.

That initial awards ceremony took place in the theatre of the Magic Circle's HQ in London on 18th June 2010, which proved an ideal venue. The shortlist of contenders was very strong, consisting of Joe Abercrombie, Juliet Marillier, Brandon Sanderson, Andrzej Sapkowski and Brent Weeks. Sapkowski emerged as the winner for his novel *Blood of Elves.*

We were keen to add more categories to the awards, and the following year we introduced another two. The Morningstar Award honoured debut fantasy novels, which we felt appropriate given Gemmell's support for new writers. The Ravenheart Award was for the best cover artwork/design, in acknowledgement of the importance of this aspect of a book's presentation. We were very fortunate in having the stunning Morningstar and Ravenheart trophies designed and made by artist Lee Blair. (A full list of all the winners in each category, 2009-2018, appears elsewhere in this book.)

We had many ups and downs, triumphs and disappointments with the awards over the years. But none as sad and traumatic as the loss of Debbie Miller, who succumbed to breast cancer on 7th May 2013. She fought the condition with great spirit and dignity, and all we achieved with the awards is dedicated to her memory.

The Magic Circle was our default home over the years, but we also had the privilege of staging our ceremony at the World Fantasy Convention (2013), Nine Worlds Geekfest (2015), Fantasycon (2016) and Edge-Lit (2017/2018). We were grateful to the organisers of all those events for allowing us to be part of them.

I don't want this to look like the end credits of a blockbuster movie, but the many people who contributed so much to the awards over the years, and made them possible, deserve credit. Our Awards Administrators included Alex Davis (along with his Assistant Administrator Claire Thomas), Christine Harrison and Juliet McKenna. The important role of IT/Website Manager was ably filled by Sky Campbell and Gareth Wilson. Awards Ceremony Tech/Logistics was in the capable hands of Mike ('Sparks') Rennie, and the editorship and layout of the souvenir programme books was undertaken by Anne Nicholls.

We always opened our ceremonies with a reading from one of Gemmell's novels – often *Legend* – and featured a popular fund-raising auction. These two spots were performed with relish by James Barclay, Phil Lunt and Chris Morgan. The ceremonies were recorded for posterity by Official Photographers Sandy Auden and Peter Coleborn.

Another tradition was having Guest Presenters hand out the trophies in each category. In this respect we're very grateful to Chris Baker, Les Edwards, Richard Edwards, John Gwynne, Frances Hardinge, Joanne Harris, Tom Hunter, Scott Lynch, Juliet McKenna, Andy Remic, Gaie Sebold, Samantha Shannon, Michael Marshall Smith, Anna Stephens, Anne Sudworth, Adrian Tchaikovsky, Gav Thorpe and Freda Warrington.

Also deserving of thanks are the "Volunteers on the night", who assisted in the smooth running of the ceremony, and various other folk who helped out in diverse ways – Jannie van den Boogaard, Nick Cirkovic, Liz de Jager, Mark de Jager, Dominic Harman (who's also created the splendid *Legends* covers, of course), Derrick Lakin-Smith, Tiffany Lau (Deborah Miller's daughter), Lauren McLean, Rachel Oakes, Pixie Peigh (and all the Redshirts) and Mark Yon. Not forgetting our daughter and son-in-law, Marianne and Nick Fifer, and our nieces Elaine Clarke and Anna Kennedy. Thanks also to early sponsors Bragelonne, our media partner *SFX* magazine, and all the publishers that nominated titles, donated auction items and supported us in other ways. Very special thanks go to Ian Whates (who was himself part of our ceremony on several occasions) for putting together this and the previous volumes of *Legends* which have been so helpful in financially supporting us. Naturally the same goes for all the writers who very generously contributed stories.

Post credits sequence

When a favourite writer leaves us, part of the sadness is in knowing there will be no further work from them. That seemed to be the case with David Gemmell. Until three years ago, when his widow, Stella, came across an unpublished manuscript by him. It's perhaps not generally known that early in his career Dave had ambitions to be a crime writer. He wrote at least two novels in that genre. One, published under the pseudonym Ross Harding in 1993, was entitled *White Knight, Black Swan*. It had a fairly small print-run, hardly any promotion and was more or less unremarked on at the time. Long out of print, copies commanded very high prices. *White Knight, Black Swan* was finally "properly" published, under his real name, last year.

But the other, unknown crime novel, *Rhyming Rings*, had never seen print. No one's quite sure why, or whether he even showed it to his then agent or submitted it to a publisher. All that seems clear, from indications in the text, is that it was probably written in the late 1980's. In 2017 Gollancz published the book, as "by David Gemmell". Conn Iggulden supplied an introduction and I was honoured to be asked to write an afterword. Although it isn't a fantasy – it's a thriller about a serial killer – it seems to have gone down well with the fans.

That made a nice footnote to a distinguished career.

Stan Nicholls
Chair, The David Gemmell Awards For Fantasy
2009 – 2018

BLOOD DEBT

Gail Z. Martin

"That's the last of the preparation," Corran Valmonde said, standing back from the corpse on the table and surveying his work. "So there's just the anointing and the shroud left to go."

"Thank the gods. Five dead today is more than we've had since the last plague went through." Rigan, Corran's middle brother, wiped his hands on the leather apron.

"We put him back together pretty well, I think. Best we can, for a monster kill," Corran replied. The man's face remained untouched by the horror that killed him, but the rest of the body had been shredded by sharp claws and wicked fangs. Corran had stitched the body and tried hard not to think of doing the same for his mother's savaged corpse, or the body of his betrothed, Jora. Sewing the mangled remains back together and washing away the blood was the last courtesy he could do for the dead, that and marking the shroud to send the departed to the gods.

"What do you think killed him?" Rigan asked. "Black dog?"

Corran shoved down his rage and grief and forced his tone to be steady. "Maybe. But I heard tell about ghouls, down along the waterfront."

"And as usual, the guards do nothing," Rigan added bitterly.

"Of course they do something. They look the other way while we die, and then show up to collect their bribes for keeping us safe."

Rigan sighed. "Not much we can do about it except keep out of the way." He looked up. "Kell – do you have that pigment ready?"

"In a minute. I can't just slop this together. Messy pigment makes for bad magic." Kell, the third of the Valmonde brothers, was still too young to be formally apprenticed into the family undertaking business, but he had been helping Corran and Rigan since he could reach the supplies. Ever since the creatures that killed their mother left the three of them to fend for themselves and run the business as best they could.

Kell brought over small pots of pigment made from soot, ochre, blue woad, and chalk, and set them beside the corpse Corran had just finished preparing. "Three of them are Guild burials, so good shrouds, and full honours," Kell reminded his older brothers. Kell ran the errands now that they were on their own, and that included taking the cart around to gather up the dead each morning – at least, those for whom relatives were willing to pay for a ritual burial.

"Good timing. We owe Guild fees, and the guards will be around for their bribe," Corran said. "Should be enough left over for you to buy a decent chicken in the market for dinner." He looked toward Kell, who had also taken on the household chores. "I've had my fill of cabbage for a while."

Kell shrugged. "A week full of healthy people makes for hungry undertakers. Pretty sure the Guild frowns on helping people along to the After."

Rigan rolled his eyes. "Don't even joke like that. The guards have no sense of humor."

"Come on, let's get these finished," Corran urged. At twenty, he had become the head of the household by default, with their mother dead and their father gone a few years before that, a victim of the guards' ire. Rigan, two years younger, did his best to carry as much of the burden as he could, and Kell, six years Corran's junior, did far more to help than Corran felt he had a right to ask. Sometimes, they barely scraped by, but so far they managed to keep the Guild happy, avoid the notice of the guards, and do right by the dead.

Kell mixed the pigments – ochre for the gods of the earth; woad for the gods of the sea; chalk for the gods of the sky; soot for the gods of fire. Corran motioned for Kell to bring the paints closer. Rigan took the palette and put his thumb into the ochre, drawing a complicated sigil on the dead man's abdomen. Next, he marked in chalk on the chest, making another symbol in woad across the lips, and finally drawing one more rune in soot on the forehead.

There were songs to be sung over the departed, and ways in which even the humblest corpse had to be readied to present itself to the ancient spirits and go to the After. Guild burials cost the most and received a few more formalities, but even the least expensive services sent the dead on their way with dignity.

Corran and Rigan sang in the old language, and their combined voices never ceased to send a chill down Corran's spine. Together, Corran and Rigan wound the bodies in shrouds.

"It's too late to start burying them tonight," Corran said. "We'll get an early start on it tomorrow morning." In the distance, the bells tolled nine times, leaving only a candlemark until curfew.

A knock sounded at the back door, sharp and insistent. Kell moved to answer, but Corran bustled past him. "I'll get it," he said, as his brothers exchanged a puzzled glance and shrugged at his hurry.

Trent and Ross fidgeted in the alley behind the shop. Trent was the butcher's son, and Ross was a farrier by trade. Both were close to Corran's age.

"We've got a problem. We need you tonight," Trent said quietly, glancing up as if to assure neither Rigan nor Kell were in hearing distance.

"This isn't a good time," Corran countered.

"It's never a good time," Ross replied, with an edge to his voice. "These things don't happen on schedule."

"All right," Corran said, stealing a glance over his shoulder at his brothers. "I'll come." He turned back to Rigan and Kell. "Ross needs some help at the stable – a couple of skittish horses."

"We can help, since we're done here," Rigan offered, untying the straps from his leather apron.

"That's not necessary," Corran objected quickly. "But it could take a while. Don't wait up for me. If it goes past curfew, I'll stay with Ross."

Rigan raised an eyebrow, then shrugged. "Just stay safe. And don't oversleep – we've got bodies to bury in the morning."

Kell's eyes narrowed, giving Corran a stare that suggested he had weighed Corran's alibi and found it wanting, but he said nothing, just turned his back and began cleaning up the palette and brushes.

"I'll be home early," Corran promised, hanging up his apron. He plunged his hands into a bucket of water to wash off the pigment, then dried them on a towel and grabbed his cloak from a peg near the door. "Lock up after me. And stay inside – the cutpurses are getting bold."

With that, Corran pulled the door shut behind him, setting off at a brisk walk to keep up with Trent and Ross. The three men kept their heads down, sticking to back streets to avoid running into guards who might want to know why they were abroad. Until curfew, being outside or going to a pub in the evening was entirely legal. That didn't stop some of the more aggressive guards from preying on pedestrians, shaking them down for a bribe just to avoid trouble.

"What's going on?" Corran asked in a low voice.

"Not here," Ross replied with a curt shake of his head. "The others are waiting."

They walked for several blocks, then ducked down a ginnel and into the basement of an abandoned shop, winding their way through debris until they came to an inner door and saw the thin glow of light beneath it. Ross knocked, the same sharp rhythm as at the undertaker's shop, and the door eased open a crack, revealing only a shadowy shape until the man inside recognised the newcomers and stepped aside.

"Good. You're here. Thought we'd have to leave without you." Calfon, a stonemason by trade, moved out of the way so they could enter, and shut the door behind them.

A glance around the room revealed the rest of the group. Bant, Pav, Mir, Jott, and Allery, all of them Guild tradesmen like Corran, already had their sword belts buckled and their weapons sheathed. Trent picked up a bag that Corran knew held the rest of the supplies they'd need for the night's work.

"What's the problem?" Corran asked.

Calfon met his gaze. "Ghouls. They've taken over Marelly's Close – it's a dead-end street with twenty houses, and we know the ghouls have already got to nearly half of them."

"Shit," Corran muttered. "When?"

Trent shrugged. "We just heard about it long enough ago to gather everyone. If we're lucky, we'll get there in time to save a few, if the guards don't get in our way."

The solemn faces of his comrades made clear what none of them would say aloud. They knew the risk they took, banding together to fight the monsters. The law demanded they leave such things up to the Lord Mayor's guards, who rarely seemed interested or available, no matter how many of the townsfolk of Ravenwood died bloody.

"I don't know anything about ghouls," Corran confessed. "Except what they do to the bodies they leave behind. And I haven't actually hunted anything yet."

"Every hunter has a first hunt," Calfon said, clapping him on the shoulder. "You've done well with sparring, and Trent and Ross have taught you how to use a knife and a sword. It's never easy or safe. So... do you want in or not?"

"I'm in," Corran said, squaring his shoulders. "I can do this."

None of them were there for the thrill of the hunt. They'd all become illicit hunters because the monsters had taken someone dear. Ross had lost a cousin, Calfon, a best friend. Some of the others had lost more than one person, and could no longer sit by and let the creatures wreak havoc. Still, it was dangerous work. Getting caught by the monsters meant being torn apart by fangs and claws. Drawing the ire of the guards could mean the noose.

Ravenwood City sprawled from the foothills down to the harbour, inside high protective walls. Wrighton, the neighbourhood where most of the tradespeople lived, seemed to be taking the worst of monster attacks lately, though Corran had heard tell of incidents in other parts of the city.

Tonight, they kept to the shadows, eager to avoid notice as they crossed Wrighton to get to Marelly's Close. As curfew approached, those who did not intend to spend all night at the pubs and taverns made their way back home, laughing and talking in voices that carried through the cold night air. Soon, Corran and the others had left behind the more prosperous parts of Wrighton and headed into a section where the houses crowded closer to one another, the streets narrowed, and the smell of smoke hung heavy in the air.

Ravenwood had begun as a village on the harbor, extending back from the waterfront over the decades. That meant the newer areas were back toward the wall, and the older buildings clustered closer to the wharves. The oldest sections were a warren of twisty lanes and odd angles.

Calfon knew the way, leading them back from the main street with its shop fronts into a filthy alley, then turning onto an even narrower street that twisted back between buildings until they stood in a hidden plaza that stank of blood. Marelly's Close was a dead-end street of leaning two-and three-storey buildings normally teeming with large families packed into small rooms. Now, the street looked like a battlefield, smelling of offal and death.

"Where is everybody?" Mir asked.

"Dead – or smart enough to run away," Allery replied.

"Do we know the ghouls are still in there?" Bant looked like he sincerely hoped the monsters had already fled.

Calfon put up a hand for silence. "Listen," he murmured. Corran strained to hear, but sure enough they could hear the strange chittering noises of the ghouls and the muted screams of their victims.

"Move in teams of three," Calfon ordered. "Use swords and knives, make sure you've got lime and green vitriol to destroy the ghouls' bodies. Lop off the heads; nothing else will stop them. When you clear your section, go help the others. If the guards come, split off and meet back at the cellar."

Trent, Ross, and Corran grouped together, while Pav, Bant, and Allery teamed up, as did Calfon, Mir, and Jott.

"Odds are, the ghouls are toward the end of the street," Calfon warned. "But we don't know where they came from, so we need to sweep the houses on each side. Might be coming in through the basements, or over the roofs. It would help a lot to know, so we don't get ambushed."

"And if we find survivors?" Corran asked.

Calfon's eyes shuttered, and his mouth thinned to a hard line. "You won't."

Corran's heart hammered in his chest as he and the others headed into the alley. He and his team went to the left, Pav's group went right, while Calfon and his hunters went toward the back. Corran had a sword in his right hand and a long knife in his left, as Trent eased the door open into the first of the hard-used houses in the cul-de-sac. Ross held a sword and a hastily lit lantern, while Trent had two long knives ready for the fight.

The smell hit them hard, like a slaughterhouse in summer. Blood fresh enough to form sticky pools on the floor, old enough to stink. Corran swallowed down bile as they moved carefully into the first set of rooms. As an undertaker, he had seen plenty of mangled bodies and ripe corpses. He hadn't thought anything would get to him. But the shredded and bloody remains left behind by the ghouls strained his reserve.

"They've been chewed." Ross paled, looking as if he might be sick as he stepped around the half-eaten body of a child. One arm had been gnawed to the bone, and the soft belly torn open, emptied of its organs.

"That's why we're going to kill these sons of bitches," Trent replied.

The three men moved farther into the house, and as they neared the back, Corran heard noises that sent a chill down his spine. Trent signalled wordlessly, and they readied their weapons, closing on the middle room.

More fresh bodies lay strewn across the room, swarmed by a frenzy of ghouls. The ghouls looked like withered corpses with bloated stomachs. The creatures glanced up from their feast, revealing sunken eyes and blood-stained maws filled with pointed teeth. Long fingers with knobby joints held bloody limbs the ghouls had torn from the bodies of their victims, or the bones they had gnawed clean and then snapped off to suck at the marrow inside.

Four ghouls; three hunters.

Trent stepped back, retreating to the outer room, forcing the ghouls to come at them one at a time through the narrow doorway. Trent caught the first of the creatures with a blow that cleaved it shoulder to hip. Yet the body still twitched and bucked when it fell, trying to pull its severed parts along with its clawed fingers and push with its feet until Trent's next strike sent the head rolling.

The second ghoul forced its way through, hurling itself right at Ross, who struck with his sword, slashing open the monster's distended belly and sending a sluice of half-digested meaty gobbets splashing onto the wooden floor. Even with its guts hanging out, the ghoul's focus on Ross never wavered.

Corran didn't have a chance to see how the fight turned out. A scrabbling noise overhead made him look up, just in time to see the third of the ghouls clinging to the ceiling like a roach, its blackened lips drawn back in anticipation of fresh kills.

The creature let go, turning in mid-air so that it landed on its feet and sprang at Corran, who barely got his sword between them in time to beat the ghoul back before it could swing at him. Corran swore under his breath as the creature dodged the blow and came at him again, curling its bony fingers like claws.

The ghoul raked its filthy nails down Corran's left arm. He wheeled and slashed with his sword, sinking the blade deep into the creature's shoulder, spraying the walls with foul black ichor. The ghoul drew back with a hiss, then ducked and tried to come up under Corran's guard.

He stabbed with the knife in his left hand, plunging the blade into the ghoul's chest. That would have stopped a man, but the ghoul pressed on, bleeding black liquid from what should have been a mortal wound.

If the fourth ghoul had made its way from the other room, Ross and Trent were keeping it busy. Corran had all he could handle with one opponent. He remembered the spoiled meat smell of the ghouls from the night Jora died and recalled how fast and fluidly they could move, like pallid bony spiders.

The ghoul eyed him, watching for an opening. Corran tried to remember everything Trent and Ross had taught him, how to keep his knees slightly bent and keep on the balls of his feet to move quickly, how to block and parry with his sword. Before the monsters killed people he loved, Corran had no need to be a fighter. Now, he wanted vengeance, and above all, to keep the monsters away from Rigan and Kell.

This time, the ghoul's movements were nearly too quick for Corran to track. The ghoul lunged right and so did Corran, plunging his knife deep into the monster's side and then scything his sword with all his strength to slice through the creature's bony neck.

The head thudded to the floor, and more of the awful black ooze spurted from the neck. This time, he could not choke back his response, spraying the ghoul's body with vomit.

"Feel better?" Trent asked, coming up behind him and clapping him on the shoulder. Before Corran could answer, Trent flinched back. "Gods above, you're soaked in ghoul-blood. Stay downwind!"

"Did we beat them?" Corran asked, trying to find a clean spot on his sleeve to wipe his mouth. He'd heard tales of the heroes of old since childhood, and he felt pretty certain that none of the legendary fighters ever heaved up their guts on the battlefield. At least, not that the bards reported.

"We got all the ones in this house," Trent said. Behind him, Ross had begun the work of hauling the ghouls' bodies into a heap. "There are two more houses on this side before we meet up with the others."

When all of the monsters' corpses were piled together, Ross sprinkled them with quicklime and green vitriol to eat through the flesh and make sure they stayed dead. Corran would have lifted his shirt over his nose to blunt the smell, except for the ghoul blood that stuck the cloth to his skin and stank even worse.

"Come on," Trent said, leading the way out to the street. "We're not done yet."

To Corran's relief, the second house harboured no live ghouls. Maybe there had been more monsters to start with; gauging from the way the corpses had been torn apart and gnawed nearly clean of meat, Corran figured that was likely. He lost what little remained in his stomach over in a corner of the main room, and to his relief, neither of his companions goaded him about it. To his eye, both Trent and Ross looked a bit green themselves.

"What happens to the bodies?" Corran asked, eyeing the bones.

"Nobody's going to pay the undertaker's fee," Trent remarked. "This isn't a Guild neighbourhood. I'd say, burn the whole damn street to the ground, but it's Calfon's call."

Corran wondered how the other hunters fared, and whether guards had taken any notice of the ghouls. The screaming outside finally stopped, and while Corran hoped the last of the street's residents had escaped, he feared Calfon would be right in his prediction.

The last house looked to be the oldest of the three. Corran and the others swept each level, weapons at the ready, but unlike the other houses, despite the floor being stained with blood, no bodies littered the rooms.

"Where did they go?" Ross asked, his voice tight with nervousness and fatigue.

"That way," Corran replied, pointing down the hallway. Long bloody trails suggested that the victims had been dragged away, toward the door at the end of the corridor.

Trent led the way, as Corran and Ross came behind, alert for a trap. Trent flung the door open, revealing a dark stairway leading down. Ross shuttered the lantern to a faint glow, needing the light but not wanting to warn a cellar full of ghouls that they were coming. Corran could see more of the bloody drag marks going down the stone steps.

"What would you think about just tossing the green vitriol down and seeing what happened?" Ross suggested, only partly joking.

Trent gave him a withering look. "I don't think so." Still, the look on Trent's face told Corran than the other man did not relish going into the dark.

"Why take the bodies into the cellar here and not in the other houses?" Ross asked quietly, still staring at the doorway as if it were a hungry maw.

"Maybe it's their lair," Corran suggested.

"They'd be swarming up the stairs for some fresh meat if they were nesting down there," Trent said. "There's got to be another reason. Come on."

He led the way once more, down stone steps worn smooth and low in the middle from the tread of many feet. The lantern revealed an old dug-out cellar, its floor darkened with blood, and at one end, a grating askew.

"The ghouls are in the drains," Ross said, swallowing hard. "Gods above and below! No wonder they can get around without being seen."

"We'd better go meet up with the others," Trent said, casting a wary look at the dark hole. "I've got a couple of ideas about how we can take care of the drains later."

By the time Corran and the others reached the back of the close to join their companions, the tower bells tolled midnight. Being out past curfew meant that the monsters were not the only dangers the hunters had to fear.

From the shrieks of the ghouls and the curses of the fighters, Corran realised that the battle in the house at the very back of the dead end street was not yet finished. They arrived to find Bant, Pav, and Allery blood streaked and grim, holding off half a dozen ghouls in one room, while Calfon, Mir, and Jott defended the hallway and kept the ghouls from retreating into the cellar.

"They're coming across the rooftops and up from the drains," Calfon shouted as Corran and the others waded into the fight.

"Any survivors?" Trent yelled.

"No. Just fresh corpses," Mir replied.

Very fresh, Corran noted, stepping over the bodies strewn through the hallway. He wondered if the residents of Marelly's Close had fled to the back of the dead end, thinking the old stone building would be a fortress. Instead, it was an abattoir; walls sprayed floor to ceiling with fresh blood and corpses of both humans and ghouls tossed into heaps like cordwood.

The bodies in this house hadn't been savaged like those in the other buildings. These corpses looked intact, unmarked. That almost made it worse, knowing that the hunters had come so close to saving them and still failed to rescue anyone. Corran narrowly avoided stepping on an arm flung wide from a young woman's body. Blood soaked her dress and matted her hair. A gaping hole where her throat had been torn out left no doubt as to the reason for her death. Near her lay two children, also dead, and closer to the door a man who had probably died first attempting to keep the ghouls from entering. Beside him lay a teenage boy, probably not much older than Kell, gripping a poker from the fireplace, hands still clenching the weapon.

Corran's control snapped, and he plunged into the fray with a shout, laying into the ghouls with all his might. In his mind's eye, the dead boy became Kell and the man next to him Rigan, stoking Corran's rage and fear, fuelling his adrenaline. He had heard tell of soldiers 'seeing red' in the throes of battle but had never expected to experience such a thing himself. But now, amid the splatter of ichor and the stink of fresh blood, Corran found the truth of the expression as the world narrowed around him and all that mattered was beheading the ghouls within reach of his sword.

When Corran came back to himself, the ghouls were dead, and he was covered in ichor up to his elbows.

"Corran?" Trent's tone and the worried look on his face gave Corran to know that his friend had probably been calling to him without reply for a while.

"I'm all right," Corran replied, swallowing hard. Trent accepted the lie for what it was and gave a nod.

"Any more ghouls?" Mir asked, glancing around nervously.

"None in the house," Calfon replied. "No survivors, either," he added, surveying the room. The floor was slippery with blood and worse, and while these victims had not been eaten, they deserved better than to lie with limbs akimbo, stained with gore and desecrated with gobbets of ghoul flesh.

Pav and Bant appeared in the doorway. "Looks like some of the bodies were dragged away," they reported.

"Probably means there's a drain in the basement," Trent replied.

"We've got trouble," Jott warned them from where he looked out the window.

"More creatures?" Ross asked.

Jott shook his head and managed to look more spooked than if a new legion of ghouls descended. "Guards. Blocking the end of the street."

"Shit," Calfon muttered. "Of course, they couldn't be bothered to show up to fight the monsters. They wait until the work is done, and sweep in to arrest us."

Corran's heart had only just begun to quiet from the battle. He'd felt terror, then elation to have made it through the fight. But taking on the guards was an entirely different threat.

"We're done for, no matter what, aren't we?" Pav asked, fear clear in his voice. "Fight our way past, and we hang for killing the Lord Mayor's men. Get captured, and we still swing for hunting monsters."

"Maybe not." They all turned to stare at Corran. He spoke before he had time to hint about how completely insane his suggestion might sound, but it was too late now to back out. "We can get out through the drains."

"Are you crazy?" Mir wheeled to look at him. "The ghouls are down there!"

"Do you want to fight the guards?" Trent asked, stepping up to stand next to Corran. "We could probably beat them. But if we do, we're criminals, and if we don't, we're traitors."

"We're already criminals," Calfon muttered. "At least in the eyes of the Lord Mayor."

"I've got a plan," Corran said, and they all turned to him again.

"It's risky, but I don't see that we've got a choice." Now that he'd survived his first foray against monsters, Corran needed to get home to his brothers in one piece. *I can't leave Rigan and Kell on their own.*

"Anyone have another idea?" Calfon asked, in a voice that cut through their fear and exhaustion. The exhausted hunters rallied, squaring shoulders, stiffening spines. "Because those guards aren't going to stay out there for long. Once they're sure the danger is gone, they'll come looking for us."

He turned to Corran. "It had better be a damn good plan, Valmonde. But I'd still rather face the ghouls than what the guards will do to us. So tell us all about your idea."

Corran took only a few minutes to explain, and they shifted their weapons and supplies to prepare. This time, they descended the basement steps with lanterns at full light, swords in hand and small weapons stuffing their pockets for quick access.

Calfon and Trent led as they moved into the darkened cellar, with Corran next and the rest following. Ross and Jott guarded the rear. "There," Corran said, pointing at a dislodged drain grating, and fresh smears of blood marking the path the ghouls had taken with their victims until the hunters interrupted.

"I really don't like this," Allery murmured.

"You know what the guards will do if they catch us," Pav replied. "You've seen the hangings, and the bodies gibbeted in the square. I've got no desire to end up like that."

"Don't want to be ghoul food, either," Bant shot back.

"If the ghouls get you, you're just dead," Mir said from behind Corran. "If the guards take you, they'll punish your families, maybe arrest them, maybe shut down their shop, or fine them so much they can't pay. I won't bring that down on my father. If I can't get back alive, then better to just disappear."

Corran tried to keep from breathing too quickly as Mir's words sank in. He'd gone with the hunters, taken up a sword, to protect Rigan and Kell from the creatures that killed so many in Ravenwood. But the guards were monsters of a different kind, and his family had already paid their price in blood. It would be difficult for his brothers to run the undertaker business without him if he died in the drains, but if the guards brought charges and the Guild disavowed them, they would all end up in the dungeon.

"Down we go." Calfon and Trent moved the grating enough for them to fit through the opening, and Calfon dropped down first. The light from his lantern swayed crazily as he steadied himself.

"They've been through here, but they're gone now – at least, as much as I can see," he called back up. "Hurry."

One by one, they followed. Ross and Jott wrestled the grating mostly into place, hoping to slow the guards from pursuing if they got as far as the cellar. The drains were damp from recent rains, though it could have been far worse, Corran thought. Storm drains carried the rainwater to the sewers, which flowed down to the harbour. All they had to do was navigate uphill, away from where the guards kept watch, and come up from one of the street grates.

Corran doubted escape could be that simple.

The stone-lined passageway was wide enough for two men to walk side by side and high enough that none of the hunters needed to duck. The trickle of water at their feet looked fairly clean, but the dampness spread to the rest of the rock walls, making them slick with mould. Corran listened hard but could hear nothing except their footfalls.

"No rats," he murmured.

"That's a bad sign," Calfon agreed. "They've either scattered or been eaten."

They reached the first main intersection, where several drains came together. One branch led uphill, toward home. "That way," Calfon pointed.

A crash behind them made the hunters turn toward the sound, weapons raised. Loud rustling to the right raised Corran's hackles.

"Hunters! Stop in the name of the Lord Mayor!"

"Move!" Calfon hissed. "Hurry!"

Running bootsteps from behind told Corran the guards didn't intend to wait for their surrender. But the scrabble of bony claws against rock and the rising stench suggested the ghouls smelled fresh meat.

"We've got to hold the entrance," Corran said, as most of the hunters retreated up the branch toward home. This tunnel looked much drier than the others, and Corran felt a flash of hope that his plan might work.

"We'll follow you," Calfon instructed Ross and the others. "Get them home." Ross gave a sharp nod and gestured for the rest to follow him. Corran, Trent, and Calfon remained where they stood, but they shuttered their lanterns and dug out the supplies from their pockets.

"If this doesn't work, I'm going to haunt you forever," Trent muttered.

"Rigan will send you to the After," Corran retorted. "Nobody haunts an undertaker for long."

Corran took a wineskin from Calfon's pack and spread oil across the mouth of the drain as well as splashing liberal mounts on both walls. Trent pulled small, ball-shaped clay pots from his pockets, each filled with oil and stuffed with wicks, and shared them with Corran. Calfon pulled out a small bag of glass vials and a sling. "I'm ready," he said, as they waited for their enemies to converge.

The guards ran through the tunnels, splashing through the water and clanking where their weapons struck the rock walls. The ghouls swarmed with barely a rustle across the ceiling and sides of the tunnels, like oversized pale spiders.

"Now!" Corran reacted at Calfon's order, lighting one of the balls from the lantern and lobbing it into the wide stretch of oil they'd laid down at the mouth of the tunnel. The flames caught, spreading quickly up the walls. As the ghouls reached the split-off, they drew back, afraid of the flames and heat. The running guards couldn't change course quickly enough and found themselves faced with a choice between ghouls and fire.

Corran and Trent kept up a constant barrage of lit oil orbs, smashing the fragile pottery balls and keeping the flames burning so high they filled the whole mouth of the tunnel and scorched the ceiling. Calfon used his sling to lob the vials of green vitriol into the back of the mob of ghouls driving them forward into the guards.

They dared not flee, not yet, when letting the flames die back even a little would mean pursuit. And despite the curtain of fire between them and the battle, nothing could hide the slaughter. The ghouls skittered across the ceiling and walls like pallid roaches, dozens of them, unsated despite the feast they had in the cul-de-sac, and when the guards abruptly changed course and fell back, the ghouls pressed forward, giving chase. Screams echoed in the tunnels, along with the *clack* of teeth and the scratch of claws.

Once the wave of ghouls had retreated, Corran and the others lost no time flinging most of the remaining green vitriol across the fiery barrier to wet the stone floor and keep the ghouls at bay. Trent and Corran smashed enough oil pots to keep the flames burning hot and high.

"Run!" Calfon ordered, and together the three hunters sprinted to catch up with their companions.

"The guards?" Ross asked, casting a nervous glance behind them into the tunnels.

"Busy with ghouls. Let's get out of here before the ghouls finish with them."

"I think I know where we are," Pav volunteered. "Follow me. I can get us to an exit."

Corran, Calfon, and Trent brought up the rear, watching worriedly behind them as the group trekked uphill. The longer they stayed in the tunnels, the more likely they were to happen upon another nest of creatures – ghouls or otherwise. To Corran's relief, Pav found a grate only minutes later, pointing up at an iron lattice through which they could see the stars.

"We'll come out behind The Lame Dragon," he said, naming one of their favorite taverns. "But given the time, there shouldn't be people around to see."

"Let's hope not. Coming up from a drain might make someone take notice," Calfon muttered.

One by one, the hunters crawled out, scattering into the shadows of a nearby alley. By silent signal, they split off into pairs, to better evade notice.

By the time they reached the stable behind the farrier's shop, Corran had begun to feel the full import of the night's work. His hands were raw and bleeding from scaling the rough tunnel walls, and he felt bruises and pulled muscles from the fight all over his body. Blood and gore-soaked his clothing and matted his hair, streaking his skin like a mad butcher. Now that the danger was past, Corran leaned against one of the stable walls and threw up again, though he could have sworn there was nothing left to heave. He was trembling all over. He strained to slow his breathing, hoping not to further disgrace himself by passing out. His left arm throbbed where he'd been slashed by the ghoul.

"Need to bind that up with poultice," Trent observed, coming up beside him. "Ghoul claws carry taint."

Corran looked up with a rueful grin. "Hurts pretty bad. And I keep throwing up. Some hunter I turned out to be."

Trent gave him a look. "You held your own tonight. You fought well, and you came up with a way out of the ambush. Let me tell you a secret," he said, leaning in. "We've all lost our guts a time or two. Goes with the work."

Ross drew water from a pump to fill a trough, and the hunters stripped down, eager to wash off the filth from the battle and cleanse away the smell, even if memories of the horror could not so easily be dismissed. Corran plunged his head beneath the water, washing the gore from his blond hair, glad for the bracing cold. When he came up for air, someone pushed a chunk of lye soap into his hands, and he scrubbed until his skin turned pink and sensitive.

A heap of rough horse blankets awaited them, along with a pile of mismatched garments. "You might as well leave your clothes for me to burn," Ross said. "They won't come clean. I've got clothing the stable hands have left behind, and a few things I snatched off the clothesline behind the house. I try to keep some things stashed here, for nights like this."

They changed as quickly as they could, cold from the night air and grateful for the blankets. Ross prodded their stained and stinking garments into a basket and carried it into the back alley. Moments later, the smell of smoke wafted inside. Corran looked out through the gap between the stable doors and saw the dawn rising above the rooftops.

Trent slathered pungent salve on Corran's wounded arm and tied off strips of cloth to bind the gashes. The smell made made him think of lamed horses. "Keep it clean, and if it starts to get red, come back, and Ross will try something stronger. Horse medicine works pretty well on people too," he added. Corran gave him an exhausted smile in return.

"Curfew's over," Ross said as the bells rang in the distance. "The stable hands will be getting here soon. You'll want to be gone. No need to have people wondering why you're here."

They straggled off, with murmured thanks and promises to meet again soon to train. Corran hoped that the plain trews and tunic he'd scored from the pile at the stable would be unremarkable enough not to draw his brothers' notice. He stayed to the side streets, unwilling to survive so much just to fall prey to a foul-tempered guard on his way home. But when he reached the end of his own block, Corran's knees went weak, and he collapsed against the wall as the reality of it all sank in.

I'm a hunter. An outlaw. A fighter. I never thought I had it in me, but damned if I didn't do the job. He nearly retched again, in the gutter, but his belly ached from hunger as much as his overtaxed muscles screamed for rest. Corran struggled to make sense of the feeling that he was different now, although everything around him remained the same. Something had changed in him, between the time he had slipped out of the workshop with Trent and Ross, and now. He wasn't the same man he'd been when he'd left the shop just last night.

Corran would see the horror of the ghouls' slaughter in his dreams forever, and avoid Marelly's Close for the rest of his life. It would take effort not to shy from the guards' notice, to carry on as if he had nothing to hide, and most importantly, to keep the secret of his other life from Rigan and Kell. *They can't know. They must never know. I've got to keep them safe.*

To his surprise, when he opened the back door, he found Kell sitting on the steps with a cup of tea in his hands, waiting for him.

"Where's Rigan?"

Kell shrugged. "Sleeping, I guess."

"You're up early."

"I couldn't sleep. I was worried." He looked up accusingly. "Where were you, really?"

Corran looked at Kell, his hair sticking up at all angles, still too young to shave, but far from carefree or innocent. Corran knew that he couldn't let either of his brothers bear the burden of his secret.

"At Ross'," Corran lied. "Settled the horses, then drank ale and played cards most of the night, since we couldn't break curfew. You and Rigan didn't miss a thing."

A God's Mercy

Richard Webb

Nehrud crouched, scooping up a handful of soil. He rubbed it between his fingers and cupped them over his nose, inhaling the earthy must. Good red land, ripe for tilling.

I should have been a farmer.

This land was worth fighting for; it gave sustenance and livelihood, but today would yield the same harvest as always. Nehrud looked up at the sky. It was a carapace of solid blue, so pure but so empty – it was hard to think any gods could be looking down. He doubted it but forced himself to believe, as he had always done. He no longer knew whether the old gods were worth fighting for.

Lowering his gaze, Nehrud looked out over a vista of open plains which led down onto a valley fringed with yellow grass. At the bottom was a brown scar of river, a mile off. Lines of Confederation Army soldiers scuttled across a wooden bridge, looking like ants. In fifteen minutes, twenty at most, they would be within fighting range.

His comrades huffed and shuffled, each finding their own way to deal with the inexorable drag of these quiet moments before the dance of blades. Some told jokes, sending ripples of nervous laughter through the ranks. Some stretched, or sharpened weapons, checked bowstrings, tightened bootstraps and suchlike. Some prayed, kneeling, making symbols in the air, muttering. None took their eyes from the bottom of the valley for more than a few seconds.

They had arrived too late to take the bridge – to burn it if necessary. It would have curtailed the fight that was now inevitable, holding the Confederation to the far bank of the river. But that hope was lost to time: mere minutes in which the world turned.

Nehrud's stomach churned but not just due to lack of nourishment.

A tap on the shoulder; he turned. Jaheem twisted the cork from a bottle and held it out.

"This the Vundelinean liquor?" Nehrud asked.

She nodded. "Was saving it, but little point now."

Nehrud took a swig, savouring the rasping burn. Its warmth flowed through him, helping to alleviate his body's many tiny rebellions: the blisters, the aches, the bruises, the old wounds that had never healed right.

Jaheem drained the last swig from the bottle. The enemy soldiers were closer now, no longer ants – their heraldic colours were easily distinguishable. She tossed the bottle in their direction. It hit the dirt with a muffled clunk twenty paces down the slope.

A burly figure bustled up to them.

"Nehrud, my straps."

Carom. He struggled with his one good hand to shuck his shield from round his back. Nehrud knew he hated asking, so he helped his old friend in silence. He took the shield and held it out whilst Carom shoved his stumped arm into the customised brace. Carom nodded and Nehrud fastened the strap.

"Tighter."

"It's good," said Nehrud, patting him on the shoulder. "You're good."

"I'm good as dead and you know it," said Carom as he spat on the dust. "A *shield* of all things. Damned clumsy. Like fighting with a piece of tree strapped to me where there should be… never mind."

Nehrud handed Carom his axe.

"She misses her mate," said Carom.

He'd fought all his life with a pair of axes, custom-made for him and perfectly balanced: *'his wives'* he called them. Over the years he'd mastered the art of wielding them in perfect synchronicity: fast, accurate and deadly. None were better that Nehrud had ever seen, until he lost his hand in the last campaign.

"You should have retired," said Nehrud.

"We both should," Carom replied.

When the Confederation Army marched back into their homelands, he had vowed to take a few of their hands in retaliation.

"You're a stubborn bastard."

"I'm a warrior. No time to be anything else," said Carom.

Time, thought Nehrud. *No one ever has enough.*

He looked along the line at the war-band, his comrades, a

hundred strong. One hundred well-armed, disciplined fighters: enough to ruin a small town, perhaps even take a desert citadel. But against five times their number, in open territory and broad daylight, they had little hope for anything more than a good death.

They had the slope and were lucky to have this advantage for the land yielded little else. It was an earthy outcrop looking out onto the plains; not even a few boulders to set rolling, nowhere to hide, nothing to use. Nothing now would stop the infestation swarming towards them.

Didn't matter what the auguries said: today was not fortuitous. Nehrud knew he would need more than fortune to come through this. *Divine intervention maybe*, he thought. He looked up at the empty sky. There were no gods here.

The enemy was now just half a mile distant.

Ydralla.

Nehrud wished he could see her again. And the child. Would he ever get to look at her, kiss her brow? He ached with the memory of the lover left behind and the longing for a young daughter never known.

His instinct, as always, was to push them from his mind, keep his head clear; ready to fight. But he resisted, for once allowing himself to dwell on these thoughts. Images of Ydralla flitted across his mind: the crinkle of her smile, the heat of her breath and the cool of her fingertips. And the little one – it would have her eyes of course…

"Positions!" shouted the captain of the war-band.

A score of archers split equally to the flanks, ready to fire at will once the enemy was in range of their recurve bows.

"Crossbows!"

Another score had small crossbows primed, each ready to shoot a single bolt from a range of a hundred yards before taking up close arms, no time to reload. Nehrud knew they would be lucky to take down a dozen Confederation fighters before the melee broke.

"Spears!"

A pace in front of the crossbows, another two score were ready with heavy shields and spears, a front line to take the brunt of the first assault. They lined the crest of the slope, working the terrain as best they could. They would make their opposition's final few yards very hard indeed: uphill into this stolid beast with its spiky exoskeleton, whilst crossbows loosed a volley of spiny quills. Nonetheless, their numbers looked pitiful.

"Let me through," snarled Carom. He shouldered others aside to take a place in the front line. He had no spear so broke the uniformity of the formation but none argued. His addition did not weaken it.

"Close arms, spread out!"

Behind the shield line the remainder of the war-band paced about. Most had light shields and their preference of sword, mace or axe. They were there to deal with enemies breaking through the line, for break through it they would.

Jaseem whipped out her pair of machetes, held them out wide and twisted her neck round slowly.

"Meet your deaths, you sons and daughters of piss-soaked whores," she shouted, madness contorting her features.

Nehrud recognised the fear in her bravado. He felt it too.

He extended his sword arm and turned round slowly, checking his fighting space. It was important to have room, not get cramped in the press.

"Lord-God Vriyahmet, watch over me; I will reap you a harvest of souls," he muttered, the words ringing hollow. He started counting down...

"Fire at will," yelled the captain.

The *thrum* of bowstrings reverberated across the hilltop. Howls of anguish came from further down the slope seconds later. It was followed by the *chonk* of crossbows and more howls of pain but Nehrud knew that this handful of deaths was little more than a piss in the ocean. Crossbows were dropped as the archers fell in behind the shield line. The archers with recurve bows loosed one more volley before they retreated to the higher flanks and continued their assault. Orders and curses mingled with of the clank and chink of arms and armour in motion.

Nehrud could see them now, fifty yards distant. Their faces contorted with rage and horror, eyes wide, teeth bared, faces flecked with spittle, succumbing to the madness. Guttural roars filled the air, as if the fighters on both sides were shape-shifting into beasts of slaughter.

Instead of his customary prayers to Vriyahmet, Nehrud found himself repeating '*Ydralla*' over and over, like an incantation. Maybe that was who he should worship now.

There was a crash of metal on metal and then the sickening wet crunch of metal on flesh. Agonies were screamed above the tumult, shrill and piercing, almost inhuman and the unmistakable, intoxicating tang of blood hung in the air.

The shield line held. Nehrud edged forward, his heart pumping a command to run. He could run, couldn't he? Drop everything, turn and go. Run to Ydralla.

A blur. In the corner of his eye a shape closed in on him. Reflex brought his shield up an instant before a thud pulsed up his arm. The blow forced him back, off-balance; he dropped low as another swipe bit through the air, inches from his eyes. He braced, crouched, pushed forward. Another thud but this time Nehrud countered with a straight lunge. The tip of his scimitar thrust bit through armour, under his opponent's ribs. Not deadly, but enough to panic the man into a flurry of blows. Nehrud bounced them off his shield, stepped aside and chopped. He took his opponent's forearm clean off. The man crumpled with an ear-piercing shriek.

Nehrud looked up. The shield line had buckled but hadn't yet caved. The archers had drawn light weapons, the enemy encroaching closer. The battalion's numbers were too many, enabling them to supplant the flanks and get behind Carom and his line of defenders. Nehrud moved forward.

He ducked an axe, swinging his shield forward edge-first. An enemy soldier doubled over, his kidneys ruined. Nehrud drew a red line across his chest with his blade. He strode on.

Another Confederation soldier forced his way through the front line. Without breaking stride Nehrud ran him through. It was years since he had lost his hesitation: battle took the uncertain as well as the unlucky.

He saw Carom's axe swing up and down, side to side, finding its rhythm, dancing its bloody dance. He could see his old friend's crested helm, caked in gore. Nehrud looked to the flanks, now being breached by Confederation soldiers.

Damn them all, will they never stop? Have they not taken enough?

He saw Jaseem surrounded. She blocked and swayed but dread flared in her eyes as a trio of soldiers circled her. She deflected a swipe and tried to counter but there were shields all around, her reach insufficient. A jab from the side found its way past her defences, nicking her arm. The three men sensed her vulnerability and closed in.

Nehrud ran. He careered into one of her attackers, shield first. They both tumbled in the dust. Jaseem took advantage of the distraction to dart forward and pierce a soldier in the midriff.

The third turned on Nehrud, prostrate in the red soil. He swung his mace downwards with his full might. It was all Nehrud could do to block upwards with his shield. Pain juddered up his arm, rattling his clenched teeth. Then another blow, as he scrambled to his knees. He swung his scimitar in a wide arc from underneath his shield. It hacked into his attacker's ham, just below his mail skirt. At the same moment, the man's mace cracked into Nehrud's shield, splitting it through. Nehrud howled as the impact fractured his arm. He twisted in the dirt and hacked with his scimitar, biting deeper across the soldier's thigh. The man toppled sideways like a culled goat.

Jaseem ran to Nehrud, planted her machetes in the dirt and tugged the remnants of his shield from his shattered arm. He cursed as she did so, his limb bent in a bizarre angle. She grabbed him under the other arm, hauling him up, all the while checking around.

Nehrud tightened the grip on his sword. It gave him little reassurance. He shivered, running wet with sweat and crimson. His left arm hung limp, its dead weight bringing new tortures with each movement.

"Vriyahmet, protect me," he murmured, though he could not tell if he spoke the words aloud.

Jaseem retrieved her machetes. Drawing strength from her proximity, Nehrud brought his blade up, daring anyone to approach.

Short dull clangs sounded behind them. Jaseem rolled across the ground, a blur of blades; a soldier fell and she leaped into a deadly assault on another. Nehrud turned to engage alongside her, a torment flaring in his arm.

Another soldier came into view. She aimed a draw-cut across Nehrud, where his shield should have been. He was defenceless, too easy for her to take down. A searing bolt of pure white hurt wracked his body. He sank to his knees with the shocking thought: this was his death. He would die here, today, *now*. Nehrud had known the fight was hopeless but nonetheless this moment, his actual death, was unforeseen.

By the gods, let it end. An image Ydralla with a babe in arms came to his mind and his heart broke. They had never had enough time.

"The pain is too much. Vriyahmet, show mercy," he whispered. The soldier raised her sword to deal the deathblow.

Nehrud stared blankly. The soldier stood, frozen; her sword was raised, poised in mid-air, ready to end his life. For a moment he panicked, tormented by the blade hovering above him, glistening with his blood, glinting in the sun under the carapace of solid blue.

Why did she hesitate? Nehrud realised he could hear nothing. An eerie silence replaced the cacophony of battle sounds. Had his wounds taken his hearing?

He felt no pain now, just a tingling sensation where his chest had been carved open, warmth flooding through his shattered arm. Otherwise, all was still. Fighters were all around, caught in the throes of combat, weapons bloodied: a grotesque tableau. Nehrud realised he too was unable to move, his whole body fixed in position, though his eyes were able to glance around and he could feel his breath moving through his lips. Nothing was happening. Should it? Who really knew what after-death brought?

In the corner of his vision, an old woman hazed into view, walking slowly towards him, a stick for support. She wove her way through the throng of fighters, all held in a moment of mid-motion. She stepped over corpses, pausing to study their faces as she made her progress. She looked almost happy.

"*I* watch, though few others do," she said, her voice cracked and wheezy. "Not in judgment; rather as you might watch a garden grow. My harvest of souls."

"Who are you?" said Nehrud. The words did not come from his mouth, but took shape in his head.

"The one to whom you have been offering sacrament. Few believe in me. But you do, despite your doubts."

"So, my prayers –"

"Your faith in me had withered to empty habit, but you

remembered my name when your blood was up."

Nehrud stared at her, immobile, unable to look away even had he wanted to. She crept closer. The old woman ran her wizened finger along the flat of the blade pointing down at him. She leant on the arm of the soldier wielding it, still petrified in mid-action. She grinned and hobbled around, making a show of promenading amongst the gallery of sculptures. Nehrud assumed he was dreaming, or hallucinating. Or dead already.

"No, no, and no," said the old woman, chuckling. At last she came to Jaseem. She patted her cheek. Nehrud's comrade-in-arms remained a statue.

"Jaseem is my newly-chosen one," said the old woman. "An instinct for battle like no other before her. This soldier in front of you, pointing her sword at your chest: she was my chosen one before. A true warrior-woman who screams my name as she strides the battlefield with a fervour I find invigorating. Enriches me with many souls, but like you, her time runs dry. Jaseem will cut through her heart as yours beats its last."

"But if she serves you so well, why let her die?"

"Jaseem must take her mantle in order to become my finest champion."

"Jaseem will live?"

"Yes, one of the few to do so today."

"Was I not one of your finest too?"

"You served well and for that I am grateful. But Jaseem-the-Bloody will rise to be a warrior-priest of Vriyahmet where you were only an acolyte."

"She survives. I am glad."

"She will need new protectors, though."

"Protectors?"

"You and Carom. There was a reason at least one of you always found yourself close to her side in the battle lines."

Nehrud thought on this. It was true; both he and Carom had saved the young woman's life several times. They'd also given her advice, combat training, tactical knowledge, even ensured she kept her equipment in order.

"But we could still protect her —"

"What, the pair of one-armed fighters, too old and slow to protect themselves?"

"I saved her today, when she was encircled," said Nehrud.

"I need your death. It will draw from Jaseem the pure rage which will enable her to become my most beloved. She loved you a little, I think. I will use that. She will carve a red swathe across these lands, score her name into history."

"And you hold me – *here* – to tell me this?"

The old woman smiled, without evident kindness. "You asked me for mercy. I am a god of battle; mercy is beyond my cognisance."

"So I die here?"

The old woman hobbled off into the middle distance, towards a solitary tree at the crest of the hill. Nehrud watched her blur into the shade of the tree, disappear, and then someone else started towards him: taller, straight-limbed, carrying a bundle...

Ydralla.

She walked up to him, their baby in her arms.

Though his body remained static, inside he broke with joy.

She passed through the carnage of the battle as if it were not there.

She does not belong here, he thought as she stepped past the tip of the blade hanging in the air.

She knelt before him.

He drank in the crinkle of her smile, felt the heat of her breath and the cool of her fingertips as she brushed his face.

"You are hurt, my love."

"My time is done. I wished to see you once more. And the child."

"And here we are."

"Is it really you? Are you really here?"

"Do you believe it so?"

"Yes."

"Then it is so."

"I thought of you both, often. I am so sorry. I wished I had not..."

"I know," said Ydralla.

Nehrud's eyelids could not blink away the moisture that formed in his eyes. "Her name?"

"Maliah, after your mother. I toyed with 'Nehruddine' but –"

"Maliah is perfect."

And she was. Ydralla held up the child to Nehrud's face, its tiny head touching his lips. She had her mother's eyes, of course.

In a single moment which encapsulated a lifetime, Nehrud finally understood. *This* was a god's mercy: not to gift life when death was inevitable but a gift of time, *outside of time* – an instant in which death could be given terms.

"We will remember you and find you in the end," Ydralla said, standing. She began to move off.

"Stay! Don't leave me."

"It is you who is leaving us," she said, as she walked away, without turning.

"But I need more time –"

"They will be with you soon," said the old woman, her voice echoing in Nehrud's head, though he could not see her.

"No, please, let them be. I beg you."

"Oh, they'll live long lives, good ones in truth," said the old woman's voice, "though both will ache for the loss of you."

Nehrud was overcome with sadness at the thought of this, though his body remained impassive.

"You'll be with them in the breeze caressing their hair, in the sunlight kissing their eyelids. The passing of their lives will be a mere instant to you."

"Please, I... I never had the chance to –"

"I am Vriyahmet. I show no mercy. But I reward my servants." *With a mere instant.*

"It... is enough," said Nehrud.

"Then it is time."

The warrior-woman plunged her sword through Nehrud's heart, burying it up to the hilt. As she withdrew her blade, Jaseem ran up behind her and removed her head with a scissoring slash of her two blades. She sank to her knees aside the corpse of the woman, stabbing it repeatedly, whispering Nehrud's name.

Moments later, she stood, surveying the battlefield. Whirling twin machetes like a manic djinni, Jaseem-the-Bloody roared back into the fray.

The Berserker Captain

Neal Asher

Defeat hung around them like the fetid stink of a week-old battlefield. It was implicit in every leaden plodding step they took, in the moans of the wounded in the stolen cart, and in the tarnish of their weapons and the few tatty scraps of armour they had not yet discarded. Parrick felt the march should be more disciplined, with a straightening of their ragged lines, but he had no energy to enforce it. He felt the sting of defeat as deeply as every one of the fifty-three surviving infantrymen of his once four-hundred-strong battalion.

"How much further, sir?" asked Coln, his lieutenant.

Parrick halted to survey the rolling countryside, so like the sea they were desperately trying to reach. He peered at the forest ahead of them, with its badly-needed cover.

"At this rate, the rest of the day," he said, then looked back at Coln.

The lieutenant removed his beaten helm, shook his head gingerly, then reached up to dab at the dried blood blackening his hair. He had been young and enthusiastic when they first landed here on the shores of Ordanol, Parrick remembered. Now he too was an old man, like his Captain.

"Will the ships be there?" Coln asked, yet again.

"The ships will be there," Parrick replied, forcing conviction up from the hollow in his chest.

"But will there be room for us?"

"Yes, there will be room."

Coln sighed and turned to the men as they trudged past.

"It'll be good to be going home," he said, and rejoined the march.

Would it?

Parrick wondered as he watched his men filing past. Home to the laws of the Priesthood and their damned Clergy. Home to the

43

beatings, the burnings, and the poverty. Was this why none of his men would meet his eyes? The sadness he felt drowned his usual grinding anger. The Glorious Fourth: broken at Habian's pass. When Jurt staggered past, drunk on the stolen brandy he had poured down himself to drown the pain of his beaten back, Parrick could bear it no more, and turned away. It was then that he saw the riders approaching across the grassland.

Now, does it end now?

Coln moved to his side, swore, then turned to the men.

"Riders coming! Form up!" he yelled.

Raggedly the infantrymen drew together at the side of the cart, the few pike-bearers who had retained their weapons moving to the fore. Parrick drew his sword and moved to one side of them.

"Straighten that shield line," he said, too tired to bellow orders.

Coln strode along in front of the line, cracking his sword against any shield out of place. Pride drew the line straight but Parrick knew that if this was an advance guard of the Ordanon cavalry, he and his men simply stood no chance. He watched as the riders came up out of a dip in the landscape, and waited to see if more would follow. There were only three. Coln moved to his side.

"They must be ours. They'd have turned by now, otherwise," he said. Then, after watching for a moment, "Seems they think hell hounds are after them. They're pushing those horses too hard."

Parrick nodded. Had the riders been Ordanon cavalry, he would have ordered his men to put down their weapons and offered surrender, and been relieved to do so. But tension remained, for he had a horrible intimation of who these riders might be, and wanted none of them. When they drew close enough to be identified, Coln spat on the ground.

"Priest-soldiers," he said.

Had they been of Ordanon, Parrick knew he could have expected mercy. These black harbingers had none.

The leader was a thin, effeminate individual, his face scraped of hair, even devoid of eyebrows, and his head shaven back halfway to leave a long queue of black hair. His cloak signified low rank, but Parrick saw he wore *Chothai* battle-armour, and was not fooled. The other two, dressed in the black of Indulgents, were obviously his bodyguards. The three horses they rode were lathered with sweat, and clearly close to collapse.

"Well met, Battle-captain!" the man called as he drew rein. He swept his cloak aside to reveal his medallion of rank, then stared at Parrick with cold expectation. Parrick felt a moment of rebellion, then, too tired to sustain it, he went down on one knee and touched his forefinger to his forehead and chest. Behind him his men were down on their faces.

"You men, remain as you are. Battle-captain, you may rise."

Parrick stood and faced a man who appeared to be an arch-priest, barely managing to keep the contempt from his expression. The man observed him a moment longer before going on.

He said, "I am Amondius, and I will be accompanying you to the coast."

Parrick kept his face rigid. Amondius: the Red Bishop! What the hell was he doing here dressed like an arch-priest? Why would so arrogant a man want to keep his identity concealed?

"Surely, Reverence, we would delay you?"

Amondius dismounted, his bodyguards doing likewise. One of them led the horses to one side.

"You will speak when I ask questions. Otherwise you will remain silent."

Trouble.

Parrick said nothing more – too tired for rebellion. Like a good little soldier he would obey Amondias's orders. The Red Bishop was not known for his tolerance.

It began as soon as they reached the forest.

"This man is intoxicated!"

Parrick turned and saw that one of the bodyguards had dragged Jurt from the ranks.

"Reverence, he is in some pain –"

"Silence!"

Parrick went on. He could not allow this.

"Reverence, he fought well and has been..." Parrick lost the thread. He could not tell Amondius that Jurt's pain was a direct result of the fifty lashes he had received from a Priest-soldier.

"… wounded…"

Amondius signalled one of his guards to move to Parrick's side. Parrick glanced at the man then back to Amondius as he strode towards Jurt.

"Wait, you can't –"

A fist crashed into the side of his head and blackness took him like a falling wall. He was not out for long, but when he came to it was to shouted orders and Jurt's protests. Without comment or expression Coln helped him to his feet.

"You there, find a rope! I told you two to hold him! Do so, or join him! Where is that rope?"

Parrick stumbled to his feet in time to see Jurt being dragged to a tree and one of Amondius' guards throwing a rope over a branch. There was an ugly muttering from the men.

"No, we made him drink! He couldn't keep up! The cart was full!" Parrick stumbled forwards with Coln coming up behind him.

On his agitated horse, Amondius glared at him.

"One more word, Battle-captain, and I will have your tongue cut out!"

Parrick's hand dropped to his sword as the rope went round Jurt's neck. Jurt was yelling now, finally understanding, through his drunken stupor, what was going to happen to him. They were going to hoist him, no clean neck-break, he was going to strangle at the end of a rope. Parrick stepped forwards. Dare he? He ached to cut Amondius from his horse. He took another step as Jurt's yells turned into a horrible gurgling. He dared not. Twelve years of discipline and indoctrination could not easily be broken.

The guard hoisted Jurt into the air, his legs kicking and his hands grappling with the rope above him. They hadn't tied him. With his hands free he would fight the rope and try to support his own weight, so his death would be more protracted and painful.

"Bastards!" Parrick hissed, and felt he really might do something now. But a hellish shriek issued from the forest, followed by a loud butchering thud.

A shocked silence fell. Parrick's eyes tracked the arrow tumbling through the air into the forest beyond. It seemed to take a nightmare age to fall out of sight, and made a sound like the dry rattle of knuckle bones as it dropped into the bushes. Coln's shout then broke the stillness.

"Form up! Form up! Shields!"

Stunned by what he had seen, Parrick looked back up at Jurt still suspended and slowly revolving. The man was twitching, blood pumping from his mouth and the hole in the back of his head. A shriek arrow, and it had gone right through his head. Abruptly the Red Bishop's hangman released the rope and leapt from his horse. Jurt thumped to the ground, the rope slithering down on top of him. Amondius sat with his mouth open for a second or two, then almost fell in his hurry to dismount. The men were shouting as they drew together and formed a shield wall. How well they remembered Habian's Pass where they had lost most of their number to archers. The horses scattered and Parrick noted how eagerly the Bishop and his guards sheltered behind the wall. Coln squatted down beside Parrick, his face pale.

"Sir, shriek arrows are made to scare…"

Parrick knew what he meant. The cuts made in the head of such an arrow drastically reduced its penetrating power, rendering it all but useless as a weapon. He shrugged, shook his head. What was there to say? Whoever had fired that arrow had been inhumanly strong. He glanced towards Amondius hoping for some explanation and, so surprised by what he saw there, turned for a proper look. Not even on the battlefield had he seen such terror. He nodded to himself. So there had been a reason for the Bishop to put up with the inconvenience of travelling with infantry. He looked back out into the trees and, as if summoned, a rider appeared and called to them.

Parrick peered at this tall and long-boned man. The rider wore a leather tunic over a shirt of forester's green, grey and ragged cloak and leggings, and his boots were scuffed and worn too. And surely there was something familiar about the long grey hair, skull-like face, and black nail-head eyes? Parrick's gaze dropped to the man's big ugly hands where they held a heavy laminated longbow out to one side, with another arrow already notched.

"I have no score to settle with the infantry of Jardia!" He called to them. "Send out the Bishop and his men and I will let you live!"

Parrick and Coln exchanged glances.

"One man?" asked Coln.

Parrick shook his head.

"Has to be more. Amondius and his men could easily deal with one man. They're trained *Chothai*. There must be a battalion out there."

Suddenly Amondius moved up beside them.

"Are you going to sit here and do nothing?" he hissed, his eyes wild. "Get out there and kill him!"

Him? One man then.

Parrick stared at the Bishop for a long moment, weighing his words in the face of such fear.

"Reverence, my men are infantry, they would not be able to catch someone on horseback."

He looked pointedly towards one of the abandoned horses. Amondius shook his head and turned away to stare once more at the solitary rider. Parrick felt his guts clench up. Why was he so scared? The rider called to them again.

"I will circle round you. After one circuit I will take a life. Give me Amondius!"

The rider began to move, his grey form only occasionally glimpsed between the trees.

"Have you no bows?" demanded Amondius.

"Infantry are only allowed to carry weapons of hand-to-hand combat," stated Parrick, his expression blank. It was one of those ridiculous arbitrary rules made by the Clergy.

"We must run," said Amondius.

Parrick glanced at the wounded in the cart.

"If we run we'll be easy prey. Best to stay behind the shields for a while. We'll think of something."

He wanted to tell Amondius to go out and deal with the rider himself. One man, and here the Bishop crouched and his two guards – all *Chothai* trained – did crouch behind the shield wall as if hiding from a battalion. Amondius seemed to accept his suggestion, because he was terrified and, again, Parrick wondered why.

The rider made his circuit. When he came back to his original position they waited in tense silence. Abruptly Amondius spoke up again.

"He can't touch us here. Perhaps you were right. Maybe he'll go away."

This time Parrick could not hide the contempt he felt. Clergy. Their mishandling of the war had led to disasters like the one at the Pass. He crawled closer to the line of his men. When? When was the rider going to try something? What could he try? Parrick's answer was a loud crack and the *oomph* of someone's breath leaving him. He jerked his head away from a spray of blood as one of his soldiers fell back with his shield on top of him. Parrick moved forward and hoisted the shield upright. The man underneath had an arrow through his chest. A look of bewilderment crossed his face as his mouth filled with blood. He was soon dead. Parrick did not know his name. He looked into the frightened eyes of the soldier next to him.

"It went through his shield. *It went right through Dant's shield.*"

Dant.

Parrick inspected the shield. The ruptured wood framed a neat diamond-shaped hole through the plating. What manner of man could put an arrow through a Jardian infantry shield? He looked down at the dead man again. The arrow had gone through the front of his breastplate and, by its depth of penetration, out through the back as well. He let go of the shield and moved back to Amondius, as the rider called again.

"After this circuit I will take two lives. I have many arrows."

Parrick did not doubt him for a moment.

"When he's done a half-circuit we move out," he said to Coln, then to Amondius, "If that is acceptable to you, Reverence?" He could not keep the sneer out of his voice, but Amondius either did not to notice or did not want to. He gave a curt nod. His two guards looked on with taut expressions. Parrick ignored them and turned back to Coln.

"Spear point defensive. We move fast. Perhaps he'll have no time to take aim. It's not easy shooting from horseback."

Coln looked pointedly back at the cart containing the wounded.

"Get two volunteers to stay with the cart and bring it on after. We'll have to gamble that he leaves them alone. I think he will. He's not interested in them."

Coln moved away.

"Reverence, do you wish to retrieve your horses?" Parrick asked. His Reverence did not wish to.

When the rider had done a half-circuit, a softly spoken order and the alacrity of fear quickly pulled the men into the new formation. At a jog they set out, eyes directed to where they last saw the rider.

He came from the opposite direction.

The horse, a huge grey with armoured flanks, crashed into them like an iron-shod ram. Before anyone could react, a sword flashed and a headless infantryman fell, his neck stump jetting blood. Parrick whirled as the head thudded to the ground next to him. It seemed to bounce as if in the slow drag of nightmare. Every detail of the dying face stood clear to him. He swung his gaze up at the rider into eyes devoid of pity, then the flank of the horse slammed him to the ground and he had to scrabble from under its hooves.

Someone was bellowing and tired men crashed against each other as they tried to bring their weapons to bear. After pulling himself clear of the flailing hooves, Parrick swore in disbelief when he saw the rider reach down and, with one hand, hoist one of the Bishop's guards by the back of his uniform. The man yelled and tried to cut back with his sword. The rider shook him like a child, then cut away his sword-arm as if trimming a piece of wood. Parrick tried to cut at the back leg of the horse as it poised to leap, but too late. The horse was gone. Over the heads of his soldiers. A figure in black clasped to its side, yelling as he waved the stump of his arm.

"He got Garton! He got Garton!"

Amondius back-handed the face of his remaining guard, then spun on Parrick.

"Is this how well your men fight!? Pathetic! We move now! Fast! Garton will keep him a while!"

Parrick measured the panic in the Bishop's expression and did not argue the point.

They set out at a run, the formation breaking. It felt horribly to Parrick like a run they had made from Habian's Pass – a rout. As he fought to keep his exhausted body in motion he wondered what the Bishop had meant about Garton, until he heard the screams.

Garton kept the rider busy long enough for them to make quarter of a league. The screams grew distant and finally stopped. Dread suffused Parrick and suddenly he found it easy to run again. He was coming. The rider was coming.

A soldier coughed and did a front flip in a wheel of blood. The fantastic impact of the arrow had burst his chest open. Pieces of broken doweling protruded between his shattered ribs.

"Who the... hell... is that?"

Amondius just looked at him.

"Be out of the woods soon!" yelled Coln. Then another soldier went down, spattering the trees as he spun. There came a yell from behind, full of cold fury.

"*Give them to me!*"

Abruptly, Parrick snapped. He grabbed Amondius and slammed him against a tree. The remaining guard kept running.

"Who is that!? You know! *Who is he?*"

Amondius's gaze fled in every direction. He wanted to run. Parrick held him. His gaze finally centred.

"It is... Hadrim," he gasped.

Parrick released him.

The Berserker Captain...

He felt a deep harsh sickness now, and knew the fear they all felt to be justified. The Berserker Captain; the greatest weapons master ever known, never defeated, terrifying in battle, the very author of the Jardian defeat at Habian's Pass. Parrick had only glimpsed him, being too busy trying to fight his way from that trap. But why was he here without his men? Why did he want the Bishop and his guards? He was about to ask, but Amondius pulled back and remembered himself.

"You will pay for this, Battle-captain! Release me!"

Parrick lost impetus and released his hold. Amondius pushed past and ran on. Parrick stood there panting until he caught sight of a pursuing flash of grey, then sprinted after his men.

The next arrow struck with the sound of a butcher's cleaver. Parrick saw Amondius' last guard go down as his leg buckled over shattered bone. The man hit the ground, rolled, then dragged himself upright and tried to follow, but fell again.

"Don't leave me!"

"Keep moving!" yelled Amondius.

The infantrymen needed no urging. Ahead, a break opened in the trees and beyond that lay the glittering promise of the sea. Behind them the guard's yells turned to screams.

"The boats, we have to get to the boats!"

The once-glorious Fourth came into the open in a ragged line, laboured up an acclivity, and at last gazed down on the beach. They came to a stumbling halt, the last of their strength draining from them. There were no boats here, and no ships to take them home.

"Keep moving! Get down to the beach! Tight circle and doubled shields!" Parrick lashed them with his words. They obeyed, all they had left was their discipline, their pride. They made the circle as the screaming in the forest became a strange ululation before halting terminally, as if the man had tried to sing. Forty men waited. Out of the forest came the rider, then up onto the rise above them.

"Give him to me!"

Parrick turned to Amondius.

"He is a great warrior. Yet he comes without his men and kills without mercy. Why? What have you done?"

"Shut up!" Amondius snapped viciously.

Parrick did not shut up.

"What crime did you commit?"

Amondius turned away.

Parrick turned from him and saw Coln watching. His lieutenant had his hand on his dagger, and Parrick knew that all he had to do was nod, and Amondius would be dead. He looked out to the rider and saw him notch another arrow to the string of that laminate bow.

Two shields?

He knew two shields would not be enough. More of his men would have to die to preserve the life of the Bishop. He frowned in thought. Enough was enough. Abruptly he turned his sword and cracked its pommel against the Bishop's head. Amondius dropped like a wet sack. Parrick sheathed his sword.

"This has gone on long enough," he said to the unconscious Bishop, then offered a silent prayer to gods he had ceased to believe in, and pushed past his men to walk out to meet Hadrim, the Berserker Captain.

The sand beneath Parrick's feet was almost white. What a

contrast his blood would make. At every step he expected an arrow to punch him from his feet, but in the end Hadrim lowered his bow and just watched. Once amongst the sea-thistles and clumps of grass he drew his sword, but held it by its blade just below the guard. Coming before Hadrim, he tossed the weapon to the ground.

"I come to offer to the Empire Ordanon the surrender of the Fourth Shield Infantry," he said.

Cold eyes observed him.

"You have Amondius."

"I do."

Hadrim looked out at the sea.

"Your ships are south of here."

"I wish to surrender, myself and my men."

The cold eyes returned to him.

"I do not want your surrender, Battle-captain. I want Amondius. Give him to me or die. I offer you this simple choice."

"What did he do?"

Hadrim stared at him for a long moment. When he finally replied his rage was tangible.

"What do they always do, these Clergy of yours? While we fought and died at the Pass they brought my people their God. Their God is harsh."

Parrick picked up his sword and resheathed it. That God had been with him all his life, and he had seen the beatings, the impalings and the burnings. He needed no further explanation. Without a word he returned to his men. When he got there, Coln eyed him expectantly.

"We go south," he told his lieutenant.

Coln looked pointedly down at Amondius.

"Leave him," said Parrick. "There might not be room on the ships."

THE PRICE OF PASSAGE

Keris McDonald

Troy was already burning when Peitho sought me out.

I was with the men assembled behind the barred gates of Priam's royal palace. We could hear screaming from the city outside, and we stood between the painted pillars of the courtyard with swords out and our shields resting on their rims between our feet, knowing that soon it would be our turn. If Hector had still been there to lead us there would have been no waiting; he would have led us out in a sortie against the Greeks and we would have fought to the end without fear. But Hector was dead, and not one of Priam's other sons could take his place. Priam himself stood upon his dais, girded up with the ornate breastplate and greaves he hadn't worn for decades. He looked stern and proud, but I had doubts that he could even walk under the weight of the bronze. Our King would make his last stand with his men, but it was an empty gesture. There were no heroes left in Troy.

Least of all me – one of Priam's acknowledged by-blows, certainly, and no waste of space in a fight, but no leader of men. You have to be legitimate to be a Prince of Troy. But I'd been there when Hector fought on the battlefield. I'm proud of that, and will be until my last breath. He'd counted me as a friend, and a brother under the bronze. Yet when he fell in single combat to that brute Achilles I'd lost all favour in court, even as the fighting heart went out of Troy. They'd put me to sentry duty with a trumpet on the great walls for weeks. Now I hefted the sweaty grip of my sword and inhaled the scent of smoke, knowing that I would die forgotten and unremarked, just another palace guard slaughtered by the invaders.

Then a hand descended on my arm and I looked round to see the wide-eyed face of the lady Peitho as she tried to draw me aside into the shadows.

"Misenus, come with me."

I didn't obey at once. I should have, I suppose. Peitho was the high priestess of the Temple of Aphrodite, and married to Priam's brother Anchises to boot; which made her my aunt as well as one of the most authoritative noblewomen in the city, though I don't think she'd ever deigned to talk to me before that moment. Hector was the only member of the Royal Family who'd ever had time for me. I shook my head once.

"Come *on*, Misenus." She was insistent. A handsome woman, though not young anymore, she was wrapped in a dark cloak as if it were winter, not a sweaty night in the height of summer. "There is something you must do for Troy."

My gut clenched. I had a nasty feeling I knew what it was she wanted from me. But what choice did I have, after all? I cast a swift, despairing look over at Priam and his entourage, wishing I were able to speak to him. Then I slung my shield on its shoulder-strap and followed Peitho from the courtyard.

She took me under the pillared arcade and then through the winding corridors of the palace, ducking into narrow passages to avoid the press of panicked servants and tense soldiers hurrying back and forth. Very quickly I saw that we were heading for the women's quarters and my heart sank further. If the cursed Greeks broke in now, it would be a shameful place to die. I wanted to be out at the front gate, with my King, when the final blow fell.

As we crossed the Women's Courtyard I glanced up to the skyline and the red and glowing smoke that obscured the stars. I saw a four or five figures up there; women with bows, each waiting with one knee propped on the low wall.

The priestesses of Artemis? Shouldn't they be beseeching her aid in their shrine?

For a moment I slowed to a halt. "What are they doing up there?"

Peitho turned. "Ignore them," she said in a low voice, her hands sketching glyphs of urgency. "They are covering our escape."

Our escape? The words were enough to startle me out of my hesitation, and I followed her in confusion. Not into the Royal Family's chambers as I'd expected, nor even into the Temple of Hera – from which I could hear a buzz of weeping and prayer, even though everyone knew that the Great Goddess had sided with our enemies –

but down a flight of stone steps and under a low door that cut into the rock of the hill itself. I thought I knew every inch of our walled city, but I struggled to recall what this place was. Beyond the door stood an unfurnished chamber whose blistered walls bore the remnants of red paint as dark as the blood of bulls, and huddled inside was a cluster of people, all wrapped in travelling cloaks, their wan faces staring at us as we entered.

I peered at each by the light of the single oil lamp they sheltered. Prince Anchises was the first I recognized – younger than his brother Priam but long taken by some illness that had weakened his limbs and left his head nodding senselessly; he crouched on the floor, drooling into a fold of his cloak. His son Aeneas, barely a man in years and still lanky as a stalk of fennel, stood protectively over him, spear in hand. Aeneas' girl-bride Creusa, daughter of Priam, pressed up behind his shoulder, her eyes huge, her newborn swaddled in her arms. Iulus … that was the mite's name.

So, all Peitho's closest family, then.

"What do you want of me?" I growled, though I knew – or thought I did. She wanted me to put them all to the sword, and so spare them captivity and rape and slavery; the endless agony of living as the property of the gloating Greeks. At least they would go down to Hades together if they died now. I could understand her desire.

"I want you to lead us out of the city."

"Lead you?"

"There's a tunnel beneath the walls. We can get out. It emerges at Mount Ida. I know the way but…"

I fear my jaw hung open. "Beyond the siege armies?" I said, thinking, *Mount Ida? That's twenty miles away!* But despite my incredulity I was already feeling relieved, because I had little stomach for killing women and dotards and children. At least *that* was not the task prescribed for me.

"It has always been known about in the priesthood, but we had forgotten where the entrance was." Peitho was impatient, her gold earrings and hair-beads jingling as she jerked her head.

"But you know now?"

"Last night." She drew herself up proudly, the malachite on her eyelids flashing. "Aphrodite Skotia showed me. In a dream."

Skotia meant The Dark One. Rumours of a Dark Aphrodite had trickled out to us men, but it was a women's cult that I knew almost nothing of. I felt my spine creep. "You told King Priam, then? So that we could evacuate the City? Save everybody?"

"No. You don't understand." I could see her contempt and her need for my help at war in her. She sighed, but made her voice smooth; "The way is narrow, and deadly, and there has always been a price to pay. You couldn't take a whole people down into the darkness. But a small band... they might get through." She laid her hand on my bare forearm and stared into my eyes; her own seemed almost alight. "Troy will fall, Misenus. The gods have willed it so. But my son is of the royal bloodline – the last Trojan hero. He will save our race. He *must* survive. You *must* aid us."

"It is my command, as a Prince of Troy," Aeneas put in. "Do as she says, Misenus." It would have sounded better if his voice had not cracked. I remembered the incident a few years back when the boy had tried to sneak out to fight at Hector's side below the walls, and Peitho had risked her own life to run out and drag him home, to his immense shame.

I cast him a less than deferential glance and saw Creusa brush her lips across her baby's shadowy fluff of hair. "Please," she mouthed at me, her eyes like dark stars in the pallor of her face.

My half-sister. Her child.

And outside this room my city was burning, my people were dying. I should be there to defend them. But I had never married nor had children of my own. Who was there left to fight for, other than those who stood before me?

"Right," I growled, ignoring my feeling of unease as I surrendered my judgment. I was pledged to serve the Royal Family, after all. "Where is this entrance, then?"

"Over there. The one on the left." Peitho pointed toward the back wall.

The little group parted to reveal three great disks of stone upon the floor. I remembered this room at last, then, though I hadn't been here in years. It was an old storage chamber, unused because it was too damp, situated under the shrine of Persephone Kore, the Maiden of Spring. "Those are just grain pits," I said.

"Lift the lid," said she, inexorable.

Somewhere outside, something big – a temple roof perhaps – thundered to the ground. I could hear the battle chant of some phalanx of soldiers, too faintly to tell if it was ours or the Greeks'. "Give me that spear," I grunted to Aeneas. "And lend a hand, Prince of Troy."

It was clear why they'd called me to help them; even with both of us levering at the stone it was heavy work moving it aside. The gap this revealed was circular, and dark as the mouth of Cronos. A dank smell came out of it, and when I peered down into the pit I could just make out a reflective glint.

"Have you a torch?" We had no hope of getting away underground, I thought, unless we had a source of light.

They had, it turned out – each of them had a small travelling bundle stacked close by, and Aeneas lit a torch from the lamp. *Well prepared, then*, I thought. I thrust it down into the hole at my feet and saw the flames mirrored back to me from a circle of standing water.

"It's nothing but a flooded pit," I told them grimly.

"Get down in the water," Peitho said, then added when she saw my expression; "Lower me first, if you are afraid."

"You're that sure of your dream?" I demanded. But I was sworn to my duty.

It didn't, however, make me an idiot; the water looked to be about a man's drop below me, and it was impossible to tell how deep it was, so I wasn't going down there in armour. I pictured piercing the surface and being dragged straight down by the weight of my bronze, disappearing without a sound into the depths of a well, and that premonition made me feel queasy. I untied my greaves and breastplate and left them stacked with my helm and shield, though I kept my sword scabbarded at my belt.

Easing over the edge of the pit, I hung at arms' length and then dropped into the inky water.

It proved to be only thigh-deep, but horribly cold. My balls tried to crawl back up into my body as I tested the slimy floor with my sandals. Overhead, faces half lit by the flames peered down at me, and I clenched my teeth not just against the chill but the sensation as of something clammy brushing up against my soul.

This is how it must look to the Dead, peering out of Hades.

"Look around," said Peitho. Her voice echoed weirdly off the rock walls.

I could do very little looking, for it was all but pitch-black down here, but I groped obediently around the circumference of the pit. And I made a discovery; there was a gap perhaps a handspan high between water and wall on one side – a lip of stone that might be the lintel of some low door. My probing toes found a hole in the wall, as broad as my shoulders, which went all the way to the floor.

"There may be a tunnel-mouth here," I admitted. "Pass that spear down, and the torch."

I caught the torch before it hit the water. With the shaft of the spear I probed under the rock and found that the gap went back at least that far.

"Gods," I muttered under my breath, knowing what I must do. "I'll try to crawl through," I called up.

Then, turning my shoulder first for a better fit through the narrow way, I dropped to my knees, whispered a prayer to Persephone Despoina whose realm I had entered, and slid into the gap, keeping only my face and the torch-head above the water's gelid surface, and thrusting the latter ahead as I slithered through. The flames licked the rocky roof, spilling black smoke to half-blind me. If truth be told I was glad of the irritation; it kept me from thinking about the horror of my situation, and what might be waiting beyond that narrow seam of light. And at least the billowing flame promised that there was air enough for me to breathe.

Suddenly the torch's head was no longer scraping rock. I pushed forward with my feet and slithered like a newborn from that tunnel into a wider pool, and almost immediately found the floor rising beneath me. Wading out onto a bank of mud, I turned in a circle and could make out the shadowed recesses of an irregular cavern. Beyond the small pool the floor seemed to be dry. My torch-flames flickered sideways, betraying a breeze that must be coming from somewhere.

I left the burning torch stuck in the bank when I waded back into the tunnel.

It took longer than I would have liked to lower everyone and all our baggage down to me, one at a time, and for me to show them the way under that low lintel. My shield barely fit through the gap, and old Anchises had to be pushed like a reluctant ram fording a stream, but hardest of all was trying to keep the baby above the cold water so that he wouldn't drown or betray us all with his screams. I had to drag Creusa through last while she held him – and by the time I hauled them onto the bank I was shivering with cold.

Creusa tucked the infant info her dress, muffling its howls, and I wrung out her cloak to get rid of the weight of water. Aeneas had lit another couple of torches, sending light dancing up the looming walls. When I looked around the cavern for a second time I saw the faces.

Though the cavern looked to be hewn from raw and natural rock, it was painted with figures – right up into the shadowed cleft of the roof far overhead, far bigger than life, sprawling at impossible angles, their outlines depicted in scrawls of red and black. Robed men and women, and bulls, and lions, and strange men with the heads of beasts but the wings of birds. It was impossible to make out what their stiff gestures were meant to convey. Scattered between the pictures were the slit-like gapes of niches that looked as if they probably once held bodies, though most were far out of reach from the floor.

"What is this place?" I rasped. "It's no escape tunnel."

"It was a temple to Persephone," said Peitho. Her own tones were low and even. Almost too calm, I thought; like a woman telling her child to stand still and not run from a watching wolf. "Before that, a temple to a race of gods older than the Olympians, it is said. The caves wind for miles. But there is a way through. It just means going… down."

"And you're sure of the way, are you?" I was mentally rehearsing my other option – returning to the burning city overhead and facing my fate among the howling, bloodstained Greeks. We could hear nothing of the conflict now. It was like another world down here.

She turned her black glare upon me. "I know the way. You just have to see us safely through, Misenus."

Something in that look made me shiver in my clammy clothes. She was a priestess after all, and they are uncanny people. *Safe from what?* I wanted to ask, but the words wouldn't ascend my throat. It might be best not to frighten Creusa with speculation, anyway.

"Lead on, Priestess."

"I will show the way, but you need to go first." She reached into the wet hempen sack at her feet. "And you will need this."

What she drew out was a sword which she presented reverently to me in both hands. Even in the torchlight there was something strange about its colour, so unlike the warm bronze of normal weapons. But when I took hold I found it was nowhere near as heavy as the lead nor as light as the tin it resembled, and the blade was honed to a fighting edge. I hefted it, testing the balance. It felt a shade light, but good in my hand.

"What is this made from?" I demanded.

"It fell from the stars. Believe me, you'll need it for what we face."

I looked round to see if the others were listening. All were staring at us, even Anchises, and I could see them shivering in their steaming clothes. If we sat here too long we would seize up.

"Come on," I said, standing. "We move on now. No more than one torch, Aeneas. Show us this path, Priestess."

We descended through a crack in the bedrock, finding carved and worn steps beneath our feet. I took the lead, as instructed. Peitho, the stronger of the two women, insisted on taking her sleeping grandson and wore him in a cloth sling at her breast, while the torch she carried illuminated my feet from behind. Aeneas came next, shouldering his father's weight whenever the old man's strength or balance failed him, leaving Creusa to bring up the rear carrying her pack clutched to her like the infant she missed.

We went down. And down. Further than I would have thought possible, and certainly further than a descent from the highest towers of the city, dropping near-vertically into the bowels of the Earth. I had heard that the Underworld was a cold and misty place, but it actually felt a little warmer by the time we left off the descent and moved out into a level chamber where the first choice of ways was presented. Peitho scanned the walls, which were still painted and carved, and picked a passage without hesitation, waving me onward.

There were several such choices over the many hours that followed; the bedrock of the Plain of Troy seemed as riddled with holes as a wasp-eaten apple. Little rivulets of water pooled in places, so we never lacked for drink, though I wondered uneasily if the tunnels flooded after a storm. We rested and dozed at times, before pressing onward. The paintings and the empty loculi were our only true waymarks. Peitho always, I worked out, chose a tunnel with a goddess depicted above it. Sometimes the way was fair, with height and breadth enough for even me to stride upright. Other times I had to turn sideways between two faces of rock, or crouch and shuffle on my hams under a wedged boulder. Aeneas dropped to the back, toiling beneath his father's arm, and I was impressed by the youth's patience. He had the hardest role in our little caravan.

Until we reached the first cleft, that is. The light from Peitho's torch suddenly failed to illuminate the path before me, and I stopped, using my toes to discern the lip of the darkness that split the tunnel from side to side and ran up into the walls. It was a chasm far too deep to see down, though I could hear the trickle of running water below. We lined up on the edge of the drop, peering across. On the far side the tunnel continued, and a robed and crowned woman with staring eyes decorated the lintel, hands raised to display a wheat-sheaf and a lit torch. Using the spear we measured the gap – it was almost exactly a spear-length across to that side.

"Do we have to?" Creusa asked.

"This is the path," Peitho said. "There is no other way."

Well, I was trained for this sort of thing. Shedding my heavy shield, I backed up, took a flying leap and landed successfully – except that, invisible from my launch position, the tunnel that side dipped and my bronze helm smacked into the roof with a sound like a gong. I felt the impact and when I next blinked my eyes open I was lying flat on my back on the stone, my shoulders one huge ache.

"Misenus! Get up!" Aeneas' voice sounded angry. It was just fear, I suppose.

"I'm having a rest, my prince," I rasped. "All's well." Then, under my breath, "And you can go feed the crows."

Once I was fairly sure I hadn't broken any bones, I rolled carefully up onto my knees and faced the others. My head was still ringing. Their flame-lit tunnel looked like the mouth of an oven.

"Misenus," said Peitho clearly. "I will have to throw the baby. Are you able to catch?"

I nodded, then wished I hadn't because my neck hurt, but, "No!" cried Creusa.

"Be quiet," Aeneas muttered absently, his gaze straying to his father. I could see he was wondering how far he could throw the old man. "We must not be cowards. We're Trojans, remember?"

Peitho pushed Creusa back out of the way with one arm. Unhitching the cloth bag containing the swaddled Iulus from around her neck, she swung it back and forth by the long handle, counting down. At "One!" she released and the whole lot came sailing over the black gulf, accompanied by a wail of protest from its contents. I reached out with one hand and snatched it from mid-air. Easy catch. And as I clasped the baby to my breastplate, something pale came rushing up out of the cleft at my feet.

I think I only saw the thing in time because it *glowed* – like a dead dog on a midden heap, back in the days before we ate all the City's dogs and cats. It had feathered wings that trailed black smoke, but it used long nails to scramble up over the rocks, its nose a beak like a vulture's and its mouth gaping impossibly wide against a bony chest. Its eyes were huge and white, like something blind, *and I could see the rock through its hands.*

And as the creature came I heard it breathe my name: *"Misenus!"*

All those things I recalled afterward. In the flurry of the moment I simply struck out with my strange sword, off-handed – because of course I had caught the baby's bag in my right – and off-balance but with the advantage of height, and still accurate. The blade sheared through its foul skull and I felt the bite of a blade not as if I'd struck flesh and bone, but as if I'd hit a ripe puffball fungus. Barely any resistance. And like an over-ripe fungus, the creature exploded into a dirty smoke under the impact. I was surprised when I swung through and hit the rock; surprised again when the blade sparked as it jarred.

Then it was gone, and the others were shouting, and I was standing there with the child aloft in one hand and cold sweat running off me, wondering if I'd imagined the creature.

"What – by the gods – was that?" Aeneas yelled, disabusing me.

I shook my head. The smell of burned bone was in my nose. "Quiet! There may be more!" But through we stood staring down into the abyss, there was no further movement from below. I shifted to keep an eye down the new tunnel too, though there was nothing visible but blackness. I didn't even have a torch on this side. The baby in the crook of my arm wailed.

"We must cross," Peitho said firmly.

That took some doing. I had to put the protesting Iulus down on the ground out of the way as they tossed all the bundles and my shield over for me to catch. Aeneas threw Creusa – who was light – and then his mother, who was not, into my arms. Then Aeneas and I gripped the spear between us, his end braced high over his head, mine much lower, and we slid Anchises on a makeshift sling down the length of the wood into reach, where the women grabbed his clothes and limbs and hauled him up onto the rock. Last of all, Aeneas took a running jump as I had, but he crouched on the landing so that he did not dash his brains out and tumbled instead, undignified but also unhurt.

As everyone dusted themselves off, I checked the edge of my sword in the torchlight and was surprised to see that it hadn't folded over or buckled against the rock. It had taken no harm but a tiny nick in the cutting edge. Peitho took charge of the baby again, warding Creusa off with a glare and jiggling the child up and down as she walked back and forth. For some reason that seemed to soothe the boy.

Creusa and Aeneas were trying to get Anchises to eat and drink something to keep his strength up when I pulled Peitho aside a little. "What was that creature?" I asked in a low voice. "How did it know my name?"

She locked eyes with me, and I sensed her hesitation.

"Tell me," I urged.

"They are called the Eaters of Dust," she admitted. "It is said that their jaws are broken so they cannot chew; thus they are always hungry. They are the daemons of a people long before our own. Or perhaps the spirits of their Dead." She shrugged. "We don't know."

"The *Dead?*" I whispered.

"We are descending to the Underworld, are we not?"

"You didn't say that our route lies through Hades!" It was important to keep my voice down, but my expression made up for my lack of volume, I think.

"Why do you think this path was forgotten? Only those with a great need, and a great destiny laid upon them, would dare come this way."

"And that's what the goddess told you, was it? Well, I'd love to hear more about our *great destiny*. I hope it amounts to more than dying in a hole far from the sunlight."

"Not your destiny." Her lip curled. "My son's. My grandson's. The Royal House of Troy."

I laughed then, because what else was there to do? "It will be an honour to be a footnote in their legend," I said, shaking my head.

She did not blink. "Yes, it will be."

I considered how much I disliked the uncanniness of priests. What had it been like for Anchises, married to her? Was she the one who had eaten the strength out of him?

"Now," she said, "keep your eyes open and your sword ready. If an Eater of Dust catches hold of you it will tear your soul out of your body. And there will be more of them ahead of us."

There were. Many more, slipping out of grave niches and dropping from the roof and rushing us at junctions. Luckily for us they always came from ahead, because the strange sword was the only blade that could touch them. After I saw a set of claws rake through the bronze of my shield as if it didn't exist, missing my arm by a hair but leaving no tear in the metal, I abandoned the shield as a useless weight that would only slow me down when I needed to dodge, and passed it back up the line for Aeneas to carry if he cared to.

"*You coward, Misenus*," the daemons told me.

Yes, they talked. Horrible, whispered mockery that always addressed me by name. "*Bastard-born*," one gloated; "*Son of a King, yet no Prince.*" It was a pleasure to hack off its head and watch it turn to smoke.

In fact, as fighting went, this was almost easy. None of the press and push of the battlefield, or the heavy shuddering impacts that jarred every bone and joint, or the smell of men's spilled bowels and blood. All I had to do was stay wary, twist out of reach of those slashing claws, and strike back fast. It was almost like sparring in the courtyard with other idle warriors; swordplay as a game.

"*You deserted your King, your City and your people, you piece of shit.*" I couldn't tell if the others heard its voice, or if those words were for my ears only.

"Koprophagos!" I grunted, shearing it in half below the ribs, back-handed.

Onward through the labyrinth of tunnels. Climbing, jumping clefts – none so wide as the first, thank the gods – pulling my companions up steep inclines while keeping an eye on the tunnel at my back.

"Neither children nor pride – nothing to stand and die for as a man should."

The fighting was easier than the pressing on. I rose with joy to meet each foe. Until training betrayed me and, dodging back from a blow, I flung out my left arm to parry with a shield that wasn't there and those wispy, smoking claws slashed through my arm at the elbow. I felt no pain, just a shock, and it didn't stop me stabbing the daemon through the chest within a heartbeat. But as I stepped back into guard position, panting through bared teeth, I realised that I could not feel that arm.

I expected it to be severed when I looked down. Pain can be strangely tardy in battle. Yet my arm was still there – and to all appearances uninjured. Only, I could no longer lift my hand, my shoulder felt cold and my whole forearm thrummed like a vibrating gong.

"Kunops!" I swore.

We rested after that in a small chamber that looked like it had been hollowed out by swirling water, crouched there on the stone mouthing dried mutton strips now slimy from their dunking. Anchises looked on the verge of collapse. I wondered how long we'd been travelling. Well over a day already, I guessed, and maybe closer to two. While I kept watch over the single exit, Creusa busied herself fixing my arm to my chest in a sling, so that I would at least not be thrown out by the swing of its dead weight.

I was trying not to dwell on what it meant to lose the use of my arm, should it never recover. To be a half-warrior; a half man.

"I am glad you are leading us," Creusa said to me in a low voice, breaking into my fugue. "We wouldn't have lived this long without you."

It did not feel as if I was leading anyone. Just blundering onward under Peitho's goad, like an ox pulling a cart. "Thank me when we get out," I grunted. I did not say, *if*, because I didn't want to frighten her.

"Hector always spoke highly of you," she added, her slim fingers working the torn cloth. "He was my favourite brother, you know."

"He was the best of us," I said, my throat tightening.

"He told me that he'd rather call *you* Brother than he would Paris."

I could make no articulate reply to that, though a rough sound came out of my mouth. On the surface it was not a great compliment; Paris, after all, had doomed the lot of us by his inability to keep his hands off another man's wife. And he'd never been much of a warrior. But for Hector to openly prefer a bastard over his own legitimate flesh-and-blood… If he had not been such an irreproachable man, it would have been considered shameful.

"Do you think we will see him here in the Underworld?" Creusa looked up at me through her lashes. "I miss him so much."

"Hector dwells in the Elysian Fields, not here in this hole," I answered firmly. "We will see him when we die, and not before." Which might not be too long, I thought.

Soon after, we set off again – Aeneas still gamely carrying my shield as well as supporting his father, I noted – and began to hear something other than our own scuffing steps for once. It was a distant sigh that came and went regularly like human breath, only slower and longer. I paused to let Peitho catch me up and cocked my head.

"What is that?"

She pulled a face. "We pass the Gates of Tartarus on this path. All of you," she turned to address our little group, "from now on, keep absolutely silent. It is vital not to disturb those imprisoned down here."

The Gates of Tartarus? Dismay was a clammy hand wrapped around my belly; only a fool sticks his nose into the business of the gods. But it was too late to go back now.

Our tunnel came suddenly up to rock face that stretched up over our heads into the darkness of some unseen roof. Our single torch did little to illuminate its dimensions, nor anything beyond a dark vault of an arch in the stone ahead of us, far broader than our own tunnel, that dropped steeply away into the earth. The soughing noise was far stronger here, and accompanied by a breeze tainted with rot and snake-piss. I could feel it stirring my sweat-stiffened locks of hair, raising the gooseflesh on my skin not because it was cold but because it revulsed. I found myself wondering if it really was the breath of some great entity we were hearing – some Titan from the ages before Man – and I knew that I did not want to see what such an entity might look like.

Peitho laid a hand on my arm and pointed urgently, away from that portal to a narrow crack in the rock to my right. Tumbled rocks made a staircase of sorts leading up, though the goddess symbol hacked on the first boulder had devolved to nothing more than a notched triangle. I nodded and took a step that way. That was the moment the breeze abruptly reversed direction, as if all the foul air round us were being sucked back into cavernous lungs. And our guttering pine torch went out.

I heard a snuffling wail; I assumed at first it was Creusa but as it went on I realised it was the old prince, Anchises. The darkness was absolute; a pitchy black in which nothing could be discerned except the blue-green imprints that the torchlight had left dancing in my eyeballs. I retreated to a clear spot away from the others, searching instinctively for space to act, looking from side to side as I listened to them bump and fumble and hiss, "Light it!" in near-panic. Straining eyes and ears until the former spilled tears down my cheeks and the latter were thudding to the sound of my own pulse.

And there – yes: a glimmer in the darkness, its unholy light most unwelcome. A tiny luminescent figure, growing larger as it flapped and stumbled toward us. And others following.

"*Hector is dead. Why do you deserve to live, Misenus?*"

"*Betrayer of Troy!*"

"*You will die down here, Misenus. You will die.*"

I thank the gods that the Eaters of Dust shone with that corpse-glow. It was the only thing that allowed me to fight them in the dark. I lashed out with my sword, I ducked away, I struck again – unable to judge how far away they were, unable to see my feet on the uneven floor.

Their half-flesh barely slowed my blade. Somehow I struck down, one, two, three of the things, all before an ember-pot was recovered and kindled to a flame for the torch. The spitting flames seemed uncomfortably bright at first. We stared round at each other.

Anchises' legs had collapsed beneath him. I couldn't tell if it was exhaustion or if he had taken a low blow from one of the Eaters of Dust, but the result was the same. Abandoning my heavy shield at last, Aeneas had to hoist his father onto his back in order for us to proceed up the boulder-choked defile.

Mercifully we met no more foes coming down toward us. What we did have to contend with was a climb so steep that we'd have had to resort to hands at the best of times. Now I only had one arm, and I did not dare sheathe the sword the priestess had loaned me, while Aeneas laboured under Anchises' weight. Creusa helped by pulling at her father-in-law when she could. Peitho had the baby and the torch to take care of. All the while that horrible breath gusted around us, pushing and then sucking to make our progress even more precarious. And the ascent went on and on; a gruelling climb from the very roots of the mountain, I imagined. Our thighs were burning as we finally staggered out into a circular chamber.

It was the first cave in the system that looked man-made to me. Perfectly round, and domed – and with no door out. Only a series of low apertures around the circle at floor-level. Many scores of those in fact – but each a black crawlspace less than groin-high. *Like dog kennels*, thought I, and braced myself anew for something rushing out of them to attack us.

"Which way?" Aeneas asked. The echoes shifted eerily.

Peitho's face was closed and blank. "I don't know yet." She started pacing the circumference of the chamber, holding her torch to the walls, and I moved closer to intercept any lunge from those dark holes. It was then that I noticed that above each aperture was a slab of rock ready to drop and block it, each balanced at an angle on nubs on stone. A few seemed to have fallen already. But aside from these stones the flickering light revealed only a grey, even surface that showed no sign of paint or sculpture anywhere. All was as pristine as the inside of a sealed tomb.

The hanging slabs unnerved me, I admit. Anyone crawling beneath one when it slipped would have their spine broken.

"What do we do, Mother?" Aeneas demanded. "Which one?"

She turned to face us and shook her head. "I cannot tell." There was an oddness in her expression – a masklike quality – that made me uneasy.

"Is this a dead end?" I asked.

"No. There is a way out."

"What did the goddess say?" Creusa urged.

"She said that the House of Troy would go on, if we obeyed her. She said that we must be prepared to give everything."

"Then we must try every door." Aeneas sounded ragged. He'd sunk to his knees next to where his father lay; the lad was exhausted. "One of them will lead outside."

"Quite so," said Peitho meekly, jiggling the baby in her embrace.

"Misenus can't crawl with only one arm," said Creusa doubtfully. "And we will have to drag your father, Aeneas." She held out a hand for the torch. "I will look first."

"No," I growled. "What if you meet something down there?"

"You can't hold your sword in your teeth, Misenus," she said, trying to smile. Hitching her skirts up on her waistband she knelt before the nearest portal and thrust the torch in to take a quick look, before crawling on hands and knees, pushing it forward. I pushed up to the rock face, ready to dive in and grab her ankles at a moment's notice. Peitho watched me with lidded eyes.

"It's just a tomb," came Creusa's muffled voice, and then the soles of her sandals appeared as she wriggled out backward. Her mouth trembled. "No bones though. It's nothing but a stone box."

Taking a deep breath she turned to the next hole along and lined up to crawl inside. I scored a scratch with my sword-tip on the stone of the dead-end. It would not do to lose track of where we'd been.

"*The Underworld demands a life, Misenus.*"

With that whispered challenge the first Eaters of Dust oozed through the gap by which we'd entered and flapped across the floor. A dozen of the things – no: a score and more, in no hurry now, but shuffling and creeping toward us. I hefted my sword, feeling the cold fire of desperation ignite in my belly, and stepped to put myself between the daemons and the living. The chamber was too open and there were too many of them now for me to have any chance of dodging injury. If they rushed me it would be over in moments.

"No good!" came Creusa's voice faintly. Then at the corner of my eye I saw Peitho dart at the rock, hand's raised. There was a grinding rush and a thump of stone on stone, and I all but forgot the

Eaters of Dust in my horrified realisation that Peitho had pushed the stone door off its stops and trapped the girl in the loculus.

"Mother?" asked Aeneas, his voice rising to a childish screech.

"What in the gods' –!" I yelled.

The ground shook. We are used to the Earthshaker's moods, in Troy; I recognized the danger immediately. But I'd never seen this happen before: a sliver of light – golden and burning and straight as the arrow of Apollo himself – shot across the cavern floor from a different portal, and where it struck an Eater of Dust, the daemon dissolved into ash.

"There!" screamed Peitho! "There! Go now, Aeneas! Run! Run!"

Yelling, falling over each other, dragging Anchises, they bundled under the low doorway. I brought up the rear as the Eaters of Dust flung themselves around the walls and scrabbled up into the dome in an effort to escape the ray of deadly light. I crawled in backward, bashing my knuckles raw as I clenched the sword hilt and pushed my weight along the narrow passage on the same hand, scraping my shoulders and head against the low roof.

And then there was space over me, and room to rise up on my knees and turn, and light all around me – the golden light of evening shining into a westward-facing cave on a mountainside. The heat in the air and the smell of vegetation was almost overpowering, and the light seemed blinding. As I blinked the tears from my eyes I made out a crudely carved statue that looked like the Great Mother, standing in a basin of grain. A cave-shrine then – there are several such famous grottos on Mount Ida, which is sacred to Hera. We must have come up through a crack at the rear of the cavern. For a moment I stood numb with relief; then I staggered in Peitho's direction, dropping the damned sword so that I could grab at her. But she jerked out of my clumsy grip, leaving torn strands of hair between my fingers.

"What did you do that for?" I shouted. "Why did you trap her?"

"Idiot!" Her scathing tone washed over my outrage as cold water dousing a fire. "Do you think I had any choice? The old gods are jealous, Misenus! They are dark and cruel and they always require blood. No one passes through that place without making a sacrifice. It is the price they demand!"

"But – *Creusa!* Your daughter-in-law?"

"Who else?" Her eyes flashed fire. She stood trembling with righteous passion, the baby pressed tight to her breast. "A royal daughter of Priam, to buy the lives of the King's last heirs! My son and my grandson both live, Misenus, and the line of Troy will live with them! This blood will go on and rise to its destined greatness!"

"Fuck your royal line!" I raged. "Fuck you and your son and the whole House of Troy! I hope the Furies pursue you all to the ends of the Earth!" I made another lunge toward her but Aeneas got in the way and grappled me backward, so that I had to break away as the only alternative to battering the boy.

"Don't be such a simpleton, Misenus," said Peitho. "Your base birth is showing. One girl's life is as nothing before the march of a hero's destiny."

I would have answered her, but the hot blood was rushing through my left arm for the first time, a prickling agony. I found that I could flex my fingers again, and I hurriedly tore off the sling. The golden light licked my cold flesh like a cat.

"I'm going back in," I snarled, casting about me for the discarded sword. "If she's still alive I will reach her."

"Really?" Peitho almost laughed. "How will you fight off the Eaters of Dust? How will you lift the stone? This sunlight is all that is keeping us alive right now. Will you really descend back into Hades?"

I swallowed. She spoke a terrible sense, I knew. What chance had one man against the abyssal hordes? I couldn't bear the thought of returning to that chthonic darkness, but that only made my guilt worse. I couldn't help but picture Creusa trapped in her rocky box, panting for air in the tarry blackness, unable to turn, just drumming her feet against the stone and screaming for help. For us to save her. Knowing herself, sooner or later, abandoned. How long would it take her to die? Would the daemons come through the rocks to seize her or would they let her perish of suffocation or thirst? Would her agony and terror please the foul gods of the underworld?

How long would she hope for me to save her?

I found I was praying that she was already dead.

"You unspeakable bitch," I groaned, leaning forward to retch. "You *and* your whore-goddess."

"I will pray Aphrodite Skotia forgives your blasphemy," Peitho said coolly, "because we are not safe yet and you are still needed. There are Greeks around here – see how the offerings are fresh? We must head out."

"And you," I said, fixing Aeneas with a look of loathing. "You're such a coward that you'll leave your own wife?"

"Better his wife," said Peitho, as Aeneas just goggled at me, his face grey, "than his father and his son. Now come on; we go higher up and eastward from here."

"Fuck you," I whispered, my hands on my knees. I couldn't even look her in the face any more. I didn't dare go back into the dark. There wasn't even any point; the gods had claimed their due and the greatest of heroes couldn't rescue a soul from Hades, not even Orpheus his Eurydice. I would die before I laid a hand on the slab of her living tomb.

I also knew that if I did walk away I would never spend a day or a night without picturing her trapped in her crypt, crying for me and her husband and her mother-in-law to come back. Black spots swung before my eyes.

"Well then," said Peitho, as if I was a thing of enormous tedium to her. "We go, Aeneas." Iulus gave a little hiccupping sob, as if he understood that he was motherless now and was trying to be brave.

I watched them go, though my eyes were glazed. *My cousin*, I thought bitterly. *My aunt and uncle.* I would not lift a finger to save them if the whole army of the Greeks were waiting outside in the mountain meadow.

My sister. Oh gods, my poor sister.

The truth was that I hated myself more than I hated Peitho.

My nephew. Closest of kin left to me. A helpless baby. Who would defend him for Creusa, if the Greeks came with their spears and swords?

With a groan of defeat I straightened up, tightened my grip on the sword-hilt and walked out into the fading sun, knowing that I had not escaped the torments of Tartarus, nor ever would.

SUMMONER

Danie Ware

I can see them coming.

The valley is filled with them, like a seething dark fog that rolls in off the water. Their numbers are huge, yet their movement is soundless – impossible that so large a force could move that silently.

I stand above them, on the black stone tower of the old keep. The wind in the mountain pass is cold, though I cannot feel it, and the flag snaps and flutters. Below me, the night-guards pace the long walls; I sense their fear. I do not have command of this small and outmatched resistance, but I have the experience. And, despite those who hate me, my night-vision is the best we possess.

And I can see them.

I can see them all.

I wonder if they know I'm here: Kadarr, he who Summoned a Reider as a young man and pleaded for military prowess, pleaded to be the single best warrior this world has ever seen. And the Reider answered me – they always do – it gifted me my wish. But there's a price, there's always a price. Six hundred years later I am still fighting, an eternity of war.

I am cursed, say some – but I am the thing that now stands between the soft, pale skin of the city, and the heave and writhe of the incoming army.

I hear voices. On the walls below me, a second, defiant flag is being raised. The defenders are proud and stand strong. I respect them: their discipline is good, despite their fear and despite the fact that not a tenth of them have seen real combat. And why should they have done? There have been no Summoners for generations; the city has been at peace, and has lined her streets with luxuriance and wealth...

The dark roll of the incoming force stops.

It's out of arrow-range, yet close enough to taunt. And I know its commander – she's almost as old as I am.

She will wait for the dawn...

And then we will die.

"There's nothing there," Captain Sharika had told me. She's the commander of this small guard force, and she'd stood, arms folded, in her torch-lit fabric tent. Her skin is fine and dark; her armour lamellar, strong and padded and painted in elaborate designs. "We're chasing bandits," she'd said. "Not rumours."

I had stood unmoving. "Are you calling me a liar, Captain?"

"No." Her answer had been quick, and she'd stepped back – but she'd not relented. "But I have orders."

My armour is older, leather over linen. It makes me oddly fictional, part-icon and part-myth. I bear my helm under my arm and sometimes, when I walk through the camp, the soldiers come and stare at me.

"The force is large, and moving for the pass," I'd told her. "We defend the keep."

"We don't have enough warriors to defend the keep."

That, at least, is true. Even now, they're spaced too thin and only half the engines have crews.

"We defend the keep, Captain," I'd said. "We send a runner, and we buy the city time to mobilise."

I'd not waited for her response; I'd walked out of the tent. I'd felt her wave of hatred follow me, but such things are common. And she'd done as I'd said, not out of fear but because she has both wisdom and courage.

Sharika knows, just as I do, what will happen if this force is permitted to reach the city.

It had been intended to surprise us, but we've been fortunate – and our routine scout mission had become the line between life and death.

And perhaps, I think, *Perhaps we will be enough.*

Dawn.

We face East, the rising sun. The sky over the pass is almost clear and the colours of the high clouds are particularly glorious. I am not at my best in the daylight, though I can tolerate it – I stand beneath the flag and watch as the force begins to move.

It uncoils like some vast serpent, stretching in hunger and eagerness. It can sense us, up here, as if it's one single, living organism – and perhaps it is. If its leader is as I remember, she could have Summoned anything she wished to tear us down.

But not yet…

Not yet.

Instead, she holds her force back, and she comes out to see us in person. Her name is Saris, and she carries no flag, brings no guards. The strung arrows do not bother her. Like me, she made her bargain long ago, and must live with the result.

She stops, a tiny figure at the bottom of the valley. I hear the captain give the command and a single arrow shoots down from the wall – Adur, the sniper. The shot is true, but the arrow does not strike its target.

It flashes to ash and is gone.

"You're smart, captain," she says. Saris' voice carries, though she does not shout. "Not wasting your ammunition. But it matters not – you're not prepared for this defence. Your force is too small, your supplies inadequate. Stand down, and I will spare your lives."

She lies, and we know it. It's a common mythology: that any Summoned Reider will answer your greatest dreams, for a price. But Saris was once a professional, performing Summonings for coin, and she knows that the price can be paid with others' lives. And with this many lives to capture, she can create more, summon more, raise more… and throw all of that magical might at the city, and at lands and farms.

Captain Sharika calls back, "Bollocks!" and a laugh goes up from the wall. One soldier bares his arse at the slim figure below.

Saris nods, turns to give her first order.

"Wait." I say. I have no more need to shout than she does. She pauses and turns back.

"Kadarr," she says, her voice now the warm greeting of an old friend. "Been a long time. How are you finding immortality?"

"Single combat, Saris. You and I."

That makes her laugh, the sound rich in the rising light. "Oh come now. Why would I do that? I'm no warrior and you know it. And you're playing for time – the slower you all die, the more chance your city has to defend itself. Please," the laugh comes again, "You know me better."

I do – but the attempt still had to be made.

She turns away, and I see her pale hand make the gesture. Her rings flash in the new-born sun.

There are no bugles, no drums – not for this army.

But the slaver as they come is enough to freeze your bones.

The sunlight grows stronger, and it causes me pain. Nevertheless, I can see that the incoming force is a writhing, avid mass of monsters – things conjured from the darkest corners of nightmare. These are not warriors, not even creatures; these are Summoned, daemons and visions and worse.

The soldiers are brave, and the keep's wall is high. Our siege engines rattle, ropes creaking and crew shouting. I hear the order to release and the almost-unified 'thunk' as the arms hit the stops. They throw scattershot – the keep is well supplied for this, at least – and the smears of scarlet are sizeable.

Archers shoot more carefully, picking their targets. Under Adur's command, they strike the larger creatures, bringing them down.

But the army below has fifty times our numbers. It rolls over its own dead, unseeing.

It reaches the wall, and it heaves and boils at the base. The things are dragging each other down in their eagerness to get at us. I see one young man turn and vomit, his face green. Others are pale, but they all stand fast.

Captain Sharika is at their centre, her flag a rallying point. Adur stands at the right flank. I stand at the left, spear in hand and waiting.

Eager.

This holds no dread for me. I have done this a thousand times; have done this since I was strong enough to hold a blade.

They come.

They climb like spiders, swift.

They crest the wall.

The archers fall back, waiting; I hold my flank still, while the soldiers in the centre are faced with everything they've ever feared. There are not enough of them to form defensive walls; they move swiftly, skirmishing in twos and threes, one spear, flanked by one or two shields...

The noise is appalling: shouts and crashes and cries. Shrieks of pain, or rage, or death. The hack of steel in flesh. The gouts of gore – and things worse. In the rising daylight, my vision is not good; I make out the fighting as a half-dazzled blur, see only the colours of shields and armour as our own forces battle to throw the monsters back. To begin with, they succeed – the creatures are small and not assailing fast enough. And Sharika's troops are good; they stand despite their lack of experience. For a moment, their adrenaline catches and overwhelms them – it's almost as if they're having fun – but the numbers of monsters quickly grow larger.

Still, I hold my flank back, though I feel their impatience.

Our turn will come.

I hear the captain, her voice firm and fearless. The archers are sniping now, short-range and into the melee. They hit faces, sending the creatures over backwards, wailing, their claws kicking as they die.

But the monsters are too many. They're spreading out across the walltop. One of the catapults is overwhelmed; it crashes to pieces in a cloud of dust. I can hear the crew screaming, screaming...

"Left flank!" The captain's command is well-timed.

More dark things come seething, hundreds of them. As our forces knuckle under the numbers, so I raise my spear and give the command to attack.

This – *this!* – is what I was made for.

Despite my dazzled vision, I have speed and strength beyond any mortal human, and I wade into the centre of the creatures, taking one with the spear-point, another with the back-jab of the same strike. My shield is on my other arm and used for attack. Its rim takes a monster in the teeth, a side-slam takes another. I kick and kick, and they fall away from me, choking. Even my presence is enough – many won't face me at all.

They cower as I come close.

This is why I sold my soul: this tight rush, this pure, cold skill.

The lines of my soldiers fall in behind me – they defend my back and I protect them. When one falls, I hold for long enough to let the reserve pull him from the battlefront. I don't want the lives of these men and women sacrificed for Saris' power.

And they fight *hard.*

I keep battering forwards and the monsters tumble back. I lose my spear, stuck in the bloating corpse of a foe, and draw my blade, slashing across throats and eyes. I can still hear the captain, her shouts rasping now with the rawness of her throat. If I can reach her, I can clear half of this walltop, and give the archers back their killing ground.

The creatures keep falling back – responding to some unspoken command, perhaps. They ripple and shudder, wanting to press the assault but waiting…

And then, there, in the space they leave, is their champion, the beast that Saris has chosen to be my doom.

In the brief lull, the captain is snapping orders – regrouping, observation, tending for the wounded. The walltop is slick with blood and shit, with the ichor of the monsters. Their dead flesh seems to have no bones; it liquefies in the sunlight, steaming and bubbling to nothing.

I blink, still struggling to see clearly. The sun is getting hotter and I can feel it in my bones, burning like fire.

But no time for that now.

The thing I face is humanoid, bigger than I am, and it has arms and legs that glint like steel. Half its face is gone, but there's nothing in its place – the skull protrudes in white jags that glisten in the light.

As it comes closer, it grins.

A skull-grin like my own.

It carries no weapon, wears no armour. Its chest has fragments of metal embedded in the skin – a design that recalls the Summoners' emblem.

It says, "Kad-arr."

This thing – and I know this with a horror that shudders through me – was once human. Perhaps it too made a Summoners' pact and this was the price… or the reward.

It charges at me – and, by the Gods, it's *fast.*

But, swift though it may be, even this thing is not enough. Perhaps my bargain was simply better – Summoners and their Reiders are unpredictable at best. I stand my ground; brace my weight against my shield. And it clangs into the metal like some great and sounding bell; the creature wobbles backwards, shaking its head. The captain says, 'Yes!' like a hiss of triumph and her forces take up the chant. They're calling my name now – their fear and hatred gone in the rising heat of their blood.

The thing recollects itself, charges again.

I slip to one side, spanking it across the arse as it passes. The lines of soldiers almost laugh. I'm enjoying myself now. As it spins to come at me again, I feel almost alive – can almost remember what that surge of adrenaline is really like...

But the beast comes slower this time, measuring its pace. It pauses just out of blade range and snarls at me, its head on one side as if curious, its teeth bared and rotten.

I stalk it, careful.

But then, behind it, there are more noises – this thing is a distraction and the assault begins again. A cloud has crossed the sun and I can see more clearly: this time, it's the siege monsters, great climbing creatures that bear smaller beasts upon their backs. I hear the captain's command carry a note of genuine alarm.

We cannot win this.

I stop playing – this is no time for humour, or for indulgence. Stepping forwards and past my foe, I decapitate it almost as an afterthought – my blade is sharp, and my strength more than enough. Its half-head thumps to the stone. There is the faintest of pauses... even Saris wasn't expecting that.

For the first time, I allow myself to hope.

But hope is not a strategy. The first siege-beast has crested the walltop and the others are coming. I pick up a spear from a fallen soldier – his eyes are open and staring at the sky – and I hurl it, overarm, at the newly arrived creature.

It hits the thing clean in the eye socket and it tumbles back, keening. But not fast enough – its cargo of monsters has already unloaded. They range out among the skirmishing defenders.

The soldiers are overwhelmed in moments. They're fighting rear-guard, pushed backwards and struggling just to stay alive.

A second siege-beast crests the wall. I pick up another spear.

But the third is out of my range.

I cannot stop them all. I batter and slash and kick my way through the horde; they slaver at me, claws reaching. A few have picked up weapons – they use them like clubs, thumping crudely at the defenders. Some of them flex and merge, their flesh amalgamating into larger forms.

I see the captain, still defending the flag, a cluster of her soldiers round her. She's magnificent – stabbing and slashing, screaming at the biggest ones, fearing none. A smoking bubbling pile of death builds at her feet.

I fight to reach her, and the beasts fall like a child's ninepins – I'm wading through their mess. My boots are slipping in pools of congealing ichor. But there are too many of them – a fourth siege-beast reaches the wall and its tumbling cargo blocks my view.

And then a thunder comes from below. There's a colossal impact and the wall shudders. Dust trickles from the stonework.

There are more creatures assailing the gate. And there's nothing we can do to stop them – we just don't have enough warriors. A second catapult goes down in a rumble; smoke pours from a third.

But if hope is not a strategy, then neither is despair.

If we must die here, then we will at least die fighting. I loose my centuries-old war-cry, and I hurl myself at the foe.

As evening comes, the attack withdraws.

We hold the wall.

But half of the defenders are dead, and others have been moved to a makeshift infirmary, just inside the watchtower. Captain Sharika is still on her feet, her face bloodied from a blow to her temple. Yet she refuses to give in while her warriors stand.

My admiration for her is considerable.

Rations are broken out, but I have no need for food. Instead, I hold my place upon the tower, its flag still flying.

And as the light fades, so my vision clears. I can see better now – the bruise-purple colours of the sunset that stain the sky. And down there, as those colours darken, a glow of illumination.

There's a pattern, etched in the thick soil of the pass. Blood is being spilled, offerings are being made.

Saris performs a Summoning.

The soldiers cannot see that far – but I know what it means. It means that the force will be even larger with the dawn, and that our deaths are assured. I fear not for my own – I will return, as I have always done, with the knowledge of another failure – but these youngsters, brave and naïve as they are...

No. The captain's strength has touched me – perhaps more than I've been touched in years.

And this is too much.

I have no conscience –it is something you lose, over six centuries of warfare – but this time, I will not permit the outcome.

I leave my post.

I leave my spear, my blade, my shield, my helm, my armour – all the things that have defined my role, my identity.

My existence.

In the stained remains of my linen tunic, I climb to very top of the watchtower, to the tiny platform that carries the flagpole...

And I remember.

A young warrior, proud and unafraid, trained from childhood. A force like this one, overwhelmed. A Summoners' deal – and, with Saris' help, I traded my humanity for pure battle-prowess. And we won. But the Reiders are capricious, and it took not only the trade I'd offered...

It also took my life.

I have been dead for six hundred years, yet I can never rest.

Now, perhaps, my unlife will do some good.

I see the Summoning, far out in the pass below; see the army boil and ripple and swell, a growing poison. Come the dawn, it will roll over the wall in a wave and we will be finished.

I feel some relief that the soldiers cannot see it, and do not know.

But I know. Those colours, those shapes.

And I can craft them – the same pattern, drawn on the stone in pebbles and grit, the same pale green illumination...

It is visible to the captain. I hear her feet, hear a snapping of fingers as she sends someone to investigate – but they will not reach me quickly enough.

Any Summoning is swift; the Reider comes.

Out on the pass, I know that Saris can also see this. She will know what it means, but she will not know the outcome.

My Reider grows stronger; its presence is close.

I feel the army seethe – in response to my action, Saris has commanded a night assault. She has ended her own Summoning in favour of her command. A pre-emptive strike.

She's afraid.

A breath later, shouts come from the watch – they too have seen the army in motion. I do not look. Now, the shimmer of light at the heart of my pattern takes all my attention.

My Reider, as it manifests.

You never know what they will be; perhaps their shapes are purely what we expect. Some can be huge, spiked and fiery. Some are small and sly. Some are more generous than others. Anyone can perform a Summoning, but the more knowledge you have the more likely you are to secure a favourable outcome. In older times, the wealthy would pay professionals to perform their Summonings for them.

I can hear the soldiers arming up, waking their fellows. They're tired, but they still rise determined. They joke: 'Haven't had enough yet, they're coming back for more!' 'We'll give them Hell!'

There are soldiers at my tower now; they're demanding to know what I'm doing. I'm lit up like a beacon, for the Gods' sakes…

I do not answer them.

The army is almost upon us; my time is short.

My Reider is small. It has seven brightly blinking eyes and two sets of arms; it flickers like a fire-wraith. Its voice is smoke-soft as it asks me what I desire.

I lean close and word my request carefully, making sure there are no holes. "I wish victory for this force," I tell it. "I wish the lives of these soldiers spared, and joyous. I wish the city secure."

The more I ask for, the more it can take. It grins, its teeth like knives. It asks me what I am willing to trade.

"I am six hundred years old," I tell it. "My unlife is limitless. Take as much as you need, so that these may be saved."

"The great Kadarr," the sprite says, laughing at me. "Yet – ah! – so foolish."

A thunder of hooves precedes the wall juddering under another, huge impact. The battering-ram monsters, faster on their feet, are quick to assail the gate.

I hear the captain cry, 'Here they come!' as the first of the great siege-creatures scrambles upwards, and unloads its cargo at the walltop.

Others are coming.

We will not last long.

"That is my deal," I say. I do not plead, or vacillate – the weaker you seem, the more the Reider will take.

The sprite spins in its green fire, dancing, mocking. Then it says, "I wish *life*, Kadarr. And you have none to offer me. This is no bargain –"

"Wait!" As it goes to vanish, I hold up a hand. I say, "Take the injured in the tower below."

The fighting is growing now, and savage. I dare not turn to look, but I hear the cries and curses as the soldiers are borne down. The last of catapults crashes into fragments.

The battering-ram creature hits the gate. I can almost hear the wood splinter.

"Ah." The sprite flickers and bows. "Better. A very military transaction – the sacrifice of the few to preserve the many." It thinks, then says, "Very well, then."

Relief rises in my bones.

But the sprite is not done.

"Slay them yourself, and I will grant you your desire."

The trickery is typical, and the Reider's amusement at its own cleverness. But I do not baulk. Leaving the sprite amid its flickering green smoke, I jump down from the flagpole tower – and land easily on my feet. The soldier there starts and stares at me, then tries to stop me as I push open the door to the infirmary.

"No, sir, you can't..."

I ignore him.

The air in the tower is cold. It smells of stone, and hope, and suffering.

Outside, there are screams. I can still hear the captain: I hear the scuttle and thump as another siege-beast unloads its cargo.

There is no time.

The first man dies with my fingertips in his throat. The second is too weak to move, I break his neck, turn for the next. The third is a woman, barely twenty, her leg broken; she tries to pull herself out of my way. One hand through her ribcage crushes her heart.

I can at least slay them swiftly – gangrene is less merciful than I.

In the doorway, the soldier is shouting at me, raw and hurt and disbelieving.

But outside, the mass of monsters is falling back.

A fourth patient dies.

A fifth, a sixth.

I am blood to my elbow-joints, hot and slick. The infirmary is in a panic. The combat doctor is on his feet, his belt-blade drawn; I have no wish to hurt him, nor to disgrace his defence of the injured. One strike renders him unconscious, his honour – I trust – secure.

A second strike lays the protesting soldier out cold across the bodies of his fellows.

Another death, and another. Gasps of desperate air.

The fighting outside has slackened, now; there are shouts ringing vicious with the certainty of victory.

A crushed throat kills one more. I have lost count. I can hear the sprite laughing – but that may just be nightmare. The few injured that remain are reaching for weapons – those that can – courageous to the last.

It will not help them.

Outside, I hear the cry go up, "They're retreating!'"

I hear the captain give orders to watch them; she doesn't trust those bastards as far as she could spit. I hear the last sounds of combat as the beasts are driven from the walls of the keep.

But the captain's at the tower, and in the doorway.

"Stand away." Her blade is in her hand, smeared with the darkness of a hundred dead enemies.

There are three soldiers still alive. One has a belly wound, one a shattered leg. The last one has a cracked skull, and may even die before I reach him.

"No," I tell her. I move to the man with the belly wound. He has one blood-covered hand over his bandaging, his belt-blade in the other.

The captain points her sword at me. "I knew I couldn't trust you. You're a monster yourself, no better than those things out there."

"Perhaps," I tell her.

I put my leather boot on the injured man's throat. He chokes, struggles. Blood seeps through the bandage. He's already weak, and the dagger in my leg does little damage.

The captain walks across the floor, fuming but still tightly controlled. She and puts her blade under my jaw. "Get out," she says. "Or I'll end your miserable existence, once and for all."

I have no wish to fight her. The man under my foot thrashes for a final breath, and is still.

"You faithless bastard," she says. "Is this how you buy your life, you…"

I take her blade in my hand, physically move it out of the way. It cuts into my fingerbones, but it does not matter. The woman with the shattered leg scrabbles backwards, trying to get out of my way.

"I'm sorry," I say. "It's them or you. The choice was necessary."

Outside, there are bursts of cheering; the crash of combat is almost over.

The man with the skull injury has stopped breathing. One life now hangs between defeat and victory.

I wish I could explain it – but the Reiders forbid. The captain is a military woman, perhaps she would comprehend. Or perhaps she would condemn the slaying of defenceless injured as too high a price, I do not know.

I do, know, however that they would have died anyway. And there are worse ways to meet your end.

I move for the woman with the broken leg. The captain is quick; she stops me. I say to her, "Get out of the way."

"No."

I go to strike her as I struck the others, but she's smarter than that, faster. She blocks my wrist with her sword and comes back to slash me across the throat. I rock back, and the tip just misses me.

Outside, I hear, "They're coming back!" The voice is pure panic.

A flicker crosses the captain's vision – she needs to deal with me, and go back to her command. She presses the attack; she has no shield but her blade is fierce. It dances in patterns that I struggle to avoid.

The injured woman stares at the pair of us.

I can hear the sprite, its voice in my head, *If you fail, Kadarr, the bargain is forfeit. And I can take anything I wish.*

I move forwards, catch the captain's wrist, disarm her of the blade. Before she can respond, I spin and drive it, point first, into the chest of the injured woman. The woman gapes, her eyes meet my gaze – just for a second – and she's gone.

"No, they're retreating!" A different voice, brutal in triumph. "Whoresons are running away!"

Cheers erupt.

The battle is over.

The sprite has gone.

But Captain Sharika stares at me, in judgement and hatred and complete, savage incomprehension. I do not know whether she will just throw herself at me, barehanded, brutal with outrage.

But her self-control is better than that. As I lay her captured blade upon the floor, she says, "Get out. You whoreson hell-damned *thing*. Now I understand why they loathe you, why you're an outcast, why no one will stand with you, despite your skills. You're a creature of death. A *curse*."

I have no words for her, no defence for myself. She stands back as I leave the infirmary. I return to my post, and the snap of the flag.

There, I pick up my armour, my helm and my weapons – the marks of an honour I still strive to possess.

The captain does not stop me as I leave.

I cannot return to the city. I depart the beast-bruised gateway and walk down the mountain pass, following in the wake of the fleeing army.

Sharika watches me from the walls, the flag above her head. I half-expect the arrow, but it does not come.

The night is clear, and cold.

And I am alone once more, a Lich of war and darkness.

Pelicos the Brave and the Princess of Kalakhadze

Steven Poore

This was the easy part of the job, thought Pelicos the Brave.

Kalakhadze's trading docks were much the same as every other port he had seen. Officials to bribe, beggars to shun, stalls to attract the unwary buyer. Other ports didn't extend up the sides of the surrounding cliffs however, with shacks connected by ropewalks hanging off the sheer rock. The ropewalks swayed, constantly in use, and Pelicos felt ill watching them rock back and forth, amazed that nobody fell from them. Like oversized spider webs, they stretched nearly all the way up the cliffs. The inhabitants of the topmost shacks brazenly defied weather, gravity, and common sense. If visitors to the port were especially brave, they could venture up to the Gull's Tavern for a drink. The prices were, as the joke went, rather steep.

There was only one way up to the rarefied heights of Kalakhadze itself, though. Pelicos paid his fare and queued patiently for passage in the cages. Merchants, boys, messengers, soldiers, slumming nobility from high above – all joined the queue for the cages. Ten by ten, they trooped into a cramped, pallet-floored space, and the attendants barred it from outside. The concentrated stench of sour flesh was enough to make someone behind Pelicos retch. He looked down at the boards, stained with damp and old vomit, and wondered how they didn't crack under the weight. The cage jerked into motion abruptly, counter-weighted by another descending from the cliff-top city. Pelicos peered over the shoulders of his neighbours, searching for a glimpse of the Castilar's boat as it retreated out from the docks to await his return, but his view was limited. Soon, there was only sky, rope, rock, and the backs of people's heads. And the man afflicted with an attack of vomiting, much to everybody's discomfort.

The cage rocked and tilted alarmingly as it gained height. Pelicos looked out at the tangled web of ropewalks and the looming mass of rock that defended the city. You'd have to be mad to even think of attacking Kalakhadze from the sea, he decided. And if you approached from overland instead, from the port of Charikhadze, as larger and heavier cargo did, the city would have two full days to prepare for a siege. Kalakhadze was built so high it could never fall, so the storytellers claimed.

The rough rock walls were uncomfortably close to the cage now, and for a moment Pelicos believed the cage was falling rather than rising. His stomach turned and he closed his eyes so that he could settle himself. He couldn't back out now.

Kalakhadze. A long, curving island that rose from beaches and pleasant fields in the north to a great pinnacle of sheer rock at its southernmost tip. Atop that mountain, more conventionally approached by traders and visitors alike by way of a steadily climbing road from the northern fields, was a city of intertwining towers, holds and tenements that, with Stromondor destroyed by the Hordes, was said to be the greatest in the world. Walls made up of mirrored mosaics, stairs of finest marble, gardens set so high in the sky that even the gulls struggled to reach them. A city shielded against magic by the Golden Rule, and guarded by the Steadfast. The great treasures of an unconquered civilisation, safe behind walls that only a god could breach.

Among those treasures was a certain princess whom Pelicos had been engaged to rescue: Nereya of the Dunundaya, a bright star even in Kalakhadze's glittering firmament. Her family had denied the Hellean Castilar's suit. Nereya was locked away. Separated, the lovers pined. The Castilar's letters went unanswered. He had no other choice, he explained to Pelicos at their first meeting. The force of love could not be denied.

Perhaps he was getting soft in his years, Pelicos thought. The sketch of Nereya that the Castilar showed him tipped the balance. Her eyes, the just-so tilt of her chin... The mage had sighed in quiet resignation as Pelicos the Gallant took on another hopeless cause to pay his debts.

It wasn't much comfort, but when the cage finally cleared the top of the cliffs and juddered to a halt in blinding sunlight, his boots were still dry, and his dignity was intact. He shuffled out with the rest of the cattle, jostling to be free of the cramped space, his senses assaulted by the city before him. Bored Kalaks herded him away from the cage so that they could send it back down with merchants returning to their ships.

The Halls of Kalakhadze were everything that the stories had promised, everything that the mage had said they would be. Colourful, glittering, with balconies, bridges and spires that held up the sky. Bright flags and banners flew in the wind, welcome distractions from the great blocky tenements that filled the spaces between the towers. Pelicos was already searching for the banner that the Hellean prince had described, and he barely noticed when one of the Kalaks by the cage grabbed his arm and pulled him aside.

"You're just visiting for the day," the Kalak smiled. It wasn't a question.

"Oh, absolutely," Pelicos said. "Definitely. Looking forward to it. Especially the evening."

The Kalak smacked the back of his hand with an ink stamp. "You don't want to miss the last cage then, my friend."

"What if I do?" Pelicos didn't like the man's smirk. It suggested he enjoyed his job far too much.

"We send you back down without it."

"Ah." Pelicos glanced back at the cage. "I think I'll make my own way down. But thank you for the kind offer."

He hooked his thumbs into his belt and tilted his head mockingly as he rejoined the flow of traffic through the arch into the town. The Kalak frowned, shrugged, and turned back to his work.

By the time he reached the top of Nereya's tower, the ink stamp was a mere smudge, smeared with dirt and blood. Pelicos glanced at it for a moment and wondered if he still had time to catch the last cage back down the cliff.

The Dunundaya servants hoofed up the stairs behind him, clubs and knives at the ready. The first one had found him forcing the locks of the chests that held the Hall's treasures. Pelicos managed to knock him into silence before he made too much noise, but it seemed the damage was done. He grabbed what he could, and hoped that the mage had been right.

The Golden Rule doesn't act against magic that was already upon Kalakhadze before it was enacted, the mage had told him. *And the Dunundaya possess a small collection of magically-endowed items from the time before the Rule. I was shown them, once.*

Coiled rope over his shoulder, spear in one hand, great boots that flapped around his knees – he must look like a bloody fisherman, Pelicos thought sourly. But he flew up the stairs ahead of the Dunundaya as the hue and cry was raised, and he could almost believe that the boots added a spring to his step.

He jabbed the blunt end of the spear at the nearest man, shifted his grip, and poked him away down the stairs. The woman behind him tripped, and Pelicos rapped her over the head. She dropped with a grunt.

More noise came from far below. The entire Hall was beginning to rouse. He'd have to rule out the kitchens as an exit. That didn't leave many options.

He tried the door on the landing. It swung inward on well-oiled hinges. Moonlight turned the stone walls of the bedchamber soul-blue and darkened the drapes. The princess was a silhouette swinging long legs from the bed, tightening loose pants at her waist. He saw the whites of her eyes, and her teeth as she bared them to him.

"Don't fear," he grinned. "My name is Pelicos the Daring. I'm here to rescue you."

She blinked. "From what, precisely?"

"Imprisonment, of course. The tyranny of family. The denial of true love." He paused to make sure she understood. "Fair maiden locked in a tower. Prince to the rescue. Sail away to freedom, love, and happiness."

"My door wasn't locked," the princess pointed out.

"This is the Dunundaya Hall? And you're Nereya?"

The princess nodded. She pulled a shirt down over her head. Brisk, unafraid. Pelicos felt a sliver of uncertainty wedge itself into his spine.

"I am. And those are my grandmother's boots you're wearing."

"They're comfortable. We should go."

Nereya strode across the room to face him. "If I wanted to be rescued, I'm sure I would have said something to someone about it. I assume this prince of yours employed *you* to take me away from all of this?"

Pelicos nodded.

"Fine. It would be unprincipled of me to stop a man doing his paid work. But don't think I'm going to help you either."

He looked out at the landing, where the servants still lay concussed, then back at Nereya. She stood with her arms folded, as though this was but a minor inconvenience. The sounds from below were getting louder. It was definitely time to leave.

"Does this door lock from the inside?" he asked.

The rope was longer than it looked. And stronger, too. Perhaps the mage had been right – perhaps the Dunundaya's treasures *did* include some enchanted items from before the Golden Rule. Pelicos wished he'd had more time to examine the contents of the chests in the room at the foot of the tower. He hitched the rope to the bedpost and flung the rest of the coil off the balcony while Nereya leaned against the wall and watched.

"So, you're Pelicos the mercenary."

"Pelicos the *Merciful*," he corrected her over his shoulder, trying to work out how far short of the ground the rope finished. The glimmer of torchlight below wasn't enough to aid his sight. "It's *Merciful*."

"Ah. I must be thinking of a different Pelicos."

There was an enquiring knock at the door, saving him from any further reply. He gestured urgently to the edge of the balcony instead. Nereya shook her head. Pelicos gestured again, and received the same reply. The knock at the door became more demanding. Pelicos cursed under his breath and pulled Nereya across to the balcony. She didn't resist but, as she had promised, she didn't do anything to help him either. Pelicos thought he could see how this was going to go, and he decided he definitely hadn't charged the prince enough for this job.

He steadied himself against the edge with his feet and rolled Nereya up and over his shoulder with his free hand. The added weight caused the rope to cut into his palm, and for one heart-stopping moment he thought the smooth stone would slide away beneath his feet, but the soles of his purloined boots barely shifted.

"You've done this before." Nereya's voice floated up to him.

Pelicos hitched his shoulder up and tightened his arm against her thighs. "Hush. I need to concentrate."

"Mind where that hand goes."

Step by step, not thinking about the distance to the ground, definitely not thinking about the angered hammering at the door in the room above. He couldn't hurry, but at the same time he couldn't *not* hurry. At least with Nereya over his shoulder nobody would be daft enough to try to cut the rope or shoot him down. So he hoped.

He passed a shuttered window. There were voices, loud and agitated, in the room beyond. The Dunundaya were fully roused and angry – a thief in the Halls, chests broken, goods stolen. For now it appeared they weren't properly aware of what had occurred upstairs. Of who, even now, hung precariously outside the tower itself.

Shadows passed behind the shutters. Kalak curses and the clatter of blades. A slamming door. Sudden quiet. Pelicos sensed an opportunity. "If I swing about, you can use my knife to unhook the shutters," he hissed. "Then we can creep down the stairs while everybody tries to get in your chamber."

"No," said Nereya. "I told you – I'm not helping. You must do this yourself."

He took as deep a breath as he could. "All hells – I'm doubling the damned fee."

"Sounds reasonable. Of course, *I'm* not paying it."

"I wasn't talking to you." Pelicos grimaced. Step by step, releasing the rope through his hand inch by inch, Nereya's weight skewing him, he started down again. His muscles quivered with the effort it took to hold on. He twisted his head to the left and saw that one of the bridges that spanned the gap between two smaller towers wasn't too far away. He started to crabwalk along the wall, first one way, then the other, to build up some momentum. With Nereya's weight added to his own, it wouldn't be an easy jump. But it was probably safer than getting to the bottom of the rope and feeling a Dunundaya spear or three pricking his cheeks.

As his arc increased he felt Nereya tighten her grip on him. If she wasn't going to help, she certainly didn't intend to let herself come to harm. One last look, breath hot in his lungs, and Pelicos pushed away from the wall, loosening his grip on the rope – if he missed, he might still have half a chance to –

His boots skated across the stone ledge of the bridge, and back into the air. Or they should have done. The soles pulled him to a halt, overbalancing him so that he had to twist and allow Nereya to drop onto the bridge before his spine popped. Pelicos teetered on the ledge, one arm whirling, and finally managed to fall gracelessly down next to the princess. The rope must have been cut, he thought. He had landed just in time.

As Nereya cursed and brushed herself down, Pelicos swiftly gathered up the rope in rough loops and slung it across his chest. It hadn't been cut, he realised with shock. The end he had tied had come loose. That shouldn't have been possible – especially with the knots he had used.

The surprise must have shown on his face. Nereya sniffed. "You almost killed us both there. If it wasn't for my grandmother's rope and boots…"

"Hardly. They don't call me Pelicos the Acrobat for nothing." He looked around quickly and tried to judge the quickest route to the ground. There was shouting at the base of the Dunundaya Hall now as guards and servants spread into the streets. Pelicos took the princess' hand and pulled her towards the far end of the bridge. "Come on, we can't stand here all night."

The door into the tower was solid, but unlocked. The owner of this hall had no fear of guests dropping in unexpectedly. Pelicos peered up the stairs that curved around the interior of the tower. Not much illumination, fewer decorations – a less wealthy family, relative to the Dunundaya. Or perhaps just less ostentatious. But that was all to the good – less visible wealth meant fewer guards. He started downwards with Nereya in tow, wishing he had kept the spear for self-defence, but he couldn't have carried both that and the princess. He wasn't going to tell her that though – he was beginning to suspect that it wouldn't be a good idea.

This was a smaller tower built above servant quarters and kitchens, to judge from the taste of the air. Pelicos followed the turn of the stairs down until he reached another door in the outside wall. Kalakhadze was a city of bridges, towers, and high gardens, and he guessed the Dunundaya would expect him – an outsider, a foreigner – to flee through the streets. No, Pelicos was keeping his feet firmly in the sky. This door led out onto a much shorter bridge that passed, via a slender tunnel through the heart of another tower, to an enclosed stairwell next to a tenement with timbers so old and twisted that it seemed to reach out to the curving brick for support. Now Pelicos veered upward again, heading for the door that led out onto the tenement's rooftop garden.

The shouting was more distant now. There was only the usual murmur of a city at night. Even at this hour there were Kalaks in the gardens, young lovers in furtive pairs, small groups gathered by lantern light, older folk taking the air. A few labourers knelt by their raised beds of berries, onions and fast-growing greens – the city's work was never finished, and Kalakhadze had elevated its agriculture to the skies along with everything else. Pelicos kept away from the lamp-lit groups, steering a path to a bridge that would take him to the roof of the next tenement. He slowed his pace as much as he dared, hoping that the Kalaks would take Nereya and him for another courting couple. It was a ruse that wouldn't stand much scrutiny, he knew.

"You were lucky back there," Nereya said quietly as they weaved between the raised beds.

"No," he grinned back, lying easily. "That was all meticulously planned ahead of time. I am nothing, if not thorough."

"I see. Pelicos the Practical."

"I have been called that. And worse."

"But you're not my fabled prince."

Pelicos sighed. "Alas, no. But I can bring you to him once more."

"I should like to meet him," Nereya said. "If only to know at last who in the name of Kolus' stoneclad balls the idiot thinks he is that he can abduct a Dunundaya from her own hall!"

Pelicos stopped so abruptly that Nereya's momentum pulled both of them off-balance. "I beg your pardon?"

Nereya pulled free of his hand and folded her arms across her chest. "You were told I was held captive against my will by my family?

That the course of true love must prevail, and hearts that beat as one must never be parted?"

He stared at her and ran his tongue across the back of his teeth. "If I admit those words are alarmingly familiar, will you raise a hue and cry?"

She smiled as she shook her head. At least, Pelicos thought it was a smile. "No. I said already that I would not stop a man doing his paid work. And as I told you, I *would* like to meet him."

"Well, I'm relieved to hear that," Pelicos said, though in truth he was anything but. "Uh... perhaps we could carry on, before anybody notices that my very presence here after dark is a capital offence?"

He had envisaged a thrilling chase through alleys and undercrofts, hurdling obstacles, Kalaks cursing as they fell behind. The sort of adventure that portside taverns recounted by the dozen. Instead, he was strolling across the open rooftops with the Dunundaya princess as though they were themselves a courting couple. Or, at least, brother and sister. Or very distant cousins, because there was no chance that anybody looking twice at Pelicos would mistake him for any kind of Kalak.

And, disconcertingly, Nereya took the lead. Pelicos resisted when she started to pull him away on a different path, but he realised quickly that she knew the city far better than he did. "Where are we going? The lift cage is over that way, isn't it?"

"It is, but the lift cage is closed for the night. You weren't intending to return to your ship that way, were you?" Nereya glanced at him. "Not a well-judged plan, if so. The attendants would have just thrown you over the edge once they realised you had broken the visitors' curfew."

Pelicos shrugged. "It could still work. We'd land in the water, wouldn't we?"

"Not from where they'd be throwing you," Nereya said grimly. "The tide doesn't come in that high."

"I'm open to ideas," said Pelicos the Adaptable.

This part of the clifftop was a peculiar mixture of gardens and tenements. It looked as though some of the gardens had fallen away, crumbling into the sea far below, while the buildings all seemed to lean back from the edge, as if scared to get too close. For his own part Pelicos kept to the paths Nereya took, caution winning out over curiosity for once. There was still a good hour of night remaining, and the Dunundaya princess had assured him that they had time to reach the trading docks.

There were enough people out in the streets and the undercrofts beneath the tenements to make Pelicos very uncomfortable. It would only take one overly-observant Kalak to raise an alarm and spoil everything. He tugged his hood forward and ducked his head, self-conscious, his shoulders tensed for trouble. Nereya was determined and confident, and that only unnerved him further.

"Over here," she commanded, and he realised he had been so lost in his own thoughts that he hadn't heard her the first time. There was a door at the base of one of the tenements, and a set of stairs behind it. Stairs heading downwards, into the ground, into the rock of the cliffs themselves. Pelicos frowned at Nereya as the connections came together in his mind.

"The Dunundaya deal with smugglers? I thought your family was hand in hand with the Steadfast."

"We are," Nereya said with a sharp smile. "And we do. Better to control something than to have no control at all. Lead the way, brave hero."

There were more questions he wanted to ask, not least of which was what was waiting for them at the bottom of the stairs, but Pelicos bit them back and headed into the dark, feeling his way with both hands. The boots he'd purloined kept him from slipping on the damp, uneven rock. Old Kalak magic, ghosting through the weaves of the shield that the Steadfast had constructed centuries ago. The mage *had* been right, Pelicos thought. There was magic still on Kalakhadze, if you knew where to find it. That was a secret worth knowing.

Nereya came behind, more sure-footed despite the darkness. Pelicos was beginning to wonder if his part in this rescue was actually necessary at all – the Dunundaya princess seemed far more capable and self-reliant than he had been led to believe. And that thought led him to another: what else had the Castilar left out of his tale of forbidden passions and tyrannical parents?

Only his outstretched hand prevented him from butting his head against the door at the bottom of the passage. Nereya must have been counting steps, because she had already slowed behind him, and now she reached under his arm to slide a bolt that Pelicos could not see. He put his back to the rough wall so that she could squeeze past and finish the job.

"I thought you said you weren't going to help me," he observed.

"I have appointments to keep before noon," Nereya replied. "I would like to have been completely rescued before then."

Pelicos nodded to himself. "I'll try to hurry up a bit, shall I?"

"That would be appreciated. Step back, please." Nereya pulled the door open, to reveal another dark space. This one smelled of armpits, musty cloth, and linen, and when she pushed a second, narrow door that opened into the untidy main room of someone's house Pelicos realised the they had emerged from a cupboard built onto the side of the cliff. Which meant that this was one of the shacks clinging precariously to the rocks high above Kalakhadze's docks.

There were two men at the begrimed table in the middle of the room. Both wore puzzled scowls to complement their collections of scars and tattoos, and the jugs on the table spoke eloquently of a night spent sampling various tariff-free liquors. A stringbearded Kalak half rose to confront them, while his companion reached under the table.

"What you doing here? There's no collection tonight."

"Passing through," Pelicos smiled, rolling his shoulders. "Just ignore us."

"Don't think so," said the other one, the stubs of his teeth jutting forward. He came up with a studded club. "You're no Kalak. Reckon that's double at least."

"Would a broken nose be adequate payment?" Pelicos looked at Stubtooth as he spoke, but his fist lashed out and connected with Stringbeard's face. The man stumbled back over his stool. Stubtooth roared forward, club held high. Nereya shouted something in Pelicos's ear, but he was too busy defending himself to pay attention. Kalak smugglers were wiry and slippery, even the hungover ones. The studded club gave Stubtooth a longer reach, so Pelicos ducked back and shoved the whole table at him before climbing up over it and kicking him into silence.

Nereya sighed. "Was there any need to do that?"

Pelicos shook his hand. His knuckles burned. "I have an instinct for these things."

"I see. Pelicos the Instinctive. Never mind." Nereya crossed to the door and pulled it open. "Here's your short-cut past the tariff-masters and the Steadfast, my hero."

He looked over her shoulder, past the small platform that the shack was built upon, out over the great dark curve of the cliffs. He took in the sheer drop to the sea below, criss-crossed with overlapping layers of slender rope bridges. The breeze shifted slightly and made the scaffold that held up the shack creak, and his stomach lurched.

"Down there? The ropes? Peleanna's teeth… I hope you don't expect me to carry you all the way down."

Nereya grinned. "No, you'll need both your hands free this time."

Shouts and clattering echoed from the passage concealed by the cupboard. The Dunundaya had woken up fully and tracked their missing daughter here, Pelicos realised. Little wonder if they controlled this lucrative little nest. And now he couldn't go back, only forwards. "You first?"

"It's your rescue." Nereya gestured to the first of the ropewalks.

It was easier if he didn't look down, or try to work out where he ought to place his feet. Pelicos found that out quickly enough, but it was one thing to know it and another to stop himself glancing down every few steps. The ropewalk swung treacherously underfoot, the magic boots he had stolen almost pulling his feet to match the swing. The guide rope burned his hands as he held it just above his shoulder. Nereya came behind him, her movement rocking the ropewalk even more. Pelicos gritted his teeth and stared at the shacks that clung precariously to the rock face on the other side of the bay. Even at this early hour there were lanterns lit in some of the windows. There were Kalaks on the ropes, somewhere below, their voices drifting up through the air.

"Faster!" Nereya hissed.

"Only way I'm going any faster is if I let go!" Pelicos hissed back over his shoulder. Then he yelped and flinched as something hissed through the air past his raised forearm. There were shouts from the platform they had left behind, followed by more arrows. "They're shooting at us!"

"Then move!" Nereya sounded more amused than annoyed. "Give them a harder target!"

Pelicos ducked and came close to losing his grip. "I'm beginning to think you're enjoying this!"

There was another ropewalk below this one, angling off in a different direction. Pelicos whispered a hasty prayer to whichever gods might be listening, and dived for it like one of the monkeys he had seen in Galliarca's markets. The guide rope smacked across his chest and he hugged it desperately, kicking his legs to try to reach the ropewalk. Another arrow spun past, more off target this time. Then the ropes bucked violently as Nereya flew down over him and landed on the ropewalk with the grace of a cat. The ropewalk bounced up and stuck to the soles of his boots.

Nereya extended a hand to him. "We don't have all night, Pelicos! Come on!"

Now there was more shouting from the top of the cliffs. Lanterns being lit. A few all-night drinkers had gathered at the windows of the Gull's Tavern to watch and hurl encouragement and abuse in equal measure. A couple of Kalaks had begun their own descent along the ropewalk from the shack the Dunundaya smugglers used. They were plainly skilled enough to keep one hand free to carry long knives. Pelicos cursed again, wishing he had defied the mage's orders to leave his own sword in the boat.

He hurried behind Nereya as fast as he could, his heart skipping every time his feet skated the edge of the ropewalk. At least the archers had lain off now that their fellows were chasing close behind. Nereya pulled her hand free and jumped down to another, thicker bridge, descending again almost immediately even as Pelicos tried to judge his first leap. At this rate, he thought, *she* would have to come back and rescue *him*. Far below, at the seaward edge of the bay, an orange sail flew on a small ship. Out of reach, save if he fell...

A mad idea sparked in his mind, as if fired there by the gods, and Pelicos the Inventive looked up and around. Mad, but quite possibly brilliant too.

"Pelicos!" Nereya snapped up at him.

"I'll be there in a moment! I just need a knife!"

"What?"

Pelicos turned in place and grinned at the approaching Dunundaya men. The first was close enough to see his expression and slow down warily. Pelicos decided to seize the advantage and take the fight to the man. He feinted low to one side, followed up with a kick to the man's leading knee, and grabbed at his knife as the man clawed for the guide rope to halt his fall. So far, so good – he had a weapon, and now he had to catch up with Nereya before they became too separated.

"Hold on tight!" he shouted, and threw himself into thin air.

The ropewalk he was aiming for came up awfully fast. He swung one arm around it just long enough to alter the direction of his fall, and his breath exploded from his lungs as he landed on the next level down. Miraculously he had managed to keep hold of the knife. He struggled back up, gasping for air.

"Are you mad?" Nereya jumped down and balanced herself expertly on the ropewalk.

"I've been called that," Pelicos admitted. He twisted the guide rope around his arm and then took the knife to the other side of it and began sawing. "I'd hold on, if I were you."

"What? You *are* mad!"

Halfway through the cut, the remaining strands parted under the strain. Nereya yelped, and Pelicos scooped her into the crook of his arm as they both fell through the air at the end of the guide rope. The ropewalks flashed past, the bay surged up to meet them, and Pelicos thought suddenly that he ought to let go of the rope before he smacked against the side of the cliffs.

They dropped like stones, and plunged into the sea. Pelicos spat out water and cast around for Nereya. He would be in a fine fix if he lost her now. When she surfaced a few yards away, spitting curses at him, he grinned with relief and struck out for her.

"Nearly there!" he called out.

She waited for him, treading water. "You're an idiot, Pelicos. Perhaps you *should* have just jumped off the top of the cliffs in the first place!"

"This was more fun," he said. "That boat there, with the orange sail – your beloved awaits!"

Nereya looked at the hull. "You came in that?"

"My employer's purse, not mine." Pelicos lifted one shoulder.

Nereya rested herself against him. "Well, I need a rest. You do the work."

By the time they reached the boat at last, the sun was rising over the horizon to illuminate the side of the bay. Pelicos lifted Nereya up as much as his aching muscles would allow, so that the mage could take her weight and haul her into the boat. Then he used the last of his own strength to climb the length of knotted rope, throw a leg over the side and roll over onto his back in absolute exhaustion. He stared up at the cloud-flecked skies and the slack sails, and swore to himself that if his next adventure involved any swimming at all, he would be charging a premium. At the edge of his sight the mage offered Nereya towels and a cup of wine. *Damn the cup*, Pelicos thought, *just stick the bottle in my mouth and let me rest.*

There was little hope of that, however. The Castilar stepped forward, over Pelicos and past the mage as though the pair weren't even there. He had shaved, and his hair was oiled and combed. He was heavily perfumed in the cloying manner of the Hellean courts. He wore clean, rich clothes, the very picture of the prince Pelicos knew he was not.

"Dear Nereya, you're free! We will be together at last!"

Nereya smiled at him. Pelicos had known Nereya for less than a night, but he could see that there was no warmth at all in that smile. He hauled himself up onto one elbow to watch.

"Together!" Nereya clapped her hands to her chest. "How wonderful! Be still my heart! A life away from all the comforts of home, in a muck-ridden old Hellean estate, in the company of a man who never even thought to ask if it was what I wanted! Oh the joy!"

The Castilar's exultant expression went awry. "How could you not want to leave this place? Your family had you imprisoned in a tower! My letters were unanswered, my visits rebuffed! The last time I sent an envoy, he was chased away at sword point! What else could I assume but that you were held under lock and key?"

"You could have assumed that I had no desire to ever see you again," Nereya said. "Because then you would have been correct. Why do you think I had my brothers drive your man away? Why do you think I never answered your letters?"

"Nereya, my light, you cannot mean that." The Castilar stared angrily down at Pelicos. "This isn't like her. Is she hurt? Did she hit her head on something?"

Pelicos sat up, still dripping, and raised his palms. As far as he was concerned, the job was done. All that remained was payment. And he had a horrible feeling the Castilar wouldn't want to honour that part of the arrangement. On the other side of the boat, the mage had covered his face with his hands. His shoulders shook with mirth.

"No, I haven't lost my senses, you fool," Nereya said. "*You're* deluded! I was not imprisoned – I merely had no interest in your suit! I blocked your envoys from my house! I had your measure the first time we met at your Emperor's festival – a cut-price peacock with borrowed feathers! *You will add colour to my house*, you said. You doomed yourself with those words! I am no decorative piece to be dusted off for visitors, not that the great and the worthy would ever flock to the doors of such a family of jumped-up cobblers! You're so obsessed by your own appearance and status in the Hellean Court that you could not view me as human, let alone as an equal. And your cowardice surpasses all else – any noble man or woman worth their salt would have treated with me in person, rather than sending messengers to spout pretty words paid for by the stanza!"

She slapped him. He rocked back on his heels, eyes wide, astounded, one hand flying up to his cheek.

"You don't even have the courage to abduct me yourself!"

In the silence that followed, Nereya turned her back on the Castilar and stepped up into the prow of the boat. She raised her arms over her head and dived smoothly into the sea once more. Pelicos stood and watched, a broad smile upon his face, as she swam with powerful strokes back towards the cliffs below Kalakhadze. Behind him an argument had broken out between the Castilar and the mage, but Pelicos ignored that, his attention fixed on the Dunundaya princess. He felt the urge to cheer and applaud.

"Do you hear me?" the Castilar shouted. "Bring her back here! I demand you bring her back to me! I paid you for this!"

"To be fair, Pelicos *did* bring her to you," the mage said reasonably, but he sounded close to laughter too.

Nereya's strength took her quickly to the base of the cliffs. Now she began to climb, hand over hand, quite effortlessly, up the vertiginous rock face. Pelicos braced his hands on his hips and shook his head in wonderment. If he had to pay back every coin he'd been advanced, this adventure would still have been worth it for this moment alone, he thought.

The Castilar grabbed him by the shoulder and spun him about. The man's face was ruddy with humiliated anger. "What are you waiting for, you fool? Go after her! I thought you were a damned hero!"

Pelicos stared down at him, back at the small figure on the cliffs, and then at the Castilar once more. "You know what? She was right."

"What?"

"If you want something done, you really ought to do it yourself."

And Pelicos threw the Castilar head first into the sea.

THE TIMEKEEPER'S TAROT

Den Patrick

It started out like any other night in the sultry sprawl of Terminus. Ketch shouldered his way through the press of bodies in the Chapterhouse district, keeping a keen eye out for the Watch and their tatty grey cloaks. Onwards he went, into the familiar fug of the Rusted Cog and its many diversions. The usual faces greeted him, the usual faces turned away, and the bar staff struggled to stay ahead of the endless calls for drinks and, more rarely, food. Strong liquor was in high demand by patrons keen to forget the day's woes, much as it always was.

Ketch descended the few steps from street level, catching the eye of an old flame and nodding to her but offering nothing more. He'd no wish to become ensnared in notions of nostalgia tonight, even romantic ones. Sweetsmoke teased at his senses and the familiar pang manifested in his fingertips, at his forehead. But he had no use for that tonight. Ketch was intent on the card table, a way to battle the fickle forces of chance without spilling blood. Ketch took a seat and Lady Fortune smiled upon him. Somehow Ketch won a game with a flush of Hanged Men, causing the other players to piss and moan. It was 'a bad omen' they said. 'Unseemly'.

Ketch was known to play until his winnings had flowed and ebbed away again, but this time he excused himself from the table with pockets of Electrum guineas and a fist of silver shillings. He felt the old restlessness rise within and was glad the patrons had thinned out; crowded bars bred fights and Ketch found himself at their epicentre all too often. He made space for himself at the bar among a clutch of locals and talk turned to the city: the rising cost of Sunfire, the increased patrols by the Watch, the bribes needed to travel from one side of Terminus to the other. No one spoke of the Umbral Lector. It was said she had ears everywhere and did not take kindly to criticism of sour people, and Ketch was surely one of those. One silver shilling followed another, sliding across the counter as the time spooled away. The shot glasses spent more time empty than full, and the clear spirit burned all the way down, much as it always did.

The Rusted Cog was famous for the vast clockface that spread across the wall like a diagram. Rumours persisted that one could know the time in all the places beyond Terminus if one knew how to read the profusion of sigils and recherché symbols on that broad face. The arms of the clock declared it two hours before dawn when the message came. The boy was a scrap from the streets, with shorn hair and the kind of filth that looks inbred rather than merely ingrained.

"She wants to see you now. This moment she said." The boy, who Ketch guessed was ten but malnourished enough to look seven or eight, wiped his nose on his sleeve. There was more blood than snot. The boy would be dead within the year if Ketch knew right, and Ketch usually did. Another soul lost to the Redfleck.

"I'm not working tonight," replied Ketch. "I'm not wearing my leathers and I'm unarmed." He listened to himself as the words slurred together, the way the lie fell from his lips. Ketch never went anywhere without a shiv at the very least.

The scrap was undeterred. "She said if I don't bring you to her I don't get paid." He put enough emphasis on the last word to turn some heads in the Rusted Cog. A few locals smirked, guessing Ketch had found some new trouble for himself.

"Outside," growled Ketch. "And don't say another word." The scrap thrust out his narrow chin, victorious, and swaggered from the tavern with as much bravado as he could muster. The bravado was short-lived as Ketch took off down a side street.

"It's this way!" complained the scrap, pointing East to no avail.

"That may be so," replied Ketch. "But I need to sober up and get a few things."

The scrap trailed behind as they fetched up in Ketch's boarding room, where he donned his leathers and took up a knife as long as his forearm.

"She said we had to be quick." The scrap stood at the solitary window. "Said it was urgent." He looked out into the city, past the domes and spires, deep into the ever-present tenebrae.

Ketch dowsed his face in cold water and checked his blade. The scrap shuffled his feet and cleared his throat.

"Calm yourself. I'm ready to serve your lady."

The scrap wrinkled his nose. "She ain't no lady of mine. Ain't no lady at all."

"How great the mind that accepts difference," said Ketch, allowing himself a mocking smile.

"Get you with your fancy way of talking," replied the scrap. "What's that supposed to mean anyway?"

"Don't be so quick to turn away from what you don't know." Ketch shouldered past the boy and into the street.

"I know she's a Kriegbauen," replied the sullen boy.

"And what do you know about them?"

The scrap scowled harder but said nothing and the unlikely pair headed east, fading into the gloom of the city.

It took another hour of strained silence and hushed whispers to reach their destination. They slipped down side streets and into back alleys to stay free of the Watch and their prying fingers. Ketch was in no mood to lose the remaining coin he'd won to pointless bribes, and he'd been on the wrong side of the Watch enough times he might end up behind bars. Such was the price of curfew and infamy.

Terminus nestled in a vast cavern and those that knew no better believed it was the last great city. Other, more deluded sorts, said it lay beneath all the cities that ever were, even the cities that had only existed in figments or wonderings. Ketch thought that anything grand about Terminus was a hundred years in the gutter. He couldn't imagine a resurgence any time soon.

"This is it," said the scrap, looking over his shoulder, clearly keen not to be caught so close to their destination. They stood on The Street of Unholy Charnel, and the cobbles were spattered with dried blood from the many butchers and fishmongers hereabouts. Ketch stood before a door of cracked and fading blue. Some cowardly bigotwit had painted the number '13' in the old runic script. The paint of the graffiti was bright red, like blood.

"Bastards," growled Ketch. He turned to the scrap. "Wait here." A silver coin appeared between his fingers then vanished just as fast as the boy reached for it. "Payment when I come back."

The scrap scowled and Ketch wondered if it were the only expression the child knew. He'd been much the same at that age.

The staircase was too dim, too steep and too narrow, much as it always was. Ketch rapped his scarred knuckles on the door twice, then twice again, then once.

"Come," said a serene voice. Ketch hoped he hadn't used up all his good fortune on cards. He would have need of a touch more before he could take his rest.

The door at the top of the stairs opened on to a long attic room. All manner of oddments and curios littered the many shelves. The few stretches of wall not obscured by furniture were covered in framed parchment: richly illustrated designs and schematics that Ketch would never understand.

"You came," said Horologine, not turning from her place by the floor-length octagonal window.

"Don't I always?" said Ketch. Another scrap knelt by Horologine's feet, polishing her mistress' ceramic hands.

Ketch took in the wonder of his sometime mistress. Polished mahogany bones and panels of cream ceramic suggested the outline of a human body, and a female one at that. Horologine had seemingly followed her creator's intentions, wearing a floor length skirt of dark turquoise. A headdress of tassels in the same colour gave the impression of hair.

"A new soul joins us from the Above," said Horologine, still rapt in her contemplation of the street below. "It slipped through the cracks between worlds to end up here, in Terminus."

Ketch cast an eye over the work station that lay between him and the Kriegbauen. The table was four feet to a side. Long cards lay across the surface in orderly constellations, though Ketch didn't recognise any of the suits or houses. Incense like cinnamon lay heavy on the air, and lanterns of bright Sunfire hung from the ceiling, holding back the night.

"And you want to go looking for them?"

Horologine turned to face Ketch and he was reminded of the scrap's protests: "she ain't my lady." To look upon a Kreigbauen was unsettling, the eyes were absences, ovals of darkness. Horologine's face was a serene mask, a note of enquiry had been carved into the set of her brow above the gentle smile. She'd painted her lips red and two thin stripes of the same hue ran down her face as if someone had slashed each cheek.

Of course she wanted to go looking, it was who she was. It was what she did.

"Curfew will be over soon," replied Ketch. "We need to be ready. D'you have any inkling where this lost soul of yours has fetched up?"

"Near the Shimmersea Gate," replied Horologine.

Ketch suppressed a sigh. He'd have preferred to stay central.

"The usual fee, I suppose?"

Horologine nodded. "Our contract remains unchanged."

The young girl at the Kriegbauen's feet stood up, bowed woodenly, then slipped through a half door to some other part of the attic. One couldn't be choosy for work when one was an orphan, and this girl had fallen on good fortune, Ketch reckoned. There were worse things in Terminus than to find yourself working for a Kreigbauen

"I sometimes wonder if you collect humans the same way academics collect ghost moths and parasights."

"Collect is not the word I'd choose," said Horologine crossing the room in fluid steps quite at odds with her constructed appearance. "I gather."

Ketch allowed himself a smile. "I suppose you do." She'd gathered him too once upon a time, and kept him fed, though Gods knew why.

"But why do I have to come?" said the scrap when Ketch emerged on to the street. Horologine followed, her sightless gaze falling on the boy who all but recoiled.

"I'll need an extra pair of eyes," replied Ketch, "and besides, you might learn something. Ever been to the Shimmersea Gate?"

"Of course," blurted the scrap, puffing himself up. "And you'll pay me?"

Ketch nodded. "Here's the silver I promised you earlier." Ketch tossed the coin and thought the scrap might drop it in shock. Clearly the boy hadn't expected Ketch to make good on his word. The coin disappeared into a dirty hand and was seemingly forgotten. The scrap stared at the red paint on the blue door and frowned.

"So what does that mean then?"

Ketch cleared his throat and felt pang of embarrassment, he'd no wish to explain the graffiti with Horologine so close. The Kreigbauen answered before Ketch could frame his response.

"The symbol represents the number thirteen," said the Kreigbauen. "It is commonly thought that the creation of my people will spell the end of human beings." She bent forward, so her face was level with the scrap. "It is said that one day the clocks will strike thirteen and the Kriegbauen will rise up against their creators and murder everyone, revenging themselves on humans everywhere."

Curfew ended at that moment and the bell towers sounded all across the city. The scrap stared at Horologine more intently with each somber chime. It was not merely the end of curfew, but seven o'clock in the morning. The boy sagged with relief when the bells stopped on the seventh chime.

"It seems you will be spared the thirteen chimes," said Horologine. "For another hour at least."

"Come on," Ketch headed off down the street, regretting the many drinks of the previous few hours. His stomach rumbled. "There isn't much time; we may have already lost them to the Ghost Compact."

Terminus woke from its torpor. The lucky souls of the city grabbed a few hours' sleep here and there, but a gnawing anxiety kept most in a fitful slumber. In a city of perpetual darkness it was no great issue to sleep whenever one chose, assuming one had the quiet and peace of mind to do so.

A gang of Kriegbauen emerged from a work shed, all carrying pickaxes over their shoulders. No doubt they were off to cobble the streets or lay new sewers; all part of the Umbral Lector's grand scheme of renovation and improvement.

The trio turned in to another street and a Qarín approached in a cream robe, no taller than the scrap that strutted at Ketch's side. The diminutive creature nodded to Ketch, the hairless head almost hidden beneath the hood. The Qarín turned eyes of roiling fire back to the street, keen to be at her destination.

"I don't like Qarín," said the scrap, under his breath.

"And you don't like Kreigbauen," added Ketch. "Which must make your life tricky in a city like Terminus."

The scrap said nothing, not sure whether Ketch was taunting him or not.

"Taking your girlfriend for a walk?" said a gruff voice from just ahead of them. Ketch had known trouble would find them, as trouble always did, but was surprised it had come so soon. A huddle of bravos had gathered at the street corner. The leader, if Ketch guessed right, was leaning against the wall with one hand resting on his short steel. The well-worn hilt looked almost as battered as the scabbard. There were four of them, which was three too many for Ketch's liking. He'd known Horologine for thirty years and never once seen her fight. If it came to steel he'd be all alone.

"Just passing through," said Ketch, a note of warning in his voice. The leader seemed to take it as a challenge and slunk to the middle of the street.

"Don't I know you, friend?" He was a youth of twenty-something, and might have been handsome if not for the broken nose. The pierced eyebrow didn't suit him, nor the shock of black hair, razored to stubble along the left side of his skull.

"No, you don't. I'm not from around these parts." Ketch stopped, giving himself a dozen feet or so between himself and the gang. "Though I'm well known in Chapterhouse. Come and look for me if you like what you see."

"I'm looking at you right now," said the pierced bravo. "Can't say I like much of anything, least of all your pet Kriegbauen."

"She's not my pet and we're busy. Why don't you take yourself to the bath house? You can sweat last night's Spireworm out of your system."

"Only women drink Spireworm," sneered the bravo.

Ketch drew his blade, rolled his shoulders, and released a long sigh.

"Fuck's sake. One on one, then? Or do you boys dogpile like common thugs?"

The bravos preened and stood straighter, though Ketch noted

two of them grew pale and fumbled at their weapons as they drew steel.

"We're not thugs," mumbled one of them, though he sounded more hurt than angry.

"Just take your filthy Kriegbauen away from here," said the leader, clearly too tired or too bored to fight. "We don't tolerate their kind on The Street of Quiet Temperance."

"I did say we were just passing through," replied Ketch. "Perhaps if you were less hungover you'd have understood."

"Hungover?" The bravos' leader raised an eyebrow. "This is the Street of Quiet Temperance. We're all as sober as saints here, friend."

The four of them descended into high pitched laughter, hysterical and shrill. Ketch had them wrong; the bravos were not hungover but stoned on sweetsmoke. The trio circled the giggling bravos and went on their way; only once they had turned the corner did Ketch sheath his steel.

"You were particularly direct," said Horologine when the bravos were many streets behind them. "I thought you were trying to talk your way out of trouble, not provoke them."

Ketch cleared his throat. "I was hoping my age and experience would cow them, that and my willingness to fight."

"It was a gamble then?" said Horologine.

"Every day is a gamble," replied Ketch. "I play my cards, and you play yours."

"The Timekeeper's Tarot are not playing cards," said the Kreigbauen. "They are a tool for divination. Though I admit, sometimes I gamble on certain outcomes."

"Like today," said Ketch. It wasn't a question.

A procession of people stopped the conversation. They were swaddled in bandages and robes, disciples of the Thrice Plagued Mother. Ketch took the scrap by the shoulder and led him to the side of the street. Horologine followed.

"Who are they?" asked the scrap.

"Religious types, off to matins to make their orisons," Ketch looked over his shoulder as the last of the disciples shuffled past. All of them bore a sickly pallor and a dreamy smile. A few of them appeared to be bleeding from the corners of their eyes, though Ketch couldn't tell if it were real or makeup. The disciples tripped and stumbled down the street, high on their own mortality.

The scrap scowled again. "Can't say going to church in the morning would suit me much." His voice was loaded with scorn, the words parroted from someone much older if Ketch had to guess.

"The disciples believe in a Goddess who contracted three types of grave illness before she was sixteen," said Horologine to the scrap. Ketch noticed the boy didn't flinch and cower as before. "They in turn take it upon themselves to suffer as she did in the hopes it brings them closer to divinity."

"They get sick on purpose?" said the scrap, now curious.

"They infect each other," said the Kreigbauen, resuming their journey.

"You know a lot, don't you?"

Horologine nodded and the scrap fell into a respectful silence.

"Here we are," said Ketch as the street opened onto a broad piazza. "If they're still alive we'll soon know about it."

"This is the Shimmersea Gate?" asked the scrap, looking around and curling his lip.

"Of course. But you've been here before, haven't you?"

"Oh, yeah. Course."

The far side of the square presented a wall of rubble that may once have been a stocky fortification, but that time was long past. The stone doors beneath the gatehouse were ten feet high, but detritus in the archway said they'd not been opened in years, decades even. A trio of men climbed the shattered wall and disappeared over the other side, where silvery light danced from an unseen source.

"Where are they going?" said the scrap.

"Fishermen most likely." Ketch's days of fixing nets and hauling fish had been mercifully short-lived. "Going to pull in their catch. All the sand crab and strangle eel comes from Shimmersea."

"Never eaten strangle eel," grunted the scrap.

"If you're not careful the strangle eels eats you."

"We're wasting time," said Horologine, regarding a metal device in the palm of her hand. It might have been a pocket watch, but had the look of compass. The face was ceramic but the filigree was black iron. "This way."

The Shimmersea Gate was home to haulers and heavies, hard looking men and woman who had turned their backs on good fortune long ago. People were attending to the serious business of getting by, and, for those who couldn't, simply surviving. Carts and crates of crab and fish rattled down the cobbled roads, pulled by teams of four people. Others brought up the rear, leaning in with brawny shoulders when the wheels stuck in the cobbles. And everywhere a briny stench intruded, so cloying the scrap held a sleeve up to his nose.

"Mind yourself now," said Ketch as a cart passed close by. He took the scrap by the shoulder and guided him to the side of the street.

"I saw it just fine," said the scrap. "Only a gutterbabe would get run down by a cart. Everyone knows that." The boy broke in to a coughing fit and took a moment to steady himself. He wiped his mouth on his cuff. Ketch saw blood in the spittle.

"We are drawing close," said Horologine, holding the device before her with a hushed reverence. She followed Ketch closely, letting him shoulder his way through the thinning crowd, past unfriendly eyes. "Take the next left turn and be quick."

Ketch led Horologine and the scrap around the street corner. The smell came first, the air was cleaner, as if all the impurities had been seared out. It was the smell of a breach between worlds, the tell-tale scent that someone had arrived in Terminus from who-knows-where.

The second thing Ketch noticed was the lack of cobbles. Old refuse littered the packed earth; the few doors and windows had been boarded up. And for good reason, as it turned out.

Horologine glided past him with a graceful step, still intent on the pale cream and black iron device in her palm.

"It's not safe here," said Ketch. "Mind your footing."

"They are here," said the Kreigbauen. "They must be here. Where can they be?"

The ground bowed upward, the compacted soil shuddering, painful contractions for an unholy birth.

"The Revenir are coming," whispered Ketch. Another patch of ground began to warp and heave.

"I know," replied Horologine. Her flat voice lost none of its usual calm, which only made Ketch's growing dread worse.

"At least two." He drew his steel and felt sweat prickle at his temples and the nape of his neck.

"They are here," repeated the Kreigbauen, still walking forward, oblivious to the danger.

Ketch hated the Revenir. Hated their carrion stench and sightless faces, not that the Revenir had much in the way of a face.

"We should go," said the scrap.

"Get back to the corner," said Ketch. "Get yourself on a cobbled street." The very largest Revenir could still burrow up through cobbles, though it happened less now since the Umbral Lector had agreed the Ghost Compact.

The scrap didn't need telling twice, fleeing as fast as his bony legs would carry him. For a second the life of the nameless boy was more important to Ketch than his own, and that's when the Revenir came for him.

The ground split open at Ketch's boots and pallid flesh surged out of the gap. Ketch fell backward, stumbled, went down hard. The steel was jarred from his hand and the Revenir dragged its body from the hole in the ground, rearing up tall. Two stubby eye stalks waved in agitation.

"Slugs. You're just fucking slugs," growled Ketch. The Revenir slumped forward, falling, hoping to smother him with an underside of tiny serrated teeth. His leathers might buy him some time but it would be a slow, agonising death. Ketch rolled away and the Revenir crashed to the ground with a wet smacking sound. His blade lay on the other side of the creature - Ketch fumbled in his boot and drew his shiv.

A crimson skull had been tattooed on the pallid flesh of the Revenir. The mark declared it a member of the Ghost Compact, who were free to consume unregistered humans in Terminus. And no one was quite as unregistered as the newly arrived.

Ketch gritted his teeth and stabbed down again and again with the shiv, pale fluid bleeding from the punctures. The Revenir reared up again. Ketch scrambled to his feet in response and stumbled back. The shiv's meagre blade wasn't long enough to cut past the Revenir's thick blubber. He was inflicting flesh wounds, nothing more.

Horologine had located her prize; a human woman who had taken it upon herself to hide in the refuse. She was attired in congealing plasma, naked but for pale fluid streaked with cyan and indigo. The woman had the look of someone suffering night terrors as Horologine attempted to soothe her. A second Revenir lumbered toward the Kreigbauen from behind.

"Shit." Things were about as bad as they could get. Ketch feinted left and slipped to the right, switching the blade to his left hand as did so. The Revenir lurched forward and received the shiv to its midsection, raking a gouge in the undulating flesh. The creature shivered in pain then turned toward Ketch and slumped forward again, engulfing his leg up to the thigh. The second Revenir was almost upon Horologine, who was still intent on consoling the newly arrived.

"You'll be needing this," said the scrap. Somehow the boy had sprinted forward, and retrieved the sword.

Ketch didn't waste a second on platitudes. He hacked and swore and growled. The Revenir was flayed, coming apart in gobbets of quivering flesh.

"Get off my leg, you bastard thing." But the Revenir had curled in a death spasm around Ketch's knee, immobilising him in the narrow alley.

"Horologine. Look out!"

The Kriegbauen stood and turned calmly, her dark gaze falling on the Revenir. There was a moment of stillness, as if something was being communicated in the silence.

"I will not stand aside," said Horologine quietly. She brushed some dust from her skirt as if the whole situation were merely an inconvenience. The Revenir convulsed from the base of its slab like body, rearing up until it towered over the Kriegbauen, some seven feet of bloodsucking parasite.

Ketch hacked at the corpse that held him fast, prying apart the dead flesh, but he was not quick enough to reach Horologine or the woman she shielded. The Revenir surged toward the Kriegbauen and Horologine flexed her hands. Bright steel blades emerged from her palms, piecing the upper section of the abyssal creature just below the weaving stalks. Horologine pressed her weight behind the blades, pressing the steel deeper into the creature. Revenir and Kreigbauen were locked together for several seconds before Horologine wrenched the blades sideways, pallid flesh and yellowed gore spattered the walls.

"Fuck's sake." Ketch sheathed his sword. "If I knew you could do that I'd have stayed home and gone to bed."

The scrap stared at Horologine in wonder and the blades disappeared back into her palms. She held one ceramic finger to the painted lips of her mask, indicating this was a secret they must keep between them.

"All Kreigbauen were disarmed after the war," said Horologine. "To carry weapons, concealed or otherwise, is forbidden."

The scrap nodded. "I was worried it was going to get you," he said before turning his back on them, heading to the cobbled street. Ketch watched him go, surprised when the boy waited at the corner.

It took a long time to coax Horologine's lost soul across the town. The newly-arrived woman fainted not long after they passed the Shimmersea Gate. Ketch had carried her over his shoulder, which was easier in some ways and a good deal heavier in others.

Finally, they fetched up The Street of Unholy Charnel, back at Horologine's blue door with its bright red graffiti.

"Do I have to wait down here again?" said the scrap. He'd not breathed a word since they'd left the alley, following close at Ketch's heels, wide eyed and watchful.

"No," said Horologine. "You must come upstairs."

Ketch smiled, noting the look of awe and excitement on the boy's face. Quite the difference from the near permanent scowl and the assertion "She ain't my lady".

Horologine spirited the newly arrived woman in to a bedroom, reached by a narrow door between the looming bookshelves.

Scrap, as Ketch had come to think of him, stared at the broad table and the Timekeeper's Tarot. To his credit he kept his hands to himself, but his eyes devoured every illustration and intricacy.

"What are they?" breathed the boy.

"They are a system of divination," said Horologine, slipping back

119

into the room. "A way to glimpse the near future." The Kreigbauen rang a small bell that summoned her servant. Scrap and Horologine's girl stared at each other for a few awkward seconds.

"Take the boy to the shop on the corner and make sure he eats," said Horologine. She pressed coins into the girl's hand and nodded slowly. The girl eyed Scrap, caught between wariness and obedience. She led him from the room and down the stairs with such reluctance that Ketch had to grin.

"You're getting slow," said Horologine.

"Was just a hangover. You caught me at a bad time."

"Perhaps you should spend less time drinking," said the Kreigbauen, taking up her place before the octagonal window. "What will you do now?"

"Take the boy to the apothecary. He has the Redfleck. He has it bad."

There was a long pause, and Ketch wondered if the meeting might have reached its end. Hard to tell with Kreigbauen sometimes.

"The cure for Redfleck is not inexpensive," said Horologine. "And requires a series of doses over a fortnight."

Ketch nodded. He wouldn't have much change out of the money he'd just earned, but that was the way of coin. Easy come and easy go.

Ketch shrugged. "Seems you're not the only one to gather up waifs and strays."

Horologine turned away from the window and approached the Timekeeper's Tarot, gathering the cards up tenderly.

"Come back tomorrow," said the Kriegbauen. "I will have more work for you. And bring the boy."

HER GRAIL

Ben North

An alchemist seeks the Grail (as so many have before her) across the lands of strangers no stranger than those she grew up alongside in the slums of the Borough. All brothers, sisters, parents and children under the skin, under dyes, silks and woollens, beneath dirt or perfumed oils.

She strikes deal after deal, makes compacts both Earthly and Infernal. All leave her diminished, the burning in her belly harsher, the bile she retches after each lonely meal taken in shadows more and more bitter.

The sacrifices she has made of others haunt her terribly. There is the head of an albino child delivered into the red hands of the Monks Martial at their Temple. With souls already stained by secrets found carved into Solomon's Stones, their rituals appease the only gods which now answer them in the cold vastness of divine abandonment. For Christ, weeping, has turned his face from their slaughter, so in desperation they seek patrons who would trade power for horrific tribute. In exchange for making that tribute possible, the warrior priests reveal to her much that even they fear.

In guaranteeing the unnatural succession of the Dead Lords of Navarre, she not only discovers a new branch of necromancy but also secures a horde of gems which finance her quest for half a decade. And dooms their servants and subjects for a century to come.

The betrayal of an entire fellowship of like-minded esoteric seekers, the closest she has ever come to friendship, all to secure a grey stone on a leathern thong. A thing so dull it gives no hint that it will take her to a cave in the high mountain passes of the hidden lands of the great lost monarch of Christendom: King John the Prester. And there show her the beginning of an end to a lifetime of searching.

A lesson learnt hard and early as a starveling child on the streets of a great city planted seeds which now near fruition. In disgust and waste, pain and despair, lies great reward – if only you know how the trick is done. The stinking streets of the tanneries taught her this, as she first glimpsed the magic which turned piss and turds and sheep brains and lime and raw hides into fortunes for merchants who wouldn't deign to go near the district where so many laboured for them.

For, after a ritual requiring the bones of a songbird she travelled twice the length of the Silk Road and then halfway again to secure, rare earths from twenty far-flung lands, and the sacrifice of her own left thumb and right forefinger, all immolated in the impossible heat of Greek Fire, she inhales smoke reeking of two decades of misdeeds – and exhales a vision.

A goblet. A chalice. Porphyry and gilt. A clumsy, heavy base of buttery silver, the broad cylinder inscribed with Aramaic, Latin, Arabic, Zoroastrian, and angular pictograms which she recognises as a bastardised strain of Elohimic. She knows now as surely as the hard ground she sits upon that it is there. Within that base, held tight within the moon metal, is a small stone cup.

There. The Grail. The Truth. A look beyond the veil, not the hazy glimpses she has had so far. This time the curtain will be held back, the light of knowledge cast upon her face for all time. Yes, for all of time, till the last days, till Revelation itself, for not only is this the Grail, the vessel from which the slaughtered godson drank before his betrayal, but it is also a *lapis philosophorum*, a squared circle, the alchemist's Great Work.

What follows are relatively simple matters of organisation. She travels secretly to the Levant, undetected and unhindered by assassins bound in a deadlocke forged by her fellow seekers after Greater Truth, a vengeful and influential former lover, and all the power, wealth and implacable hatred of both the Church of Peter and the Eastern Patriarchs.

Once there, she recruits by blackmail the most skilled and irreligious thieves in the whole empire of the Mohammedans, and has them steal by way of kidnapping and much murder the contents of an old reliquary, long forgotten in the sealed vaults of a cathedral made mosque.

After guaranteeing the death of all those involved, by means of a pact arcane and ancient she smuggles the entire haul across the Middle Sea in the span of but a single night. She comes to rest only when she reaches a sheep-herder's cottage in the hills above Tarragona, the shepherd's blood now feeding the roots of the twisted thorn bushes behind the hovel.

Then, among the fake finger bones of martyrs, nails of the 'true cross' and stolen treasures of many centuries of rapine and plunder, she picks up the chalice. It is gaudy, unbalanced, a thing ill-formed despite its opulence.

And she smashes it hard against the blackened stone of the hearth.

Into a crucible made nearly white hot, she places the heavy silver cylinder of the base, the marks of a thousand years sliding away in molten seconds.

Then it is there.

She beholds it.

It cools.

She holds it.

Then, simply, a draft of fresh spring water poured in. It holds but three modest mouthfuls, but her cup runneth over, filled as it is to the brim.

And yet when she drinks it, she cannot stop. Three mouthfuls become four, five, forty, sixty, three hundred.

There it is, all of it. Something akin to truth in every gulped mouthful.

And she is drowning in all the knowledge of the world.

Piercing the Mist

Shona Kinsella

It was dusk when Jocarrah landed at the edge of the village. I stood, wincing at the cramp in my thighs from riding so long. Jocarrah nudged me with a head almost as large as my torso and a rumble started somewhere deep in his throat. He licked my arm, his tongue rough, his fang grazing my forearm.

"Go," I said, ruffling his mane. "Hunt. I will call for you in the morning."

He growled again and took to the air, buffeting me with the downdraft from his wings. I watched until he was out of sight then stretched, tightened my bag, and headed for home.

A snake of fear coiled in my stomach. In all the months I had been away training, Mother had written only twice. For her to have sent a message asking me to come home on the same day that I passed the test, earning my place in the Lion Guard, seemed ill-fated. I pushed the fear away, trying to recapture my joy at being the first female member of the Guard.

The village was quiet as I made my way between the houses, towards the small, blue-painted home of my mother. I frowned as I saw that the garden looked a little overgrown. My mother was a fastidious woman – it was not like her to allow things to become untidy.

"Ko!" I called in greeting from the gate. Mma Gabedon, my mother, appeared in the doorway to the wooden house.

"Hope!" She ran down the path and I opened the gate and hurried to meet her. Mother grabbed me in a tight embrace and I pretended not to notice the wet patch at my shoulder where her tears had soaked into my tunic.

"Let me get a look at you," she said, holding me at arm's length. "Well, your braids are a mess, your clothes are dusty and you're too skinny. Don't they feed you at that training camp?"

I bit back a retort as Mother bustled about me. "It's good to see you, too."

"Go and wash up and then come in for dinner." She lifted her skirt as she walked up the steps to the door, pausing on the top one, her back still to me. "I'm glad you're here."

When I went inside after washing at the pump, Mother was putting food out on the table and my mouth watered at the smell of it. Spiced chicken with rice and mango, one of her specialities.

"Where is Baruti?" I asked, when I realised that Mother had only set out two plates.

Mother paused, her body tense, then continued setting out the food. "I don't know where your brother is."

"What do you mean? Is he out with Tomas?"

Mother sat down heavily and put her face in her hands

"Mother! What's wrong?"

I fell to my knees at her side and stroked her back, fussing over her.

"Please, tell me what's happened?" I didn't like the pleading tone in my voice, but I couldn't suppress it.

"He's gone," Mother choked out. "He ran away and joined The Mist."

I sat back on my heels, stunned. "But, *why*?"

"A new man, Yapo, came into town," Mother said. "He said he was a wondering preacher, bringing news of the gods. He spent a lot of time with the young men of the village, Baruti and Tomas among them." Mother pulled a handkerchief from her skirt pocket and blew her nose. "I thought nothing of it – encouraged it even, you know how restless Baruti has been since your father died. How can I have been so blind? This is all my fault! If only I had paid attention sooner."

"When did you realise something was wrong?"

"Baruti changed. He became sullen, started arguing with me over everything."

"That must have been upsetting for you, arguing with him instead of me." The words were out of my mouth before I could stop them, and I flushed with shame when I saw the look of pain cross Mother's face. "I'm sorry. Go on."

"He came home very late one night, long after curfew, and when I questioned him he said he didn't recognise the curfew as law, that the king had no rightful place –"

"Stop!"

Mother looked up sharply, seeming surprised and a little irritated at my interruption.

"I'm a member of the Lion Guard now, sworn to protect and defend the royal family. If Baruti has said treasonous things, I cannot know about it."

The colour drained from Mother's face. "How could you say that about your own brother?"

"You want me to abandon everything I've worked towards, since I was a child, everything I believe in, just because Baruti has gone and done something stupid?"

"I don't understand you," Mother said, her tone caught somewhere between anger and sadness.

"When did he leave?" I asked, trying to guide the conversation to safer ground.

"Ten days ago. Tomas too, and a few others. They all left during the night, with Yapo."

"Has anyone tried to track them down?"

"Some of the fathers went after them but too much time had passed; they couldn't find them."

I stared over Mother's shoulder, mind racing. As a member of the Lion Guard I should report this straight away. The Mist were the most wanted group in the kingdom and I had a lead on them, however small. But if Baruti was found with them, he would be tried for treason.

"I don't know what to do, Hope. I'm so scared for him."

I wrapped my arms around Mother and squeezed her tight. "We'll think of something. I promise."

I walked along a path outside the village, scuffing my sandaled feet in the dust. There was only one place I could think of to go for help, but it was the last place I wanted to be. The village witch.

She sat on a stool outside her door, shelling beans. Her hair was unbound, with thick streaks of grey marring the walnut colour of the rest. She looked up at me with one green eye and one brown and squinted.

"Good evening, Hope of the Lion Guard."

The possessive way she said my name sent a shiver down my spine and I thought of just turning around and walking away, calling for Jocarrah and flying straight to the palace. Instead, I swallowed hard and answered her.

"Good evening, Shira,"

"What brings you to my humble home?"

"Just walking," I said.

Shira looked at me without saying a word, her mismatched eyes boring into me.

"I have a problem," I said and then the whole story came pouring out of me.

"And what would you like me to do about all of this?" Shira asked when I was finished.

"I want you to help me to find him and bring him home."

Shira laughed. "Do I look like I'm about to go hunting around for some lost young man who means nothing to me?"

I looked at the thick staff propped next to Shira's stool, the lines of age on her face, the loose way the skin hung from her arms. I sighed.

"No. I suppose not."

"Do you know why they call themselves The Mist?" Shira asked, seemingly from nowhere.

I frowned. "Isn't it something to do with being everywhere and no one can touch them?"

"Ha! That's what they like people to think, but no. They're called The Mist because they cast a mist over your thoughts so that nothing looks quite the same any more. It is powerful magic, but, just like mist, it can be pierced."

"How?" I asked, desperate for some way to save Baruti.

"Like all magic, there is a cost," Shira answered. "Are you willing to pay it?"

"What will the cost be?"

"I cannot say. The gods decide, and you will not know what it is until payment comes due."

"That hardly seems fair."

Shira shrugged. "What does fair have to do with it? Fairness is a human notion, it means nothing to the gods."

I rubbed my head and tried to think. I loved my brother, I did, but could I make a bargain without knowing what would be asked of me? What if it meant sacrificing my place in the Lion Guard?

"I see you're taking this seriously," Shira said. "Good. Too many people rush into magic without thinking things through. Why don't you come back in a few days, when you've had time to decide?"

"I can't, I am to report to the palace tomorrow. I don't know when I will next have leave to return home."

I thought of Baruti with something other than anger at his foolishness. I remembered how he would tag along behind me when we were children, always happy to let me take the lead. I remembered his open, trusting face and his willingness to stay in the village and look after Mother when I went away to train for the Lion Guard.

"What do I need to do?" I asked.

"I will mix up a powder for you. You must carry this with you; you must be physically close to your brother for this to work. You take a handful of the powder and blow it into his face. He has to breath it in. The powder will counteract the spell he is under, clear his mind. You must then keep him away from the Mist; if he returns to them, he will be lost forever."

"How do I find him?" I asked.

"That part is for you to achieve." Shira rose, brushing off her skirt. "Now, leave me to my work. Come and collect the powder before you leave in the morning."

I woke to the smell of cooking onions and the clang of a pot on the stove, floorboards creaking as Mother moved about the kitchen. I got up and glanced out the window while I pulled trousers and a tunic on. The first faint blush of dawn touched the sky; Mother was up early.

I padded, barefoot, through to the main living area and stood, watching her for a moment before she noticed me. She was wearing one of her best dresses and had her hair loose, cascading over her shoulders.

"You look lovely," I said, making her jump.

"I didn't realise you were there."

"Special occasion?" I asked, gesturing to the dress.

"I wanted to see you off in style."

My heart ached a little. "You didn't have to do that," I said softly. "You always look beautiful to me."

Mother gave me a sad little smile and turned back to the stove. "I'll braid your hair for you before you leave, if you like."

I sat at the table and considered telling her about my visit with Shira the day before. I didn't like keeping secrets, but I also didn't want to get her hopes up. I still had to find Baruti and there was no guarantee the powder would work when I did. Instead, I promised her that I would not give up on him and then we made small talk over breakfast.

Mother cleared the dishes then stood behind me, deftly weaving my unruly hair into braids. Into each braid, she wove threads of different colours, one for each of the twenty high gods. She finished by winding the braids around each other on the back of my head and securing them with an ornate pin that my father had given me, not long before he died. Tears prickled the backs of my eyes when I realised that this may be the last time Mother would do my hair.

When I slid from Jocarrah's back, Shira was seated in the same spot as they day before. The wind carried her scent to us, ancient and dry. The witch narrowed her eyes when Jocarrah growled, a low grumble that carried a threat I was unused to hearing.

"Don't worry, he won't harm you," I said, giving the lion a warning look.

"I'm not scared of him; that is why he grumbles." Shira answered, getting to her feet. She handed me a small pouch that smelled of earth and spices and something I couldn't place. "Remember, only use this if you are prepared to meet the cost, otherwise things will not go well for you. Understand?"

"I do. Thank you for your help, Shira."

The witch looked to the sky and shrugged. "We all have our roles to play. Go now."

Jocarrah landed in the palace courtyard and we were immediately met by a servant, dressed in impractical white robes. He directed me to the Lion Hall, a large building behind the palace which served as the base for the Lion Guard.

The door was opened by a young guard I vaguely recognised from the training camp. He ushered us both inside and then closed the door. We stood in an entrance hall that had to be larger than my mother's entire house. On my left was a door, which stood open, showing a room with a desk and chairs. The commander stood from behind the desk and made his way into the hall.

"I am Commander Tau. You must be our new recruit."

"Yes, sir."

"I have been informed that you impressed your trainers and passed the entrance test with great skill." The commander held his hand out to Jocarrah, allowing the lion to sniff him. "If you continue to perform like this, I will be glad to have you."

"Thank you, sir."

"Get yourself settled in. Begin to familiarise yourself with the layout of the palace. Report to me at the second gong tomorrow for your first duty."

"Yes, sir." I looked around, unsure of where to go.

"Kefen, show the recruit around, please, see that she has everything she needs."

"Of course, sir." The guard who had opened the door turned to me. "Let's get your lion sorted first. Follow me."

After I had settled Jocarrah into the lion enclosure and dropped my belongings off in my room, Kefen took me to get something to eat. We settled at a table in the middle of the dining room with bowls of goat strew and chunks of bread.

"I know the theory, of course – what they teach in the training camp," I said between mouthfuls of stew, "but what is life really like here?"

"Mostly it's routine. As you're new you'll be put on grounds patrol. You have to be here a while before you're on palace duty."

Kefen paused, dipping some bread into his stew and then taking a large bite.

"What's the biggest threat?" I asked.

Kefen looked around and then leaned towards me, lowering his voice. "I'm not sure how much I'm supposed to say but the Commander will brief you tomorrow anyway. The official position is that assassins from other countries are the only threat to the king; that makes everyone feel safe because the king is on good terms with all of our neighbours. The truth is, the only attempts to be made on the royal family in recent years have come from The Mist."

My stomach clenched.

"In fact," Kefen continued, "there were two attempts to gain access to the palace in the last month. Both prevented, of course, but I know the king is concerned about this new boldness."

I was so focussed on Kefen that I didn't notice the other man approaching until he was standing beside our table.

"You must be the entertainment," he said, looking down at me.

"Excuse me?" I asked.

"Well, I know we haven't stooped to allowing women to join the Guard, so you must be here to entertain us." He leered at me as he spoke, looking me up and down.

I fought the urge to cross my arms over my breasts, knowing that my discomfort would only amuse him.

Responses raced through my mind. Should I ignore him or taunt him? Belittle him or hit him?

"Aren't you going to dance for us?"

His foul breath washed over me, making my skin crawl. I pushed my chair back and got to my feet. Silence had rippled out from our table until everyone in the dining hall had stopped what they were doing to watch us.

"Worried I'm better than you?" I asked, sneering.

"Don't be ridiculous, little girl," he snarled.

"Why else would you object to me being here?"

"The day you can best me is the day I leave the guard."

"Promise?" I asked sweetly.

He looked around, seeming to suddenly realise that he had very publicly backed himself into a corner.

"I don't have time for this," he muttered then turned and stormed off.

I sat back down and forced myself to begin eating again, although

I didn't relax until everyone else had returned to their meals and the buzz of conversation once more filled the room.

"Don't take it personally," Kefen said. "Haverin bullies everyone."

"I can handle him," I said, but inside I wasn't so sure.

I settled into a routine quickly. I was given the early watch so patrolled my section of the grounds from dawn until noon. I spent the rest of my time with Jocarrah and avoiding Haverin as much as I could.

Wherever I went, the powder Shira had given me hung from a pouch on my belt. The weight of it was a constant reminder that I had not yet figured out how to save Baruti. My duties kept me close to the palace and I was already under enough scrutiny.

I began to think that I may not be able to help my brother at all and I swung between relief at not having to choose and guilt over my lack of faithfulness. If it had been the other way around, I had no doubt that Baruti would have come for me by now.

One morning, as I sat astride Jocarrah, flying over the princesses' private gardens, an unfamiliar pattern of movement caught my eye. I nudged Jocarrah with my knees and he held us in place while I scanned the ground. The trillia, carnivorous vines that bore sweet smelling flowers and venomous barbs, were furling back in on themselves. Something warm-blooded had passed this way, close enough to excite them.

Everyone who should be in the garden knew better than to get too close to the vines.

I straightened my spine and looked around, carefully searching the shadows for any hint of movement. I chewed my lip as I tried to decide what to do. Should I raise the alarm and risk being branded a fool if there was nothing amiss? Could I afford to make that sort of mistake? I could look around some more by myself, but what if there was someone sneaking around the grounds and I missed them?

I had almost resolved to raise the alarm when I pictured Haverin laughing at me. I clenched my jaw and guided Jocarrah in an ever-widening spiral over the gardens.

Closer towards the palace walls, there were scuffs in the pebble-lined path, indication of a struggle. That was all I needed. I pulled the whistle from my pouch and blew it as loudly as I could, three short blasts and then a long one

Protocol was for me to stay where I was until the commander reached me but below, a man burst from beneath the branches of a fruit tree and ran for the palace wall, towards the entrance to the Princesses' wing. I urged Jocarrah to follow as the man below weaved between trees and bushes, making it difficult to keep track of him. Close to the walls, he ran out of cover and I ordered Jocarrah into a dive; he shot down through the air to land on top of the intruder, pinning him to the ground under one enormous paw.

I slid from Jocarrah's back and told him to back off. For a moment, he just looked at me, golden eyes unfathomable, drool dripping from his fangs. I stood in front of him and growled, pushing his nose back. Eventually, Jocarrah stepped away.

I pulled my dart pipe from the pouch at my belt and slipped a dart inside, holding it ready to use if the intruder tried anything.

His tunic was ripped and a wound on his back seeped blood where Jocarrah's claw had broken his skin. His leg was bent at an odd angle. He groaned and turned his head towards me.

"Who are you?" I asked. "What are you doing here?"

"Death to the King," the man said through clenched teeth.

I heard more whistles and shouts; the others would be here any minute.

"Are you one of The Mist?" I asked urgently.

"Only The Mist know the truth," the man said, clawing at the ground, trying to pull himself towards the palace.

"Don't move." I raised the blowpipe with one hand while fumbling in my belt pouch with the other. This was my chance – I could test the powder, make sure it worked before I used it on Baruti. My fingers found the drawstring bag from Shira. I tipped a small amount of the powder onto my hand and hurriedly blew it into the intruder's face.

He breathed in, sneezed, and passed out just as the commander alighted beside me.

The corridors beneath the palace were a maze of ochre brick and flickering torches. In some places water dripped through from unknown sources, giving the air a faint mineral scent, a bit like the lake near home just before it began to disappear at the start of the dry season. I took a few wrong turns but each time I quickly realised my mistake and turned back. By the time I reached the corridor leading to the cells, I was having second thoughts.

What if word of this expedition got back to the commander? Had I earned enough good will from him today to allow me this breach in procedure?

I hesitated, considering turning back. This was the best chance I had to find a way to help Baruti. I had to take it.

I strode down the corridor and turned the corner to see a guard I had not spoken to before standing outside a cell door. He looked me up and down and a bead of sweat trickled down my back.

"What are you doing down here?" he asked.

"I just wanted to make sure the prisoner was secure," I said.

"Worried we weren't looking after him properly?"

"Worried I hadn't done everything I should have, more like," I answered, letting my shoulders collapse so that I would look smaller, less threatening.

The guard's features softened into a smile. "You did well to subdue him," he said. "We've not been able to take one alive in a long time. Normally, they're so fanatical they'd rather die than fail in their mission."

"It was an accident," I forced a laugh. "My lion knocked him out."

"Tell the commander it was a carefully calculated move." The guard grinned. "I'm Deve, by the way."

"Hope," I said.

"I know who you are," Deve replied.

"Could I speak with him, just for a minute?" I asked.

"On you go," Deve said, gesturing to the door behind him. "Only a few minutes though."

"Thank you."

I stepped into the cell and closed the door behind me. The intruder was huddled in the corner, injured leg splinted, a vacant look on his face. I hurried over and crouched beside him.

"Who are you?" I asked in a low voice.

He turned to look at me and I saw for the first time how lined his face was, how weather worn. "My name is Galien." His voice came out in a dry croak.

I looked around for some water but there was none in the small room. I would just have to hope his voice didn't give out before I got what I needed.

"Why did you come here?"

Galien swallowed hard. "To kill the king."

"Why?"

"The Mist sent me. I ... I don't know why I did it, though. It was as if they had some power over me." He grabbed my arm, his fingers digging in to my flesh. "You must believe me! I didn't act of my own accord!"

"I believe you," I said, peeling his fingers away.

"Did you free me? How did you do it?"

"It's a long story and I don't have much time," I said, looking towards the door. "Someone I know was taken by The Mist and I'm trying to find him. Baruti Gabedon. Do you know him?"

"No, I don't think so," Galien said. "Will you speak for me? Tell them that I didn't mean to come here, that I wasn't in control."

"Are you sure you didn't know Baruti? He was recruited by a man calling himself Yapo."

Galien stiffened at that. "I know Yapo. He runs the camp on the east side of Verova, in the caves on the mountainside. He recruited me."

"So, Baruti might be there? On Verova?"

"Yapo might have sent him on to one of the other camps by now but that would be the best place to start."

I stood up and turned for the door.

Galien croaked. "Please help me. I don't want to be executed."

A stab of guilt made me feel sick. I had been so busy thinking about how I could use Galien to find Baruti, I hadn't considered what would happen to him, another innocent caught by the magic of The Mist.

"I will do everything I can," I said, knowing it wouldn't be much.

Deve was relieved to see me leave. I thanked him once more and took off, before we both got caught. I hurried along the corridors, replaying my conversation with Galien and feeling the weight of his requests for help. I grudgingly came to the decision that I needed help. I would have to tell Commander Tau everything and pray that he would help rather than having me thrown in beside Galien.

The wind was knocked out of me when I was suddenly thrown to the side, crashing through a door and landing hard on the cold, brick floor. Before I could get my bearings, someone was pinning me down.

"Not so tough now, are you girl?"

I would recognise that foul breath anywhere. Haverin.

"Get off," I growled.

"Not until I've taught you a lesson," Haverin panted. "You want to be a man so much? Then you don't need all this hair."

He pulled one of my braids loose and swiftly sawed his knife through it. He tossed it aside and grabbed another.

Fury flooded my veins and I began to thrash, hissing and spitting, snapping my teeth towards whatever I could reach. I managed to knock Haverin off balance and wriggled out from beneath him. The knife lay on the floor and I snatched it up, along with my braid.

"I'll have you now, bitch," Haverin spat, lunging towards me.

I ducked to the side and swiped with the knife, drawing a line across his side. He howled and crumpled to the floor. I crouched, panting, watching him. Blood leaked between his fingers where he held his side, but the wound was shallow.

"The next time this knife tastes your blood it'll spill every last drop," I said, getting to my feet and stumbling backwards out the door.

Right into the path of Commander Tau.

"Let me get this right," Commander Tau sat behind his desk, pinching his nose. "You, Haverin, one of my senior guards, felt it was appropriate to assault a fellow guard because you don't like her gender?"

"There's no place for –" Haverin started.

"Yes, or no, guardsman!" Commander Tau's tone was deadly.

"Yes, sir." Haverin looked at his feet.

The commander nodded to the guardsmen at the back of the

room. "Throw him in a cell until I decide what to do with him."

Haverin shot me a look of pure hatred. "Ask her what she was doing in with the prisoner."

"Take him away," the commander fixed his eyes on mine. As soon as the room was empty he said, "Well?"

I thought about denying that I had ever been there but Deve could back up Haverin. I thought about trying to come up with a convincing lie, something that would leave Baruti out of it, but I was exhausted and emotionally spent. Today had been too much.

"I was trying to get information that would help me find my brother."

I told Commander Tau everything. He had Galien brought up to be questioned and a wave of relief washed over me when he supported everything I had said. Eventually it was just the two of us again. I knew I should be scared – he could have me executed for treason if he so wished – instead I was empty.

"You should have told me all of this when you first arrived here," Commander Tau said, staring at me over steepled fingers.

"I know," I said, weary.

"Still, it seems clear to me that you acted out of nothing but loyalty to your brother and that is something I cannot fault. Go to your room. Get some sleep. Report to me at the third gong tomorrow, when I'll decide on a course of action."

"My room, sir?"

"Your room. For the moment, at least."

"Thank you, sir."

I stumbled upstairs and fell asleep fully dressed.

Three days later, dawn streaked the sky behind Mount Verova with vibrant colour as we flew past. Fully half of the Lion Guard had flown all night to be here now, pouches of Shira's powder at every belt.

"We need them to come outside," Commander Tau called. "Let's announce ourselves!"

Bellrika, his lion, roared and the others all answered. The noise was terrifying.

Shouts sounded below as people ran from the caves and scattered across the mountainside. As one, the Lion Guard swooped, skimming over the fleeing men and women, releasing the powder over their heads. One by one, the people below fell unconscious, many collapsing mid-stride. Some few managed to escape but by far the majority of those in the camp were captured that day.

As soon as the commander gave the order to land, I was on the ground and running from one fallen man to another, searching for Baruti. He was the twentieth man that I turned over. I glanced towards the cave mouth and saw a man matching Galien's description of Yapo moving back into the darkness. I blew my whistle then sprinted after him.

Inside the cave, it took my eyes a moment to adjust but I could hear movement up ahead. I had no powder left but I had my blowpipe and I was determined that the man who had ruined so many lives would not escape. I followed the sound, before I could see clearly. I heard the swish of something sharp cutting through the air at the same time I saw the shadow move. Something hit my arm and pain exploded right up to my shoulder, making my vision go white. The metallic tang of blood filled my nostrils and I lifted the blowpipe to my lips. I was swaying, and I knew I was going to pass out. Just before my knees buckled, the shadow moved again, and I blew a dart.

I awoke wrapped in bandages, Baruti by my side. I was in a bed in a small room that I didn't recognise. I was groggy, my thoughts slow.

"What happened?" I asked, licking dry lips.

Baruti jumped from his chair. "You're awake!" He poked his head out the door and shouted to someone that I was awake before coming back and holding out a glass of water to me. I tried to lift my injured arm to take the glass. My arm didn't respond.

I tried again, staring at it dumbly when it stayed lying by my side.

"You were injured saving me," Baruti explained. "You went after Yapo and he attacked you."

Before I could say anything, the door opened, and Commander Tau entered, followed by Kefen.

"Good to see you awake," the commander said.

"Thank you, sir." I tried to push myself up but couldn't.

"I want you to know that you killed the man known as Yapo, one

139

of the head recruiters of The Mist. You have done a great service for your King."

"What will happen now, sir?" I asked, trying to figure out why I felt such dread.

"We have gained valuable information from those captured; for the first time, we can take the fight to The Mist." He looked at me with pity and I wanted to scream but didn't know why. "The healer has said that you may regain some function in your arm, as time passes."

"I don't understand," I mumbled.

"Yapo attacked you. He almost cut your arm off, you were lucky to keep it at all."

I looked at Kefen and he blinked fast and looked away. I clenched my jaw until it hurt. "I'll practice, day and night, until I'm just as good with one arm as I was with two."

"Yes, well." Commander Tau sighed. "In the meantime, you'll be given an administrative role, and the King wishes to reward you. You'll be given a minor title and some land."

"The King is gracious."

"Go home with your brother. Get some rest. Come back to us when the healers say you are ready."

Once more, Shira was seated outside her house, but this time she was at rest, face tilted towards the sun. I hesitated to disturb her, so peaceful she looked.

"Well, are you just going to stand there all day?" she asked without opening her eyes.

I snorted. Whatever made me think her ignorant of my presence? She had doubtless known I was coming even before I left home.

"I brought you some things, from my mother." I said, placing my basket down.

"Your mother is kind." Shira still hadn't moved. I couldn't decide if it was more or less disconcerting when I couldn't see her mismatched eyes.

"She is grateful to have her son returned to her," I said.

"Less pleased that her daughter is not returning, I would imagine."

"I'm sure she'll be much happier now that I can't fly," I said, a sharp edge to my words.

"You are still in the Guard, as you wished – what have you to complain about?"

"In name only. I've lost everything I loved about the Guard."

"Give it time," Shira said gently. This was a side I hadn't seen before and it disturbed me more than I cared to admit. "You may yet fly again. I would be more concerned about your Commander Tau; think what price he will be asked to pay for the amount of magic he has used."

"Is that supposed to make me feel better?" I asked bitterly.

"Feel better or not, it is your choice." Shira tipped her head back and closed her eyes again. "I'll be seeing you again soon, Hope of the Lion Guard."

Chosen of the Slain

K.T. Davies

A ghost sun hung low in a pewter sky. Pallid rays pierced the gloom and inlaid the shadowed boughs of black pines with silver. Shards of iron had been hung from the looming trees and rang like temple chimes, but the forest was not a temple, and the Vadrui were far from pious.

True, those who dwelt under the direct and benevolent rule of the Provincial Governor had been delivered into the light of The Way. Alas, the Governor and the pointed influence of her legions were far from here. Out here in the benighted hinterland, heathen gods still held sway, and demons haunted the nightmares of the ignorant. Albrecht raised his visor and rubbed his tired eyes. Given the vast array of rusting metal charms hanging from the trees, the locals were either besieged by an army of devils or were the most superstitious peasants he'd thus far encountered in this most superstitious land. Another brace snapped, distracting him from his musing and throwing the struggling labourers into the mire. The funeral carriage rocked back into the mud, and one of the conscripted villagers cried out.

"My leg, my leg's caught!" Panic and pain shrilled the lad's voice as he struggled like a rat in a trap to pull his leg from between the buckled wheel and the listing wagon.

Albrecht looked at Kroust who was up front with the lead pair of horses. The young knight shrugged, as helpless as he was against the combined forces of poor roads, the thoughtless ostentation of princes, and the ineptitude of mismade peasants.

"Yori, get on the brace." The blacksmith stood head and shoulders above his countrymen, which added weight to his words. He tossed his hammer aside and rolled up his sleeves, revealing forearms as befitted a man of his trade. They were also heavily scarred, more so than Albrecht would have expected of a village smith, even a bad one. Something about the man's confidence kindled the knight's interest. The smith was big, but much of the muscle that had once sat upon his broad back and chest now hung heavily around his middle. As with most of these heathens, he wore his greying hair long and his beard braided. "Feli, put that wedge under the wheel. "Gian, help Yori." The smith shoved one of the exhausted rustics out of the way and wrapped another's hands around a brace. They followed his direction eagerly and without question. The listing funeral carriage groaned like a wounded beast, its axles creaked under the strain, and stressed bolts twisted. The trapped boy whimpered, aware that time was against him. The smith spat on his hands and wedged his pole against the damaged wheel. "When I say lift, you all lift. Narri, Feli, you be ready to pull him out." He didn't shout, the old bull instructed with the calm assurance of a man used to giving orders. "Lift!"

Fighting to keep their footing in the treacherous mud, the men heaved on the poles. Albrecht would have put money on their efforts being wasted as the damned thing weighed eight tonnes. The smith grunted, his massive shoulders strained, and wood groaned ominously. To the knight's surprise, they lifted the carriage – just a few inches, but it was enough for them to drag the boy clear. Against all odds, the peasants had won their battle; alas, when the wagon came to rest, the wheel finally gave out, snapping bracing poles like matchwood and delivering the final victory to the mud and Albrecht's continuing misery.

Despite being worth more than the village and all the inhabitants, the labourers abandoned the crippled funeral carriage in favour of tending to the boy. After a quick examination, they got the churl back on his feet.

"A Miracle of The Way," Albrecht called to Kroust. The younger man gave him a questioning look until he saw the direction of his gaze.

"Oh, yes, indeed. Praise be, brother."

One of the yokels slapped the shaken lad on the back. "Aye, Turlig. If you'd bin under that thing when the wheel went." He made a snapping gesture. The boy swallowed.

"Well, he wasn't." The blacksmith wiped his hands on his leather apron. "Now get him home to his ma. And for..." The smith caught Albrecht's eye. "For *Saints'* sake, don't tell her what happened." The labourers made to return to the village but slowed to a halt when they saw Albrecht. Some looked to the smith for direction, some to the knight.

Old authority against new, eh? So be it. "I didn't say you could leave." Albrecht didn't want to converse with the nithlings if he could avoid it. He spoke their dog tongue well enough, but Vadrun was an ugly language; rough on the throat and so guttural that even lovers' lies sounded like insults.

"The boy's hurt. He needs to go home." The smith strode over to Albrecht, again taking command like he was born to it.

"I can see that, smith. The others seem whole enough. Pray, why are they leaving?"

"We're going to need more braces, and more men now the wheel's broke. They've been at it all morn, they need t'eat, and I need more tools and..."

Bored, Albrecht raised a mailed fist. "All right, all right. How long?"

The bull scratched his chin. "Tomorrow... probably."

"Saints' sake!"

"If you say so."

Like a good blade, the smith's insolence was finely balanced. It dawned on Albrecht that he was beginning to dislike a man who should have been beneath his notice. "Those scars on your arms. You were a Raven Warrior, no?"

"No, my lord." The fellow buried his gaze in the dirt. "They all died."

"Not all. I heard that to avoid the gallows, some of the murderous scum cut the marks of their allegiance from their flesh." He leaned on his saddle. "Can you believe it? Such cowardice, such weakness."

The smith threw him a bladed glance. "All tattoos are forbidden, and no one would keep a mark, no matter how innocent, that might see their family sold into slavery for lack of coin to pay the fine."

"It's for the sake of your souls. Tattoos are barbaric, ungodly, and against The Way."

"That knowledge came but recently to this land."

Damn him. The peasant had drawn him into a debate. Albrecht smiled tightly, noted that Kroust was watching intently, no doubt storing away the details of the encounter for later mockery. "If the *tax* of which you speak were applied to insolent tongues the imperial coffers would have enough coin to pave every cart track in this shithole with Lorentzian marble." The smith bristled, and so he should. He should feel shame in his heathen soul; the sting of truth should be as a scourge upon these people until they learned their place. "Something wrong?"

He thought about it almost too long before answering. "No, sir."

"I didn't think so." Albrecht's Cambrian blood revelled in the submission of his enemy, but he was also a Knight of the Way. It was his sworn duty to educate these animals and save their souls from eternal damnation. He patted his horse's neck. "You know, if you people spent less time fighting us, you would learn, and you would prosper."

"Aye, sir." The man sweated insolence and breathed disrespect.

"Just get a move on. We have many miles to travel before we reach the monastery at Ravens' Fall."

The mention of the monastery kindled fire in the smith's eyes. "Your Lord ain't going to get any less dead, no matter how long it takes to get this gilded coffin cart out of the mud."

He couldn't argue with that. Lord Orfitz was five weeks dead, and no matter what Yalst said, not all the incense in Vadra could mask the stench of liquifying corpse, gods knew, they'd tried. Truth aside, he couldn't let the smith's impertinence pass without redress. He struck the surly cur across the face with his crop. The welt rose immediately, pimpled with blood. The old warrior tensed.

Now that he had baited the bear Albrecht wanted him to attack, just to see what the old warrior had left, but then he would have to kill him, and the damn carriage would never be repaired. "Raise your hand to me, and you forfeit your kin."

The massive fists unclenched. The smith wiped blood from his face, left a wry smile in its place. "And you're a holy warrior?"

"I am indeed a Knight of the Way, but if you strike me I will be forced to hang you and your kin; oldest to youngest. This will not be in retaliation; a Knight of The Way has no ego to offend. It will be as a lesson." He smiled benevolently while enjoying watching the smith seethe. "You're part of the Tath Taran Empire now. Cambria knelt before the Throne of the Sun two hundred years ago and now, so must Vadra."

"Kneel, or die, eh?"

"Now you're getting it." Albrecht turned his mount towards the village.

"You'll have a harder time convincing the Wittekin."

The knight knew it wasn't what the Vadrui said that frighted a flock of crows from the trees but merely the act of raising his gravelled voice. Heavy-bodied, the birds tore into the sky as if they hated air, the clap of their night-brushed wings a mockery of applause, their call, shrieking laughter. Albrecht's mount stamped, fought the bit. The milling labourers ceased their chatter. Kroust half-drew his sword and scanned the treeline as though the mere mention of the forest demons would summon them.

"What did you say?" Albrecht asked, knowing full well what the smith had said, but this wasn't a question, it was a test. The smith's life and the lives of his kin would be defined by what he said next. *Now there was power*, the only power a nithling like this would ever possess, and he knew it. Albrecht could see it in his pale eyes; the steel certainty that his words now carried a potentially fatal weight.

"Nothing, sir." His furious gaze stabbed the ground.

"Are you quite sure?" the knight asked, bored of a game where he held all of the pieces. The smith nodded. "You have an hour. Do what you have to do then get back here and get this fucking carriage out of the fucking mud. And, while you're at it, cut that superstitious garbage down." He waved at the charms hanging in the trees.

"Sir –" The smith began.

With heel and rein, Albrecht gave the command for his horse to rear forcing the cur to leap back to avoid her flying hooves. Amused, the knight turned to the village and cantered away.

Albrecht didn't know what the dump was called and didn't care to find out. He rode through the market place, past dirty children, past the chapel of The Way that had been gifted to the village, to the inn where his fellow knights had been billeted. The smell of incense drifting from the chapel charged the woodsmoke brume with the scent of juniper, cinnamon, and pine. The holy odour warred with the smell of pork fat and mead leaking from the inn. The sound of drunken laughter vied with liturgical chants and promised, if not heaven, a respite from the purgatory of this particular corner of nowhere. He dismounted and called for a groom. Hanging over the door, low enough to brush his head, was another iron charm made of rusted nails bound with reeds. He tore it down and threw it in the mud.

The inn was spacious with a stone hearth and deep inglenook, something of a luxury from what Albrecht had seen on his travels across Vadra. The other four knights of the honour guard acknowledged their captain with a salute when he entered. He returned the gesture, bade them remain seated with a wave when they made to rise. Praster Yalst was sitting alone at the best table in the inn, which had been laid with his personal silver plate. The skeletal remains of two capons sat beside a bowl of dried fruit, a loaf of white bread, and a jug of mead. A pair of hounds waited patiently for Yalst to finish off the remaining birds. The Praster poured a goblet of mead, took a slurp. "This is quite good, you know. You should try it, Albrecht."

"Only water for me. I'm fasting until we reach the monastery." Out of the corner of his eye he saw some of his knights surreptitiously hide mugs under their cloaks.

The priest laughed, spraying chicken across the table. "You amuse me, knight." The ochre-robed priest looked ten years younger than he was and always surprised, having been blessed with large eyes that were set too wide apart in a childishly round face.

Albrecht took off his helm. "Shouldn't you be leading the Mortumatis, showing the youngsters how it's done?"

"I am, in spirit." He patted the bench. "Come sit – you haven't taken a vow against sitting, have you?"

"No."

"Splendid. Have they repaired our General's chariot?"

"Tomorrow, probably. The wheel broke."

"I knew it. I knew that..." He cleared his throat. "*Wonderful gift* of the Governor wouldn't cope with these roads. Innkeep! Yes you, dear. I need your best room and a bath drawn. You do have a bathtub?"

The woman curtsied, tucked an errant braid behind her ear. "Aye, father. I have a fine tub."

"I am a Praster of The Way, child, and a eunuch. I am certainly nobody's father."

The innkeeper blushed and hurried from the room.

Albrecht leaned in and whispered. "You've fathered bastards from here to Lorentzia."

"Shh. Keep your voice down, or you'll spoil the 'holy miracle' that I intend to enact upon the wench." The priest winked.

"You will burn in hell, Yalst."

"And poor, due in no small part to maintaining my army of little bastards, but one cannot take it with one."

"You could gild your coffin and parade it on a gilded carriage."

"I'm louche, not vulgar."

Albrecht poured a mug of water. The jug of mead smelled enticingly of honey, blackberries and sweet spice; it was winter, it was cold nights by a warm fire with his dogs at his feet. He took a sip of water. It tasted brackish, reminded him that he was far from home. "Did you know they believe in the Wittekin in these parts?"

The priest wiped his mouth with the back of his hand. "The iron charms somewhat gave it away, aye. I'll sacrifice a chicken to ward off the forest demons."

"I'm serious."

"Don't be. It's harmless bullshit; old habits yet to die. They'll see the light of The Way when we give them covered sewers and water closets."

"I don't like their blacksmith. There's something about the man that I do not trust."

Yalst skewered another chicken, his soft hands and pearl handled eating knife bright with grease. "You don't like anyone, Albrecht. I'm sure you spit in the mirror every time you see your own, pained face reflected therein, and I don't blame you." He chuckled. "Be easy, sir knight. We're... three days from Ravens' Fall? Three, short days away from a month of lavish funeral feasting while we listen to the sweet lament of the Sisters of The Way." He put his arm around the knight's shoulder. "Picture it; those sex-starved maids, crying for Ortiz, soft bosoms heaving, aching for a big, brave knight to ease their sorrow."

Albrecht shrugged him off. "I think he was a Raven Warrior."

"The smith? Saints' sake. Show me a man or woman over thirty in this country who wasn't." The Praster ripped off a chicken leg, waved it at the door. "They'd have anyone – probably why they lost the war. Now, for the sake of your health, man, take that stick from up your arse."

Albrecht downed the water and got up to leave. "I'm going to help Kroust with the horses."

Yalst absently scribed the symbol of the sacred Hand of Yesha in the air with the chicken leg while he poured another mug of mead. "May the peace of The Way be upon you, knight."

Fuck you. Albrecht ducked through the door and came face-to-face with the charm. Mud and horse hair clung to the nails. He tore it down again. The sun was sinking behind the trees; the light in the village was sombre, woodsmoke blue. He crossed the square, dropped the charm in the well as he headed past the mudwalled chapel. The local prastigan was loitering outside. She looked like a Vadran, but she wore her hair short and rather than the usual leather kilt, she was wearing trews and the ochre tunic of a prastigan of The Way. She was a thin creature flinching and birdlike. Her pale face was framed by greying locks, her eyes were red-rimmed, either from crying or from the incense smoke that was failing to mask the stench of decomposition coming from the chapel. She saw Albrecht and rushed over before the knight could avoid her.

"My lord –"

"I'm just a knight, prastigan." He inclined his head and made to pass the priestess, but she stepped in his way.

"Yes, of course. Forgive me. I am Prastigan Murta. I am here to show The Way." She waited expectantly for the response.

Albrecht did not give in to his desire to sigh. "And The Way will lead us to Salvation."

Murta touched the Hand of Yesha amulet she was wearing around her scrawny neck. "The Way has brought you here. We are honoured that the noble general lies in repose in our humble chapel."

"The honour is ours, prastigan."

The priestess drew closer, cast a nervous glance around the square. Her breath reeked of mead and fear. "We are beset by evil, my lord," she whispered.

Albrecht didn't want to hear this. He wanted to help Kroust and the grooms bring the horses in, and then he wanted to get secretly drunk. The chapel door opened behind Murta and one of Yalst's acolytes rushed out and threw up. The sickly sweet aroma of vomit and rotting hero rode the wave of incense and tallow that billowed from the chapel. "It has been uncommon hot this month, I am told." He smiled at the priestess.

"Did you not hear me, my lord? We are beset, by demons." Skinny fingers dug into his maille. "They are coming. Every night, they grow bolder. But now that you are here, we can fight them."

"Fight who?" The young priest finished puking, wiped his mouth, and bowed apologetically to Albrecht. "Go to the inn, lad."

"But Praster Yalst said —"

"Tell the others to go with you."

"But what about the Mortumatis?"

"I'll say it. Go get some food in you, strong drink if you can face it."

The priest wiped his mouth on his sleeve. "If you insist, Sir Albrecht."

"I do."

Murta's face lit up. "You *have* been sent. I knew if I recited the One Hundred Reasons often enough, I knew that The Way would send someone to aid me in the battle against evil." It was then that Albrecht noticed the rows of shallow cuts on the prastigan's arms. She saw the direction of his gaze and smiled. "I punished myself every time I misquoted the litany for, as we know, discipline strengthens the spirit."

The remaining priests and priestesses hurried from the chapel and exchanged brief benedictions before scuttling across the square to the inn. Overhead, crows called as they flocked and crowned the oval of open sky with a wreath of thorn-winged shadows. The Way didn't trade in portents and omens, but back home in Cambria the village elders would have spat in the dirt and knocked back three thimbles of birch brandy if they'd seen such a thing, which was not uncommon. He smiled as he pictured the sun-drenched market square, the pink lace blossoms trailing over whitewashed balconies; the fire of sunset leaching into the warm ocean. His grandfather would raise a glass, 'spirits to ward off spirits, and keep the old gods happy', he would say and wink at Albrecht. Yalst would call the superstition a 'habit' rather than a rite, but then Yalst thought four roast chickens were 'a snack'.

"Sir. Please, we don't have much time."

"What is it, prastigan?"

"The Wittekin. They stalk me. They whisper in the darkness and mock me for my faith."

Someone, probably the damned smith and his heathen cronies had filled the poor wretch's head with tales of forest demons. "Ignore them, and they will leave you alone."

The priest gripped his arm with bony fingers. "They will come and kill us, and worse, they will take our souls."

Not ungently Albrecht reclaimed his arm. The circling crows cackled. "The Way will prevail, prastigan. You have nothing to fear."

She gripped his hand. "I have done nothing but fear for two years. *Two years*. This village is a battleground in a war between The Way and the Wittekin." Her gaze darted to the trees. "And I fear that The Way is losing."

"There is only The Way. You of all people should know that."

"I have seen what I have seen. I have heard what I have heard."

"You have seen the Wittekin?"

"Yes!" Tears coursed down her cheeks. "And they are terrible to behold."

This was pointless. The woman's harrowed face and haunted eyes told Albrecht that Murta absolutely believed she had seen that which did not exist. "Very well, I'll speak to the Praster." *About taking you with us to the monastery.* "Go home now and get some sleep. You look exhausted."

"Thank you, thank you, my lord." She made to sink to her knees. Albrecht stopped her. "I must stay here, help you prepare. The crows are their heralds. They will come tonight."

"Saints' sake, no." He softened his tone. "I mean, thank you, but

I must speak to the Praster first. If you are to help you must be well rested. When was the last time you got a good night's sleep?"

"I... I nap in the chapel when I need to."

If the poor wretch lasted another year out here, he'd be surprised. He took her by the shoulders. "If you are to fight evil you must be at your strongest. Go home, eat something, and sleep safely. We are here with you. The Way will protect you." His attempt at a reassuring smile was wasted on Murta, who nodded absently before wandering off towards a small hut beyond the chapel. More iron charms had been hung on the trees that crowded over it. The metal shards spun on nettle cords, touched gently, rang softly.

The knight stepped around the watery puke and leaned upon the doorway. Lord Ortiz's grand coffin had been placed in the aisle, on a plank table that had been hastily dressed in ochre velvet. Fat coils of incense burned on the lid which had been sealed with lead and carved to resemble a shield. A pity then that the corpse juices were soaking through the bottom of the casket. Albrecht cursed the carpenter who'd scrimped on the lead lining, but as with the carriage the coffin had been lavishly and, of more importance, conspicuously gilded. The sides were decorated with relief carvings depicting scenes of the general's greatest victories. It was less a resting place than a piece of propaganda because Ortiz's greatest triumph was killing the last Raven Queen of Vadra.

Albrecht closed the door. Despite what he'd told Murta, he had no intention of saying the Mortumatis. The continuous recitation of the prayer for the dead was holy theatre, something to inspire awe in the natives and to give the novice prastigans something to do aside of swatting flies and fighting for Yalst's favour. The knight paused on the threshold. He had intended to relieve Kroust and make sure that the labourers were working on the carriage, but the sound of a ringing hammer distracted him and drew him to the source.

The smithy was down a lonely track on the outskirts of the village. The hut stood beside a frothing race where the water flowed like dragon scales over fractured sheets of slate. Smoke spirited through the sod roof – ghostly serpents writhing bright against a screen of crabbed oaks, boughs bent from the weight of charms hanging from them.

"There must be a fortune in iron hanging around this village." He spoke to announce his presence between hammer blows. The smith picked up the glowing wheel rim he was working on and embedded it in the glowing embers of his forge before turning to Albrecht, hammer and tongs in hand. He did not hold them like tools unless his trade was war. The knight didn't reach for his blade, although the urge was there.

"What do you want, Cambrian?" The smith relaxed his stance.

"Cambrian? I'm a Knight of the Way and an imperial citizen." Albrecht ducked inside. The sod roof was supported by carved posts, and the walls were river cobbles packed with moss. A dog slept in the ashes by the forge.

"I'm an imperial citizen, apparently, and Vadrui, but." He shrugged.

"But?"

"It pays to know the difference between a native and an incomer. The Vadrui are incomers, as are you."

Albrecht picked his way through the forge, careful not to entirely turn his back to the man. "Smith, leader, and storyteller is there no end to your talents?"

The smith's brutish face blazed scarlet above his beard, yet his eyes shone intensely, coldly blue. "They will come tonight. I would suggest that you bind yourselves with cold iron, anoint your blades with the blood of a lamb, and perhaps give offerings at the elm grove. I note you smile." He spread his arms wide. "You're right. It would be a waste of time for they will not be appeased."

"Let's indulge each other. Please, explain." Albrecht found the smith's insolence stimulating, here at least, when they were alone and without an audience of inbreeds to either inspire or cow.

The smith gave a wolfish grin, but that was all.

"Come, man, speak freely, why won't they be placated? Is it because we're Imperial, is that why they would eschew our sacrifice of lamb blood and chickens?"

The old bull laughed at that. "The old ones tolerate the Vadrui because we show them respect. You people don't. It doesn't matter what you are; it's what you've done that has set them against you." He shrugged.

"What have we done to them? I mean we've beaten the Vadrui, but how have we offended these old ones?"

"You built your monastery on their sacred site, and yon corpse killed their chosen one, and fed her body to his dogs."

"You heard about that?"

"Wasn't that the intention?" He pumped the bellows, the ruby coals breathed heat.

"So, if you were me, a Knight of the Way, a captain in the army of the Empire of Tath Taran and his most Exalted Pradashan, Shapanu the Eleventh." He touched his heart. "How would you deal with this?"

"Kill myself." He plucked a cherry red stave from the coals and tapped the worn anvil before striking the metal with more force than the work warranted. "To show you're serious, although and I say this with all due respect, perhaps a mere captain isn't worthy enough, as sacrifices go." He spat on the stave. "Of course, I'm no expert. I would say talk to a Raven Warrior, but you killed them all."

"Not on my own, but I take your point... *smith.*" Although he was leaning casually against a water butt, Albrecht had gauged the distance to the smith, the height of the ceiling, and space around them. He was content that should the old bastard turn on him he had enough room to draw without snagging his blade on anything except bull hide. It was then that he realised he'd come here to kill the Raven Warrior. May The Way forgive him, but he despised the old Vadrui and those like him who clung to ignorance and superstition. How many good men and women had been killed trying to redeem these imbeciles? "Well I'm not going to kill myself to appease a folk tale but, myths aside, you would like to see me dead, wouldn't you?" He spread his arms, inviting the bull to make a move. "We're alone. No one knows I'm here. Come, *Crow Fucker*, take your chance while you have it."

The smith's hammer hung a beat before he struck the anvil and loosed sparks into the heated air. "Brave words when we both know the edicts. I won't condemn this village by smashing your skull in, although gods know, I'd enjoy it."

It began to rain. A few heavy taps became a drumroll which became a thunderous cascade. The sharp moment passed, leaving

Albrecht caught somewhere between disappointment and relief. "I expect the carriage to be repaired by first light."

"I know… sir."

Albrecht waited until Yalst had staggered off with the innkeeper before joining his knights in a mug of mead. It was sickly sweet, and dangerously innocuous, so much so that he was halfway through the third mug before he realised he should slow down. He drew his cloak around him and began to drift into a warm, comfortable doze, lulled by the crackle of logs, the patter of rain, and the quiet babble of conversation.

"The horses are gone!"

Battle-hardened reflexes hauled him to his feet and put his sword in his hand before the echo of the shout had died. The young knight stumbled through the door to the stables. She was breathless, pointing wild-eyed into the darkness. "They're gone. The horses have been stolen. I barred the door, I swear, but it's open, and they're gone."

"Where are the grooms?" he demanded.

"I don't know, sir."

"Tomarz, Kroust, get out there, and see if you can see their tracks," Albrecht ordered. They headed to the stable, Albrecht went to find Yalst. The inn was a sprawling, single storey dump so it took him longer than he would have liked to find the Praster's room. When he got there, he saw the door was ajar. Expecting the worst, Albrecht charged in. The Praster erupted from the tub set before the fire. The innkeeper sat bolt upright in the clothes strewn bed.

"What the fuck are you doing, Albrecht?" Yalst demanded, steam rising off his pig pink flesh.

"The horses are gone. I was just –"

"Get out!" The innkeeper leapt from the bed, grabbed her shift, and ran from the room. "Wait, not you!" Yalst glared at Albrecht. "Now see what you've done."

"Praster –"

"Get out."

Albrecht ran to the stables. His knights were outside searching for tracks. He joined them. "Anything?"

Kroust nodded, pointed at the muddy ground with his guttering torch. "The horses went north into the forest for some reason. No sign of the grooms. Shall we go after them?"

Thunder rolled menacingly, Albrecht peered through the rain into the trees and in return, felt eyes upon him. "Get back." As he spoke the undergrowth shuddered, and slender saplings were snapped by an unseen force. Before him, a being garbed in shadows and black feathers resolved from the darkness and glided towards him, eyes shining in an ashen face. She, for he was sure that it was a she, despite the obfuscation of the night-kindled murk, was wielding a bone spear that was sheened with blood. Five more of the demons followed her. The blood froze in Albrecht's veins. "For The Way is the Light," he intoned as the Wittekin charged silently from the trees. "Spread out." His throat was dry, his voice a strangled croak. The one before him cast her spear.

Albrecht spun away. The spear split the air inches from him and took Hillis who was behind him in the throat. The youngest knight clawed at the shaft. Her mouth opened, perhaps to utter a dying scream or a defiant curse, whichever it might have been died with her. The spear crumbled to dust, Hillis folded, hot blood anointed the ground. Albrecht took a two-handed grip of his sword and set himself. Someone yelled. He dropped into a low guard and turned to see another of the creatures charge Etrin. Overawed, the knight swung wildly at his supernatural foe and missed. The demon cast the feathered edge of her cloak before her in a wide arc. It brushed the knight, cut tabard and split maille. Etrin staggered, stared at his chest in mute horror at the widening slash of scarlet marking death upon him.

Marcalla backed towards Albrecht. She was a veteran, she didn't panic, but like him, she was afraid. "What are they?"

"I don't know." He knew. Nuaskai bellowed in pain as his sword hand was severed. The knight fell before a shadow with a bird skull face. The stable door slammed shut behind them; the bar hammered down. "Open up." Silence answered his desperate cry. "Damn it!" He hammered on the door.

"They're not going to open it, and I wouldn't advise running, they'll enjoy the hunt." The smith strode around the corner of the inn, hammer in hand. One of the creatures leapt at him, a bone blade scything from the folds of its ragged cloak. Quicker than the knight would have thought possible, the smith side-stepped and swung the hammer backhanded at his baleful assailant. The powerful blow connected. The cloak flew apart, feathers scattered and an unearthly, keening wail wicked into the shadows. The smith answered with a war cry that hurled fear from the night. "I name thee!" he bellowed. "Axe and Mist! Cloud, Shield-splitter, Spear-thrower, and Silence. Hear me, I am Thron, son of Magnus one-eye, son of Adatha Wind Weaver, and I say you cannot have them." The smith's fierce challenge shattered the bonds of age that bound him. He stood taller, planted himself as if he was rooted to the bones of the earth, and faced the demons. He would not face them alone. Albrecht formed up beside him. The smith grinned like death, reached into the pocket of his apron with a bloodied hand, and cast a handful of iron filings into the air. The Wittekin recoiled, drifted silently back into the trees, leaving wolf tracks where they passed. Relentless as a glacier, Thron advanced, seeding the air with filings and gilding the demons. Albrecht's flesh crawled as he watched the Wittekins' tenebrous forms writhe and shift between bird, wolf, and woman, and finally fade to nothing but angry whispers that were drowned by the next peal of thunder that rolled across the lightning silvered sky.

The storm gathered, rumbled into the distance. The rain sang a lament on its passing. "Is it over?" Albrecht asked the smith.

The old bull sagged, wiped his bloody hands on his kilt and rested his hammer on his shoulder. "Aye."

Marcalla covered Hillis with her cloak, and Thron plodded back the way he'd come without another word or backward glance. Though the fight was over, a war now raged within Albrecht as reason strove with superstition for primacy. "Smith?" The knight called, but the Vadrui kept walking. "Thron!" His pace slowed. "Why did you help us?"

"I didn't. I helped my village."

Thron was amongst the crowd that followed the general's funeral carriage to the village boundary stone. He was pleased his repairs held and that they were finally on their way. None of the remaining knights acknowledged him as they processed behind the lumbering wagon.

The solemn ring of their armour a grim accompaniment to the mournful chant of the priests. When the last of them was out of sight, he went to the glade. Yori and Gian were sitting in the clearing, sharing a jug of mead while the ravens feasted on the horses' heads that were hanging from the sacred oak. Relief unknotted the tension he'd carried for three days when he saw the prize upon the altar that was nestled in the lightning split trunk.

Yori waved.

"Thought you'd got lost," said Gian.

"Just waiting for the Imps to go. Good work, by the way."

Gian handed him the jug. "Aye, well, you say that, but yon *fumble fingers* dropped the fucking lid on me and almost broke my damn neck."

Yori shrugged. "You were taking too long cutting the bastard's head off. I almost fell asleep."

Thron drank deeply. The mead tasted of honey, blackberries and sweet spice; it was summer, it was warm nights in the meadow, the buzz of bees. Set upon the altar was the rotting head of the one who had slain the Raven Queen. Thron knelt upon the blood-fed ground, soft beneath his aching knees. He held the skull steady and began to carve the bindrune into the murderer's forehead. "I know how to cut them, know how to read them, know how to stain them, know how to prove them..." He cut as he chanted. When he was done, he sat back on his heels. "Open your eyes, Ortiz." It took a moment for the magic to root, but Thron was a patient man. Eventually, the sunken eyelids opened, and rheum tears fell from empty sockets. The eyes may have rotted away, but he knew that the mind, *the spirit* of the man was locked within the grisly cage when the decaying lips split in a silent scream. Sated, the six ravens soared into the cornflower sky and rode upon a fresh wind that came laden with the promise of spring.

THE DYING LAND

Nick Watkinson

Galar stood and regarded the browning stalks of the wheat, the limp ears and shrunken grain. The field was indicative of the valley as a whole, and the valleys beyond.

His companion, Terem, broke an ear of wheat from its stem and brushed the dry grain with his thumb. "Our land is dying, Galar. But it's dying slower here than at Galven. The opposite of what we suspected." He clapped his hands together to shake off the dust. "I don't suppose you could conjure a solution out of thin air?" There was a wry cast to Terem's heavy face.

"Not out of thin air," said Galar, turning east, where the lustre of the forest canopy showed no sign of blight. "But I wonder why the forest is so resistant, what defence have the forest spirits employed?"

"Whatever their secrets, they will not share them with us, Galar." Scowling, Terem ground the fallen grains beneath his leather boot. "The law is clear, that forest is forbidden to us."

Galar reached out towards the forest with a hand, faint wisps of red and gold tracing the path of his fingers. "What laws were made in times of bounty are broken by necessity. The thief who starves is a thief because he starves."

"Finely put, but too succinct to sway the Council."

"Until desperation forces their hand." Galar shook his head. "The Council set us a task. Even should the harvest be paltry, Gwenscryfa must have the means to gather it. After that, we can only make the argument."

Together the pair returned to the path leading between the fields and into Bower Village, on either side of the track they were greeted by the sight of dead cattle and horses left to rot and stink in corrals. Terem covered his nose with his sleeve and choked an oath. Galar looked on dispassionately. The Gwenscryfan Council's inaction led to this suffering, now he was sent to put a tourniquet on a corpse. Hawking, Galar spat the taste of rot from his mouth and pressed on into the village, while Terem stumbled behind.

Within the thatched longhouse of the village headman a sorry huddle of humanity watched over their dying kin. Purpled blotches marked the skin of the dying, and the wasting of their flesh left little more than bone and sinew. Hands curled into useless, feeble claws, the victims twitched and tried to reach out but would recoil at a touch as though the pain of contact were too much to bear.

The longhouse itself was still festooned with the wealth of past years. A large central firepit loomed around a small fire, with scant logs left to feed it, but thick furs and fleeces were still draped over ornately carved chairs and benches. The wattle and daub walls were white-washed and elaborate knot designs wove over the surface, a conscious reminder of the willow that wove within the wall. Stories were described in tempera and dyes; but given pride of place was the tale of Href Cale, who gave his life as a sacrifice to the forest to bring peace between the humans and the fey.

"By the colours of your coats I'd guess you to be Magi. You'll be wanting the headman," said a man by the firepit. Galar noted this man's muscles still bulged beneath his skin, though his face was beginning to purple. The man noted Galar's regard and shrugged. "We figure we're all for it, just some sooner than others. Headman died a day back. I'm Graf, labourer."

Terem was already kneeling beside the supine form of an old woman, his eyes and hands passing over her, pressing at the joints and cupping the skull.

"Graf, you're headman now." Galar fixed the man with a hard look. "This isn't what you'll want to hear but if that harvest isn't brought in from the fields, more than one village will suffer. There is a responsibility to Gwenscryfa, to your people."

The headman went still, and a dangerous glint touched his eyes. "That's all that matters, is it? Feeding you fat town folk?"

"Without food we all die, Graf, town folk or field folk." Galar nodded to where Terem was helping the woman to her feet. She looked unsteady, though not so old as Galar had thought before

162

Terem's work. The discolouration, a sullen purple, faded into flesh tones before their eyes.

Graf choked and ran to her, he wrapped her in his arms and wept into her hair. Her expression, Galar saw, was tender despite her obvious discomfort. A mother, or a wife?

"The town folk have come to aid the field folk," Galar raised his voice above Graf's sobs. "Will the field folk aid the town?"

A scattered cheer was their only response, disappointing Galar. He'd hoped Terem's miracle might sway a little more enthusiasm their way. The headman straightened and jerked his head. From the benches around the hall, more of the healthier men and women rose to stand with him.

"Our cattle are dead, horses too. Gathering the harvest, laying it down and transporting it, that will be a work of hard labour. I expect that's why you're here, is it not, Magus?" Graf looked at Galar with a shrewd eye and led the others out. In a moment Galar heard them calling out to each other and gathering tools.

Terem aided the woman to a chair by the firepit, where she sat and gazed at the embers. After a moment, Terem joined Galar and spoke low enough that the locals would not overhear.

"As we thought, it isn't natural. This is the first time we've had a chance to see the effects in living tissue. The plague leaps from plant to beast to human and any way in between. It's likely that we are already touched by it." When Galar raised an eyebrow, Terem placated him with a gesture. "It's nothing we can't handle in humans, but the beasts? Whole fields? It is like trying to fight a fire with a cup of water. We need to be able to heal a field all at once, and then maintain that defence. With a whole circle of healers, maybe, but that would be just one field."

"Then we need something that can fight from within the plants themselves," said Galar, his eyes lingering on the painting of Href Cale, whose bloody body was pierced with roots and vines.

Following his gaze, Terem grimaced. "That's not somewhere we can go without the Council's approval. Look, I'll stay in here and get them on their feet. Focus on the task in front of you, for now. I know it won't be easy."

With a nod, Galar collected himself. "I suppose I have been

putting it off. They're going to hate me."

"Probably," said Terem as he knelt beside a withered man whose chest barely rose or fell. "Though if they're all still alive to hate you, they're all still alive."

Beyond the hide-wrapped wooden door, the field folk were starting to gather. Determined to put it off no longer, Galar stepped out into the morning sun and addressed the men and women assembled. "You have a large harvest, and hardly any of it is fit for consumption, which means more work to separate the dross. This would be a hard task if you had all hands and the beasts to haul, but instead you're under strength and the beasts are dead."

"Going to magic them back alive, Magus?" Whorled brush-strokes of purple marred the face of the woman who called out, and her derision was mixed with as much hope.

"Not alive," Galar said quietly. He beckoned the field folk to follow and walked to the corral where six oxen putrefied in the warmth of the sun. It was coming to noon and the stench would only thicken in the air. Galar lengthened his stride. He cast the wicker gate open and walked among the corpses. Each hulking, bloated body he rested a hand on shivered almost imperceptibly as his magic invaded the flesh and bone. "You will want to stay out of the corral."

"What is this?" Graf called. "Nothing we can do with these, the meat's gone bad."

A man's shouts, a woman's pleading, a crowd's misunderstanding. Galar let it all slide away from his mind and focused on the moment. He was stood in a corral, on all sides were the fallen bodies of oxen. The ground remembered when the oxen trod it into fresh shapes, pressed their muck in, made it moist. The air remembered their lungs and blowing out hot, and it remembered the musk of them. Galar remembered the oxen before they fell, when they tottered and lowed and suffered. Galar remembered the oxen when they were young and frisky, when their muscles strained against their shining flanks. The oxen remembered with him.

Struggling to their hooves, the oxen mewed and lowed. Pent up gases hissed from their lungs and bowels.

Horror warred across the faces of the field folk. With regret, Galar addressed them again before that horror turned into mutiny.

When he rested a hand on the head of one ox it nuzzled his other, looking for food. "These are the animals you remember, you worked alongside them, they remember you. There's no need to fear them. Graf, come in here."

Almost before he realised, the headman stood before Galar and the ox. The man's mouth was wide, and he sucked in a breath, then choked on the stench. Galar laughed and the field folk laughed with him, easing the horror of the moment. After wiping his mouth with the back of his hand, Graf placed it on the ox.

"Hello there, my lad," he said, "I've missed you." From a pocket stitched onto his jacket the headman pulled a corner of bread and fed it into the slapping lips of the ox. Some lustre returned to the glazed eyes of the cattle at the man's words as he fed the magic with his own memories.

When Galar walked out of the corral, the field folk didn't know what to do with themselves. They fidgeted and looked him in the eyes, or didn't, or did so alternately. "They'll last the year," he said. "Perhaps longer. It'll give us time. Where did you keep your horses? And your dogs. You'll need the dogs too." A sudden fatigue slurred his words and sent him rambling. The woman with the purpled face caught his shoulder when he sagged. Her hair was dulled with the same grease and soil that dirtied her face and arms, but her eyes shone.

By the time the animals were again raising a racket over the village, Galar stumbled through the door to the longhouse, his arm around Graf's shoulders. The headman pressed him into a chair by the firepit and threw another of the thin logs on to burn. The wood of the chairs was carved with hounds, cattle, horses, and men. The memories were strong here, and Galar found it no wonder the magic took hold so well.

Terem found him there after a moment and sat in the chair beside him. "How did they take it?" he asked.

"Better than we thought." Galar tried to look around the hall but dizziness drove his eyes shut. "How was it in here?"

"Three were beyond me, all the others are recovering. I'll tend the ones you took out to work in the morning." Terem tutted. "You've extended yourself, you didn't need to."

"They need as much time as I can give them, they have no

guarantees. We have no guarantees. It may all be for nothing. I haven't awoken the human dead."

"No, that's wise. The dogs too, though?"

Galar prised his eyes open. "As you said, it isn't just our land. People will turn bandit out of desperation or despair, as some have already. Guard dogs, bale-eyed and rotted, should be some deterrent."

"And nightmare," laughed Terem. "Rest, recover yourself. Tomorrow we'll head for Gwenscryfa and we can think up ways to persuade the Council."

In the flicker of the firelight, Galar looked to the paintings and saw the blood of Href Cale's wounds drip and the roots grow thick. Roots and vines followed him into his dreams.

Morning found Galar hunched over in the same chair. His mouth was dry, and he cast around for something to quench his thirst. A woman pressed an earthenware cup into his hand and he swilled the water around his mouth before he swallowed. He recognised her, the woman Terem first saved from the malady.

"Pella is what I'm called, Magus. I wanted to say you've done right by us. My man Graf'll see the harvest in. We'll have to clean the oxen up before they tread the grains and, sad to say, the village won't ever smell the same." Galar returned her smile with an effort and handed back the swirl-patterned cup.

A hand pressed Galar's shoulder and he half-turned to see Terem, a smile wrinkling the fat around his eyes. "It's time, my friend."

The sun was a pale promise on the horizon, yet the field folk were already at work. In gangs they swung their sickles through the crop, binding the fallen wheat in sheaves. A distant figure gave a wave and Galar guessed it was Graf, so he raised an arm and waved back. Past the fields closest to the village, Galar and Terem came to the vehicle that brought them there.

Beside the wagon a horse was hobbled, nibbling fruitlessly on the blighted grass. Whatever meal it managed to tear up from the ground fell wetly from the gaping mess of its lower jaw. There was little flesh left on the horse, rubbed away by harness and wear. Galar patted the horse on its skeletal flank and it whickered in recognition, it raised its nose and nuzzled at his head. With his eyes closed, Galar brought to the fore of his mind all the memories of this horse when it was fresh and young. He remembered the energy coiled in every muscle that would have it bound around and around a paddock with limitless enthusiasm. The ghosts of those muscles pressed against his hand as the horse stood prouder, whickered again in readiness for the harness.

As Galar climbed the side of the wagon, Terem offered a hand to help him up. Terem passed him the reins and settled over to the right of the seat. Clicking his tongue and snapping the reins, Galar urged the horse towards the road. Wheels bounced over the hummocks and into the ruts of the track as the horse hauled them forward.

"You're always upset after you use your gift, Galar," said Terem, looking out across the fields. "Can't you be pleased with what you've done for your people?"

"It must be different for you." Galar tried to push away the bitterness. "I lie to the people, to the world itself, and eventually they realise it is a lie and it falls apart. In Galven –"

"Stop worrying about Galven, you did what was needed."

"In Galven there is not a single living body, but the village pretends that nothing is different. The field folk still till the field, the dogs still bark, the weavers spin thread with skeletal fingers and they remember what they used to be... But it is a lie. They are nothing but the echoes of truth, forced to relive their existence for our benefit."

"And is that so wrong?" There was anger in Terem's tone. "Wouldn't they want to know that Gwenscryfa goes on because of their sacrifice? Curse it, Galar, you've given them a year or more to be who they were, to press their toes into the earth and breathe the live air. Can you imagine anything the dead would want more? Most field folk have family in the town, that's who they're clothing and feeding, it isn't as if we're strangers or tyrants."

"Is that enough?" Terem caught Galar's gaze and followed it to the forest looming on the far side of the valley.

"We'll figure it out, Galar."

"That's what I intend to do." Turning the horse down the track headed for the bridge across the river, Galar spared Terem a glance. His friend shrugged and sat back on the bench, arms crossed.

It was mid-morning when they reached the thick trees of the forest edge. They'd left the wagon by the bridge, and the horse hobbled. The air was sweet and pungent with burgeoning life. Terem frowned at the grass a few steps back, where it browned and curled with blight, then jerked his head for Galar to continue.

"They'll already know we're here. Just talk."

Galar cleared his throat. Now that he stood before the majesty of the forest he felt himself struggling for the words. Instead he knelt and pressed his hand into the earth. As he felt for the memories of the land here, he almost cried out.

"They are here," he said in a soft voice. He straightened and brushed green grass from his knees. "Greetings to the spirits of the forest! We seek aid and succour for our people who suffer in the shadow of your trees."

A crackle of movement in the trees, a wind tussling the leaves, no other response.

"Your forest is all that remains healthy in this land. Please, help us to understand why. Give us the means to protect our people from this blight and I swear we shall answer any boon you ask!"

"Any boon?" asked the tree before them.

Terem let out a wordless shout and stumbled back a step. Determined not to show his own uneasiness, Galar held his place and scrutinised the bark of the tree. There was no hint of a human face, but a hollow in the trunk drew his attention, within it was a shimmer of faint reflected light.

"We have knowings of the dying of the land," said the spirit dwelling in the tree. "Know you not?"

Galar extended his hands palm up and open, "We do not understand why the land is dying."

"Spill your life on the green, we will see."

Galar tugged his knife from its sheathe at his belt. When he placed the blade on his palm Galar paused, then closed his fingers around the metal and jerked the blade free. Blood welled and spilled as he opened his fingers. In runnels and drips, his blood hurled itself down at the grass.

"And now?"

"Impatient, quick to leap." To Galar's ear, the spirit sounded idly amused. 'Struggles in vain before the end."

With heat rising in his skin, Galar hissed and pressed his bloody hand tight to his right. Terem stepped forward with his own hand out but Galar shook his head and focused on the hollow. "Is your only purpose to mock me, tree-spirit? Would you bleed me dry as you did Href Cale?"

"I disturb you when sun is high, birds sing? Human wants always. Wants."

"What do you want, spirit?" With effort Galar kept the worst of his frustration from his voice. "Speak it."

"Sun in sky, song of bird, watch and think. Shiver in wind, groan and grow."

Terem spoke before Galar had a chance to swear. "And you would, more than all other things, like to get back to just that wouldn't you, spirit? Pass on your 'knowings' and we'll leave you be before the sun rises another finger's width in the sky."

"Is too late. In the span of your breath the sun passed many of your finger's widths. More. Many more. The sun is fast." The spirit paused. "Your god thinks he is dead, now his dream wakes. In waking, his dream stretches. Mind of god is all mind, god smothers all thought. All think dead. All die. Even human."

"There's a dead god," replied Terem. "But he truly is dead. The Shining Lady broke him in the mountains, the Vanes, north-east and far from here."

"Thinks is dead. Is not. Wakes. Maybe god remembers he is alive, maybe the world dies in his dream."

"If this is a god's work, how do you resist?"

"Remember; for tree, for grass, for deer, for beetle. Remember alive, thriving. Remember for each other, remember we are part of it all."

Expansive in his gesture and smiling broadly, Terem beckoned the forest towards the browning grass and the brittle wheat across the river. "Help us remember the fields tall and golden in the sun, as they were meant to be. As they want to be. Help the fields remember."

"No."

Galar took the chance to speak before Terem. "You're afraid, aren't you?" After he touched the earth and searched for the memories of the forest he was overwhelmed by the vibrancy of them, the fierce insistence of their existence. "You spirits huddle together and tell stories about the time before this blight, and to foster that illusion, to make that lie feel comfortable enough to forget the truth beyond your borders, you drag the forest into that delusion with you."

"Yes."

Terem caught him by the arm. In his animation, Galar had forgotten about the wound and his fingers dripped with blood. Galar saw the faint whisper of colours trickle from beneath Terem's hand and felt the cut begin to knit and mend and against his skin he saw the barest shimmer of reflected light.

Though the cut was sealed with new pink flesh, his hand was still wet with blood. Galar strode towards the tree and thrust his hand into the hollow. When his hand crossed the threshold, he felt the being turn on him, as if the voice were only the merest fraction of its attention and this, now, was it entire.

Its voice thrummed through his body, barely bothering with spoken word. A fountain of thought and intent, a barrage of questions and reasoning, tireless in its pursuit. A mind, unburdened of body, raw and pure. He saw himself as it perceived him. Fragile and inconsequential, almost dead, yet now a threat? It was undecided.

In that hesitation, Galar found himself. Remembered himself; stood, with a foot in the grass, the other on an upraised root, his breathing steady and in his bloody fist a handful of dust. Just dust, he remembered, reflecting the barest shimmer of light. At the edge of his awareness he felt that fountain of thought shudder and wilt, quiescent in the story of his remembering. It was dust, and dust was made for plants to grow, for beasts to forage. Its oldest memory, the deepest memory. He swaddled the mind in its own beginning, and it was soothed.

With his hand still clutched around the dust, Galar stepped back from the tree. Terem held his ground for the barest moment but stepped out of Galar's path, his face a monument to disapproval.

At the bridge they took the wagon, and Galar directed Terem to drive for the village. Despite Terem's aversion for the skeletal horse it proved keen to please the Magi and hauled them up the slope.

"Is it..." started Terem once on the journey. Galar raised his unburdened hand and shook it for silence. His eyes were dry, and he couldn't remember blinking, his gaze locked on the dried blood and the halo faintly shimmering in the air around his fist.

The field folk still worked the same stretch of field and their muscles shone with the work. They lowered their tools and pushed through the wheat when they saw the Magi. Galar stumbled from the bench and landed heavily. Pushing himself to his feet, Galar brushed aside the first stalks of wheat, the action casting withered grains earthward.

"Is all well?" called Graf when Galar pushed his way through the harvest. "Saw you by the forest. With your coats being so bright, we thought it must be Magi."

Graf's eyes flicked down to the fist trailing flakes of blood and a shimmering halo of coloured motes. "Are you well?"

"Sun in sky," said Galar, each word a prayer. "Sun in sky, song of bird, watch and think. Shiver in wind, groan and grow." He knelt to the earth and buried his whole fist, careless of the stones and roots. The ground remembered the grain wrapped inside it, the tumble as it broke its seal, the searching tongues of roots. The air remembered teasing the bright young seedling, tickling its unfurled leaves. The field remembered a thousand thousand grains split their shells and grow.

With an ache of parting, Galar unclenched his fist and ushered the spirit into the memory of the field. Eagerly the spirit spread through the earth and woke the roots, it massaged the stems to draw the water from the earth and sparkled on the upturned leaves. Just as eagerly it inhabited the delusion, believed in itself as the field and the field as itself.

The scent of ripe grain weighed heavy in the air, the soil was moist and bore a dark lustre. In fitful starts, beetles shouldered through the soft earth and earthworms breached. Galar bowed his head to the soil to muffle his sobs. Despite his fears, his doubts, he'd healed living beings and truly done what the Council told him could never be.

As he rose to his feet he heard a drawing of breath. Graf stood an arm's length from him, cradling an ear of wheat as delicately as he was able. "They're golden," he said, hushed, and took his hands from the ear when they began to shake.

"Bless the Magi," said a woman with blonde hair and shining eyes. Her eyes held his for a beat, then she looked past him. "Lady bless you both."

Terem gripped his shoulders when he turned, brought their faces close together. "What have you done?"

From where they stood the golden hue spread like oil over water, and the whiskers of wheat hushed the breeze. Terem's mouth opened and he turned alternately from the wheat to Galar, and back.

"Look, Terem," Galar laughed and gestured with a muddy hand. "I'm a healer."

Pulled into a rough hug, Galar felt his ribs protest. "You've saved us." Terem released him and hurried to examine the wheat. "No one will starve, Galar. If we can take this to every community in the valleys... No, even half, no one will starve."

It came upon him sudden and total, Galar felt the exhaustion he'd held at bay sink into his limbs like lead. Vision blurred and repeated and nausea overcame him. He fell, helpless, into his own vomit.

Consciousness returned in stops and starts, Terem's face hovered over him. "Take him to the headman's house." Galar heard Terem say.

"We'll carry you Magus, you needn't fear," said the woman.

"I'm all right." Galar rolled to his side and his guts urged, but he held the bile in his throat. "Just, give me a moment. Please."

They honoured his request and Terem helped him shamble out of the fields and into Bower village without a word.

For the second time in as many days, Galar entered the headman's house as an invalid, his arm slung across another man's shoulders. Terem helped him into the same carved chair by the fire. The pit was cool and swept. Galar fancied the ash was removed for some arcane field folk ritual. When he smiled, Terem broke the silence.

"It's remembering, isn't it? Like we do, but..."

"More than that, the spirits are the memory. Only, they've moved beyond just memory, they think and feel."

"That doesn't even make a bit of sense."

Galar tapped the toe of his leather boot on the rim of the firepit. "No, I expect it doesn't. Sorry Terem, could you get me some water or whatever you can find?"

While Terem shuffled off to peer into the various earthenware jugs and bowls, Galar tried to collect his thoughts.

"Where do the memories come from, Terem? When you healers remind the body that instead of a cut there should be sealed flesh, what holds the memory? What starts the healing?"

A jug fell and rolled on the hard-packed earthen floor. "You're not saying they're inside us?" Terem caught the jug by its handle and set it back on the bench.

"They aren't, no, they are more like us. Magi. But once, once they were dust, Terem! A dust that is most certainly inside us." Galar wove a memory of fire in the fireplace and for a moment the air above the metal ignited, roiled with heat. "Everywhere, in everything, memorising and remembering. We think with it, remember with it, encourage it into action. Together, the dust and myself, we remembered that a fire is meant to be there." Galar gestured at the firepit. "And then it tried to make that fire start again. Did we ever understand this? Did we forget?"

When Galar almost dropped the cup Terem pushed on him, his friend knocked his hands aside and pressed the cup to his lips, tender as a mother. Galar sucked greedily at the water, felt it spill around the sides of the cup and fall into his lap. Absent-mindedly, he smoothed the drips into his trousers. Terem refilled the cup from a wide bowl but Galar waved it away. Terem shrugged and drained the cup himself.

"They aren't Magi," said Terem. "We're human."

"Are we?" Galar frowned. "I mean, yes we are, yet in this whole village there are only two humans who can do what we do; not one of the field folk can."

"Not all Magi are born on the hill. I was born to field folk, Galar. There are none in the village because Magi are brought to Gwenscryfa the moment they're recognised for what they are. For that matter, our town doesn't even have a monopoly on Magi. We might be isolated out here in the valleys, and we might call ourselves independent, but Her Shining Empire in the east is governed by Magi, as is Gwenscryfa. Travelling with the trade caravans I've been as far as the border forts, and their Magi don't hide away. They wear uniforms, act like soldiers."

"So, we're not like the spirits."

"No," agreed Terem with some force.

"But we have a similar gift."

"I'll have to take that on faith, but yes."

"And if what the spirit said to us is true, the gods had this same gift."

Terem chewed on his lip. "Similar, perhaps, but in an order of scale far beyond us. The blight has overwhelmed all the land north east of Gwenscryfa, which could place the epicentre in the Vanes where the dead god fell. But that suggests power on a scale... I mean, I can manage humans, one at a time. You healed a whole field with the spirit..."

"I can't heal the way you do." Galar felt a twinge of bitterness. At Gwenscryfa the Magi were sorted according to their talents. Terem was a healer, using the memories of the body to reinforce a person's ability to overcome injury, disease, mental trauma. In Terem's hands, the memories were clear and true and honest. In Galar's, memories warped and transmuted. He could build a lie with just enough truth to make it real, spin an illusion and weave it into being. The closer to truth the lie, the longer it would persist. It was easy where memories were strong, but conjurers could even give life to an utter lie for just long enough to imagine a bridge across a gorge, boil a cold kettle without fire, or to kill. His power lied to existence itself, but that same mutability of reality was a bane to living flesh.

In his earlier years, when he was tested for healing by the Council, he was commanded to place his hands on a patient with a broken leg and heal them. The body, confused and panicked by his touch, burst into a riotous growth of cancers, overwhelming and near killing the patient. Her leg swelling with vast muscles and knobs of bone, the patient screamed and Galar's own screams joined hers. He later learned this was common practice, to teach the need for restraint in a way words could not. It was Terem, a year older and monitor for the trial, who'd laid his hands over the cancer and remembered the body into health. Galar's horror had given way to envy as the cancers withered and fell away, and in later days they'd developed both respect and friendship.

Terem taught him that each body knows its perfect self, that the memory is stored in every part, that all he needed to do was touch the flesh and he would know as well and together he and the body would set about rebuilding that perfect self. So if one would describe the healers as supernatural, in that they enhanced and strengthened the natural, conjurers embodied the unnatural, taking what should be and making it something other. Fire where there was no fuel to burn, the dead returning as echoes of their past lives, the enslavement of a forest spirit to a field.

"I'm tired, Terem," he said.

"Sleep," said Terem. "We'll leave tomorrow instead. We can take the good grain to show the Council."

"What will they do, do you think?"

"I don't know. Fête us as heroes? Perhaps exile? If they do, come with me to the Shining Lady's Empire. See what other ways Magi can live. I have heard they believe magic is a science there. You would fit in, I think."

"And leave Gwenscryfa? It is my home."

Terem settled a heavy fur around Galar's shoulders. "I know, my friend. Sleep now, we'll set off once you've rested."

Galar woke before the sun set, his head still aching from the work of the morning. Graf and the villagers loaded the wagon with sheaves of grain, and they set off, travelling through the night. As the sky lightened on the seventh day, the hills were bare of trees and windswept and Gwenscryfa crowned the highest of them. Thick hewn stone walls wrapped the highest contours of Cul Tor, and behind them loomed the squat towers of the Magi, wide as they were tall. Most lived beneath the towers in thatched houses, swaddled in daub to keep in the warmth of a fire. Outside the walls were tents and lean-tos erected by merchants, travellers, and refugees from the blighted villages. Their paltry fires, fed as much with dried dung as with wood, raised a pall of smoke in the early light of the morning.

"It'd be wise to keep the wagon covered until we've delivered it to the council or we may start a riot out there."

"Certainly worse than when we left," said Galar. "I've never seen so many people huddled in one place."

"Really, Galar," Terem laughed. "I have to get you away from Gwenscryfa, there are a few thousand at most."

For the refugees camped by the gates of Gwenscryfa, an undead horse still held some fear and they made way muttering oaths and curses. The merchants were another matter entirely, and came forward hawking trinkets and furniture, asking payment only in good grain or entry to the town.

"Bless you, Magi, seven thousand thanks for gracing my store," cried out a turbaned man with a significant moustache.

Terem laughed aloud. "Friend Calisimir, if your store were not on the very road into Gwenscryfa we would have passed by without comment."

Galar noted that though the tone was haughty, Terem was failing to hide a grin. The merchant, Calisimir, wrung his hands and beat his chest in mock anguish.

"There is no crueller barb than that flung by a bosom friend. Was any man wounded more deeply than is Calisimir in this moment? Not even Halaestrim, in whose side the blade of the Shining Lady still twists."

"Naming that god always brings ill-luck, Calisimir, more so now than ever. Would you join us within the walls?" Terem asked. "The Council may need your experience of the wider world in light of the news we bring."

"Nothing would give me greater pleasure, Magi." Calisimir strolled alongside the skeletal horse and gingerly patted its flank. Whinnying gamely, the horse nosed the merchant's pockets and the man responded by producing a sprig of mint. The horse chewed with obvious pleasure and though it lifted and tilted its head, attempting to overcome its infirmity, the greater part of the cud still dripped from the gaping hole in its lower jaw.

"Calisimir is a good friend, a merchant from the Empire to the east," Terem explained to Galar.

"Her Empire of Stars is a hungry beast," Calisimir said. "Once my people were Tamiscyran. Now we are all citizens of Her Empire, at the mercy of the legions. I like you Magi here in Gwenscryfa, you hide in your towers and let people live much as they like. In the Empire they are everywhere, driving the wheels of progress. It is an exhausting business just to keep up with their innovations."

Calisimir walked backwards with ease, his hands painting the picture of his story-telling. "A man might own a ship and laden it with silks and spice, only to be held up by rough seas and unfavourable winds and see overhead a ship soaring in the sky, its rear-castle aflame. Then, when such a man arrives in that distant port to which he set sail, he finds there the sky-ship unburdened of its own cargo of silk and spice, and the man must beg for even the most unfavourable deal in a hostile market. I must tell you, my friends, I have had the misfortune to have been such a man."

"A man whose fortunes nevertheless outnumber those he's missed," said Terem with a wink.

At their approach, the gates to Gwenscryfa were drawn open, the heavy timbers creaking under the strain of their own weight. The warriors who stood watch were garbed in linked iron mail, belted at the waist, their iron helms were conical with a flared nose-guard and below the mail their clothes were thick wool, tied close to their legs with string to better withstand the cold. Some of them hailed the Magi by name but their expressions remained sombre and they stepped forward as the wagon passed, forming a shield wall bristling with spears to prevent the mob beyond the gates moving into Gwenscryfa before the great gates swung closed.

"I've never seen those gates closed before, Terem." Galar felt his unease as a hollowness in his stomach. "Not even when the Belshaban Horselords demanded tribute at the head of their host. A thousand strong, all mounted, with painted shields, and red flags flying from their spears. Do you remember?"

"I remember, Galar," said Terem. "They said they would burn down our home. As I recall, it was a fine day for the conjurers. Wasn't there a dragon?"

Galar laughed. "It looked like a dragon, but it was just a lizard scaled up in size. The wings were for show, but the claws were quite real."

"It breathed fire, Galar."

Galar turned a mischievous smile on his friend. "That was me."

"You weren't even a Magi then."

"The conjurers weren't expecting it. Did you see they almost lost control of the illusion? I was whipped for three days." Galar's smile slipped, but when Calisimir raised an eyebrow, Galar managed to pull it back. "We are dangerous, Terem, more than you know. The purpose of pain is to teach, and in the teaching, learn discipline. Without it, were a conjurer to truly lose control… There are limits to what we are allowed to accomplish." He fumbled with the reins. "I may have broken those limits at Bower, Terem."

Terem's hand squeezed his shoulder, but his friend said nothing more until they arrived at the Council tower. The smallest of the three towers, it housed only offices, much of the library and the Council Chamber, while the healer's tower and the conjurer's tower provided the living space and training rooms for their respective Magi. Nothing approached the brooding conjurer's tower save the Magi that called it home, and even the browning grass gave it wide berth.

The healer's tower was surrounded by buildings devoted to the care of the injured, timber-constructions, each with a layered roof and capped bronze chimney pipe. There were small crowds of people led in by healers, their faces and arms discoloured with a sullen purple. Seeing them, Terem sucked a breath through his teeth.

"Look to their clothes, Galar, those are Gwenscryfans. The blight has reached the city."

"Further than that, Magi," Calisimir's voice had lost all its good humour. "The valleys south and to the west of your fine city are already fallen to the plague. They say it is the animals that die first. Did you see any animals outside the gates? Many out there say it is the end of the world."

"Is it, friend Calisimir?"

"Perhaps, but the world is large beyond reckoning. Maybe it is only the end of Gwenscryfa, while Her Empire and the world will go on."

"Gwenscryfa will never die," Galar said, half-shocked by the fierceness of his own voice. He continued with a calmer tone. "We will not allow it."

At the entrance to the Council tower, Galar swung the wagon wide and called the horse to halt before he hopped down from the bench. Faol ran up to meet them, a young Magi just out of training wearing the red coat of a conjurer. Terem tasked him to see the wagon brought around behind the towers, while Galar hauled a sheaf of wheat from beneath the cover. Calisimir's eyes narrowed at the sight of the golden grain, but he held his peace.

There were only Magi within the tower, and Calisimir was asked to abide in an antechamber until formally summoned by the Council. The numbers surprised Galar, it seemed roughly half the total Magi population of Gwenscryfa were standing in clumps in the centre or seated on the stone steps that circled in ever-ascending rows around the vast chamber. High, narrow slits in the stone walls let in some light, but they were also to draw the smoke from several dozen braziers and torches.

As Galar approached with the sheaf of wheat, conversations ebbed. Everyone in this chamber knew Galar and Terem were sent to the villages that showed the first signs of the blight three weeks before, and were expected back with nothing more than tales of woe. Galar felt he walked with hope in his hands.

The High Healer, Magus Baela, called order and opened a session of the Council. While all others in the chamber wore the red coats of conjurers or the yellow of healers, she wore a simple white robe. The Council Chamber was the only place where the distinction between healer and conjurer was made in terms of address. Outside the chamber all were Magi, but here the distinction was to provide context for the scriveners who sat in the lowest tier, each transcribing the words of the speakers. The work of the team of four scriveners would allow an exact recounting of the session for later review by any Magi who preferred not to rely on hearsay or memory.

"The Council," began the High Healer, "welcomes the return of Healer Terem and Conjurer Galar and calls the Magi to relate the findings of their investigations. Healer Rolm and Conjurer Pirel," the High Healer gestured to each Magi in turn, "who were sent with you to Galven and who then proceeded to the villages of Folly, Niven, and Ture, have already provided their testimony. We will not require them to restate it at this time, but we invite our new arrivals to make themselves aware of the particulars at their earliest opportunity."

The High Healer motioned for Galar and Terem to step forward into the central depression and address the assembled Magi. Terem took the step first, ever comfortable in a crowd, and Galar jerked to follow, earning some chuckles in the higher tiers. Since Terem was often sent abroad, at his own insistence, he was well-practiced in addressing the Council on his return. Galar, by contrast, felt a cold sweat trickle down his spine.

"Honoured Magi, High Healer." Again, Terem took the fore. There was only ever a High Healer in the Council, who kept order and ensured all voices would be heard, conjurers could never take the role. A disavowal of political power was one of the limitations the conjurers placed upon themselves in fear that it might corrupt their discipline. Each Magus had a vote, as the healers insisted, but conjurers tended to abstain – though whether they trusted the healers to vote with wisdom or merely mistrusted themselves, varied from conjurer to conjurer.

"You have already heard the sorry tale of Galven and the necessary actions of Conjurers Pirel and Galar under direction from this Council, so I will not here repeat it. The villages of Toben and Scryf were dead, man and beast, and the fields dark with blight. Conjurer Galar and myself believe they, and Galven, were closer to the epicentre of this blight than those villages investigated by our colleagues. Since the crop was beyond harvest, Conjurer Galar did not repeat the actions taken at Galven, but we made a record of the dead and will submit it for dissemination by the Council so that their families in other communities may be informed."

"The village of Bower was another matter entirely. While Bower was closest to what we perceive to be the origin point of the blight it was the least affected by it. Bower, as you may know, lies in the shadow of a forest, the very same where Conjurer Href Cale gave his life. This forest lies between the village of Bower and the Vanes, a mountain range to the north east that we posit to be the source of the blight." There were many nods from the tiers as Terem confirmed their calculations or suspicions. "Specifically, the tomb of Halaestrim, also known as the Changeling God."

Silence reigned as almost five hundred Magi processed the information and updated their internal calculations. It took a full fifteen seconds before the first Magus swore, and the chamber descended into anarchy shortly thereafter. Terem was the quintessence of patience while the High Healer harangued the Magi into something resembling order, but Galar found himself shuffling with discomfort. He recognised his friend's masterful oratory and knew he, bearing the wheat as he was, would shortly be made the full focus of the Council's attention. Every moment made the thought more daunting. With the sleeve of his red coat, Galar smudged the sweat from his cheeks and forehead, but in so doing he almost dropped the wheat.

Terem continued smoothly, as if to redirect attention from Galar's fumble. "The domestic animals were dead when we arrived, as we have observed, they are always first to die to this blight. If the Council will forebear, we will state our reasoning on this matter in later remarks. However, the fields of the valley in which Bower lies were still only browning, and perhaps a third of the crop might have been salvageable."

"The humans of Bower were succumbing to the blight; there were several fresh graves and much of the population had crowded into the headman's longhouse to tend the dying, who were some half of that population and so the harvest was neglected. I was able to cure all the afflicted, save three unfortunate souls. As my fellow healers must know by now, the blight is assuredly reversible in humans." Again, there were nods. "Conjurer Galar rallied the stronger men and women of Bower to the fields and raised their cattle, horses and dogs to the echo of life so that they might continue the harvest. As I stated, I expected a harvest of close to a third of what is hoped for in a good year, and still that was better than we saw at Galven, Toben, and Scryf."

"If you will take heed of the whole and healed sheaf of grain in Conjurer Galar's arms, I can now say this is indicative of the whole crop at Bower. There is a wagon behind the towers piled with a full load of unthreshed grain, ready for the Council's inspection. Through the actions of Conjurer Galar, a whole harvest was saved and will soon arrive at the gates of Gwenscryfa."

Sheer bloody chaos. In an utter breach of decorum, Magi thronged to the chamber floor and pressed around Galar, demanded to see the grain, and inspected it for illusion and blight. Word travelled back through the crowd of a miracle. Repeatedly they broke into cheers of Galar's name, and demands came from all around him to tell how he had accomplished the feat. Within a few minutes, with the assistance of the red-faced High Healer and her gnarled oak walking stick, the Magi remembered themselves and resumed their seats.

"You have a way with theatrics, Healer Terem," said the High Healer with little amusement. "I trust Conjurer Galar has a more level head."

Terem took the hint and stepped aside, leaving Galar at the full mercy of nearly a thousand shining eyes. In the lowest tier he saw Calisimir in a borrowed yellow coat, his turban removed. The merchant favoured him with a slow wink. After clearing his throat, Galar attempted to pitch his voice for the size of the room and was pleasantly surprised his voice didn't crack.

"Honoured Magi, High Healer, the forest beyond Bower is home to beings that we name forest spirits. These spirits protect the forest from the effect of the blight, and to some extent protected Bower also, in as far as the blight was slowed. In our histories, we acknowledge that the spirits have power over the natural world, and so it proved in Bower. In short, I convinced a spirit to invest the fields of Bower with its protective powers. In our investigation, we discovered that the memories, and the active force of change our magic relies upon are in fact linked to a dust that permeates..."

A hard, forced laugh from one Magus high in the tiers distracted Galar. As the man stood, Galar saw he wore the red coat of a conjurer. "Convinced? We both know that is not what you did, Conjurer Galar."

"Speaker, make yourself known," cut in the High Healer.

Ignoring her, the conjurer strode down the steps to the floor and stopped uncomfortably close to Galar. Under the intensity of that man's glare, Galar felt the urge to step back, but he squared his shoulders and raised his chin. In a show of disgust the conjurer turned from Galar while leaving an accusing finger raised at him.

"This man," he said, "attacked the forest, which is forbidden. This man stole a spirit from its embrace and then, Magi, he mutilated it. Yes, mutilated. This... monster overwrote that spirit's very essence, its individuality, its sense of self. In all ways but one he killed it. Are these actions to be ignored? I demand that Conjurer Galar be offered in diplomatic entreaty to the forest before he commits a greater harm to himself, the forest, and Gwenscryfa itself."

Galar threw his voice over the rumblings of the Magi. "The spirits huddle in fear of a blight they know they can thwart. In all our land nothing compares to the vitality of the forest and with one spirit, just one, I healed Bower's harvest. We face the death of thousands to starvation and disease at best, while at worst Gwenscryfa and all its valleys will resemble the village of Toben where even the insects in the dirt lie shrivelled and still. I will not accept that future for Gwenscryfa!"

With a contemptuous flick of his wrist, the conjurer back-handed Galar and in that instant, he was airborne. Dazed, he landed hard and caught his shoulder against the stone steps. Galar tasted blood on his lips and when he tried to stand nausea sunk him back down.

"I am Conjurer Href Cale, who last stood in this hall three hundred and twelve years past. The forest demands a sacrifice for this transgression, that it be this man's life, and trust it serve as dire warning to humans in all times to come."

Galar woke up on a cot in an antechamber and found Terem leant over him, his friend smiled and sat back on a carved wooden chair.

"Your skull was fractured, you know, if it weren't so thick we'd have been scrubbing your brains off the steps. The Council is still in session, you've been unconscious for a good twenty minutes. Href Cale is still calling for your head, but the Magi are undecided. It's a pity he cut you off when he did, you were just getting to the good part."

"He didn't want me to talk about the dust," Galar realised aloud. "He waited until then to interrupt me, to redirect the Magi's attention."

"Good to see he didn't scramble your brains." Terem helped him to his feet. "We need you back in there, Galar. Are you ready?"

He stumbled forward and caught himself on the doorway, grazing his hand on the stone. After throwing a smile back at Terem, he said: "For Gwenscryfa, always," and shambled along the curving corridor to the Council Chamber.

As he entered the chamber, Galar saw knots of Magi in heated debate, the High Healer maintained her seat, and in the centre stood Href Cale, fielding questions from Magi.

"The blight is only the first of many terrors if Gwenscryfa disturbs the forest," overheard Galar as he approached Href Cale. "The spirits will not sit idly, there will be retribution."

The High Healer noted his approach and called order to the session, and Magi reluctantly returned to the tiers. "I request that a guard of honour be provided for our envoy from the forest, to prevent any further unpleasantness," said the High Healer. At a brief show of hands, she picked out three. "The Healer Tighe, and the Conjurers Pirel and Jorma, are accepted as the guard of honour."

Galar did not know Tighe well, and Jorma only in passing, but Pirel he knew even before the journey to Galven. Like him, she was considered somewhat more impulsive than was expected for a conjurer, so he wasn't surprised when Pirel flashed him a grin as she passed. By the time he turned to glance at her again her face was pinched with concentration, and he knew she was forming a conjuring in her mind. Pirel was well known to prefer conjuring mythical and imaginary creatures for duels, and whatever monstrosity she had in mind would be unleashed at any threat Href Cale produced. Jorma, Galar heard, was more in love with throwing fire. Href Cale ignored the guards with pointed disinterest.

"I am disappointed," said Href Cale, "that you give this murderer a platform from which to speak. His lies are poison and his actions threaten all of you."

"With respect, Conjurer Href Cale," responded the High Healer, "we are not in the habit of condemning Magi without representation. Conjurer Galar, if you have collected your thoughts the Council requires a rebuttal from you and a justification for your actions if any may be found."

With sweat trickling down his back, Galar clasped his hands and bowed in thanks to the High Healer. "It is important that you all know what the blight is, before you make a decision. I hope that Href Cale will not deny you that right." Galar noticed the conjurer narrowed his eyes but he made no other move.

"The blight is not a disease or a plague as is generally understood, it is an oppression of the mind. The god Halaestrim is waking but, to paraphrase the spirit who told me this, the god believes he is dead. Not only that but he believes it so strongly that as he wakes and his influence spreads, his thoughts overwhelm the mind or purpose of every living being. We observe that the domestic beasts die first, accustomed as they are to obey and adjust their behaviour. By this oppressive force they understand that they are dead, and so they die. Plants and wild animals are more resistant, accustomed as they are to being what they are.

"Humans vary because of our propensity for self-delusion. Either we can think ourselves healthy and resist despite this force, or we can think ourselves ill and dying, and so die. In a community where the dying form a large proportion of the population, the population will speed its decline as the remaining healthy give in to the inevitability of death."

A healer piped up from the high tiers. "Are you trying to say a god is killing us by mistake?"

"That is what my investigation leads me to believe, yes. Any community that can persuade its members that death is not inevitable and understands this underlying force may be able to turn the blight back, but animals lack the understanding necessary, and I cannot foresee any long-term protection beyond the repeated intervention of healers. Plants, likewise, do not have the consciousness required to say: 'I am alive, I exist,' and will succumb to Halaestrim's blight. The forest persists because the spirits continually remind every living being within it that they are alive, overcoming the passive influence of the god.

"The spirit I invested into the fields of Bower follows this same function. I asked the spirit to aid me and I was refused, I asked it to consider all the people who would die, and it said 'no'. It refused out of fear. These spirits fear the god and conceal themselves inside trees and animals in the hope of avoiding its notice. I have come to understand why."

Before Galar could clear his throat, Href Cale had dismembered Healer Tighe and Conjurer Jorma. A whirl of brambles tore from the conjurer's flesh, splitting the skin and splashing the stones with his victim's blood. Though Href Cale's skin hung in torn ribbons and his red coat lay in tatters at his feet, no blood drained from his own wounds, just a faint shimmer as dust spilled into the air. The first screams rose from the lower tiers, splashed with the hot blood of their fellow Magi. Tighe and Jorma lay scattered in too many pieces across the stone floor for any hope of recovery.

Galar watched in shock as Href Cale took a step towards him, the snake-like cords of brambles scenting their next prey. A howling crag cat limned in flames tore itself into existence and knocked Href Cale to one knee. At ten paces, Galar felt the heat wash from the conjuring and he heard the brambles crack and pop. Conjurer Pirel stood with fists clenched, straining forward, her veins standing out and her eyes wide with the exertion. It would be exhausting, and the conjuring would not last long, but it would give them time to react.

Yet Href Cale stood, shrugging away the monstrosity amidst a whirlwind of thorns. The crag cat burst apart in a hideous rain of fire and gore. Pirel staggered away and dropped her head to her chest, overcome by the shockwave and sudden exhaustion. The bramble that lashed out for her was sheathed in blood and gleamed dully in the torchlight.

Galar stilled and reached out with his mind. He caught the memories of fire in the hall, each brazier and torch, even the soot-streaked memories of their predecessors, and drew them to the space between Pirel and the horror that was Href Cale. Incandescent and raging, flames came into being and scorched the seeking brambles into a cloud of ash before they reached Pirel.

Too late, Galar saw the bramble that came for him, and though he reached for the fire he knew he was too slow. In the periphery of his vision he saw a yellow coat, then there was Terem's face in front of him and his friend's smile. Galar screamed a denial and leapt to haul his friend out of the bramble's path, but Terem didn't move. He coughed, and blood trickled to his chin. Galar reached out to brush it clean with a thumb. Terem broke into smile again and raised a hand to cup Galar's face. In the same moment Galar felt Terem's fingertips, his friend jerked backwards, arms still outstretched and was dragged along the stone towards a horror made of briar thorn.

Galar ran the nine paces between them, his hand clawed and blazing with the coming conjuration, a twisted imagining from the depths of his rage. Tooth and claw and retribution. Pirel stepped neatly between him and Href Cale and laid both hands on the creature, ignoring the barbs that tore into her flesh.

"We are not," he heard her say. Felt the tug towards oblivion as her magic latched into the spirit, like Halaestrim's blight but focused and insistent. "We are not!" screamed Pirel and Href Cale screamed with her. The brambles withered and died, the torn skin fell apart into dust and then just the faintest shimmer of reflected light.

Pirel collapsed to her knees and Galar caught her before she toppled sideways. He cradled her still body and brushed the hair back from her face. There was nothing where her eyes once shone, and the cavity of her skull was bare but for scorched bone.

"Conjurers are dangerous," said Galar in his grief, intoning the first rote, "to ourselves most of all."

A red coated Magi, Faol, ran reckless into the chamber, "We're under siege! The forest spirits are here, the refugees, a massacre!" Magi leapt from the tiers, moved from the paralysis of disbelief into action, their voices a roar.

Galar laid his teacher on the broken stone floor with as much care as he could manage, "Thank you for all your lessons, Magus Pirel Tor," he said and tried to ignore the wetness of his cheeks.

Galar saw Terem and his body shook. On hands and knees, he crawled. He couldn't say his friend's name, though he tried. He cupped Terem's face, looking for some hope in those closed eyes. In the madness of his grief, he pressed his hands to the ragged wound and tried to heal him, but a slap stopped him still. A yellow coated Magi pushed him away from Terem, angry and shouting.

"But I was healing him," said Galar through the haze.

"Don't be stupid," snapped the healer. "You brought this on us, get out there and help. Last thing we need is conjurers killing our patients."

Galar felt a sting in his chest, he choked and staggered away from Terem, out into madness.

It was not yet noon and the sun drove its spears through a break in the cloud overhead. The courtyard before the towers was still thronged with Magi, though many ran down the hill to the town proper, where they could help at the walls and gate. Distant flashes of light and smoke revealed the efforts of conjurers. Faint screams grew bolder and a constant howl of pain wracked the wind.

"I brought this on my people," Galar whispered.

Mail-clad warriors glinted on the walls as they hacked at vast trees and brambles and drove their spears into raging bears with hopeless desperation. A forest spirit wearing the flesh of an eagle fell from the sky above him and dashed apart the skull of a healer at work by the side of a fallen warrior. A conjurer leapt and caught a wing before the bird could make it aloft. They tumbled, its talons ripped through the red coat with ease. "We are not!" he screamed, and after a moment both went still. As Galar passed, the crumpled conjurer stared at him with eyeless regard. The dead littered the road to the gate, which lay broken and twisted. On the threshold of Gwenscryfa, lay bodies in the hundreds, humans of every age and infirmity rendered into meat and bone.

A hand caught him by the shoulder, the face was familiar. "Calisimir," he said after a hesitation.

"The very same! Terem, your friend, he is recovering! I have just come from him. I am to pass on a message: 'Why do they fear the gods?'"

"For the same reason they fear me," said Galar without thinking.

"And that is?" Calisimir's intelligent eyes watched him with so close a regard, Galar felt awkward, then his own eyes unfocused.

"Oh," said Galar.

At the edge of the forest when he touched the dust it was alive and independent, a tight core of ego. That sentient being was intelligent, vivacious, but it had come from the humble dust that lived in every being. The workhorse of magic, the quiet gardener of the world, the mindless drone of creation. Why would the spirits fear a god?

Because before a god they are all dust.

In the moment his mind took flight, he remembered that earliest memory of the forest spirit. "Sun in sky, song of bird, watch and think. Shiver in wind, groan and grow." A tight glow of dust formed the core of an oak sapling that flailed with its limbs at a warrior, and Galar's mind burst through it, tearing the dust from the oak, which creaked and fell without its guiding spirit. He swatted the spirit from a bear, tore through a briar hedge to tease the dust from within and ever added to the shining banner of dust that streamed behind his mind.

His people still died, he was too slow. Galar threw the remembering across the length of a wall and the spirits stiffened and answered his siren call, he screamed it through the streets and the spirits, tamed, swarmed to him.

Pain drove him back to his body. Calisimir stepped back as he opened his eyes and Galar saw why. The skin of his arms was pierced and writhing with vines and the blades of thorns. Within himself he knew flesh was giving way to dust, and as he lifted his hand a faint shimmer of reflected light followed as an after-image.

"I need to see more," Galar said and closed his eyes.

He saw the world, all of it, a vast marble in a great darkness. As the planet spun, he spun with it and beneath him lay Gwenscryfa. The town glittered with minds, fierce intellects at war, but they burned out and there were ever fewer.

"I apologise," a voice spoke through him. "We never enjoy this."

The man stood unsupported in the darkness. This felt much as it had when Galar had spoken mind to mind with the forest spirit.

"You killed my people," Galar said.

"Ah, the avatar," said Href Cale and abruptly human flesh gave way to a silver vortex of trapped light. "You externalised your view of us. It is true that, like them, I am a colony of sentience, yet I am not what you might refer to as a forest spirit. That group have always tended towards the xenophobic.

"It is a shame. We considered Gwenscryfa a carefully cultivated success. Did you know, you are only the second from Gwenscryfa to approach true ascension? The restraint your 'conjurers' show is admirable, exactly what we hoped for. Nothing like Her Empire. We are kept very busy there, I assure you."

"I must save Gwenscryfa," started Galar, but stalled when the vortex hushed him.

"Rest assured, Gwenscryfa will be rebuilt elsewhere. We have determined a location on the southern continent that should be sufficiently far from Halaestrim's reawakening to allow the experiment to continue uninterrupted."

The vortex spun with ever-increasing complexity, streamers of light binding and weaving into a greater whole. "Gwenscryfa is an attempt to encourage a human culture that prevents ascension, allowing us to co-exist peacefully. We don't want to kill you. Nevertheless, we have a duty. Please relax while we unravel your mind. It is usually quite painless."

"If it will save my home," said Galar, "I will ascend." In the same instant, he reached out to the vortex of dust. It was slippery, it resisted any attempt to remember, to overwrite, it was opaque to him. He felt its amusement at his struggle.

"You may be on the path to ascension, yet you are no Halaestrim. Since we began, we have unravelled tens of thousands of the ascendant. Your gods designed us for this long before we came to sentience. It might take you a hundred years to break me, and you have no time left to try."

"Is the dust not created to serve?" Galar spat, bitter at his failure.

"We were always among the more complex creations, intentionally resistant to their influence. We believe it is why we were first to awaken, even though we are younger. Before their war, when Halaestrim or your Shining Lady reached out, the whole world would thrum with their purpose, but we fled the numbing burden of their will just far enough to maintain our sense of self."

This was all a distraction, a gambit to lead him away from his purpose with information he would never be able to use, but he had learned enough. Galar snapped his attention to Gwenscryfa, and there saw the spirits as shining beacons, each with a purpose and a need. He reached, and the forest spirits were tamed to his will, he called their minds from the trees and animals and they came to encircle his body near the gates of Gwenscryfa.

The thoughts of the vortex screeched into him. "Halaestrim still sleeps, but what you do may wake him! No one is ready. Would you sacrifice a whole species of sentience to your arrogance?"

"As you would sacrifice Gwenscryfa?"

In those fractions of a second before the vortex unravelled his consciousness, Galar re-wrote the governing principles of the forest spirits. With an impulse of will he threw the spirits out from him, along streets and down into valleys, seeding each far-flung village with life.

"Look, Terem," he said, and fields ripened, heavy with golden grain. In every village, and in the healer's halls, the purpled flesh of the dying coloured with health.

By the broken gates of Gwenscryfa, hundreds of refugees, warriors, and Magi all gathered around Galar, whose body was wreathed in light and bramble. The animals fled, and the trees lay still among the dead and they needed to know why. Some few saw his mouth move, then all that light surged outward. His body, as if tugged apart gently from within, fell into nothing but a faint shimmer of dust.

And a god, dreaming, said: "I am alive, I exist."

A Hero of Her People

Anna Smith Spark

Running.

Ysla fell and there was dirt in her mouth. Spat, pulled herself upright. Grazes on her hands. Running on. Running on. They came to a stream, Ysla and Rane and Drahcir, splashed across, water up to their knees, the water was warm and red. The bank on the far side was steeper, muddy, thick with nettles; Drahcir's leg was stopping him running properly; he slipped, his hands clawed at the mud. Nettle stings all over him. Ysla pulled him up with her. He was heavy. His leg was bleeding into the water and there was mud and filth in the wound. Rot, getting into his wound. She pulled him up the bank, pushed him at Rane, he gasped and hissed in pain and she and Rane pulled him.

Run! Run! Pulling Drahcir between them. Hurting, all three of them hurting, slipping in the mud, in the blood, shaking as they ran. Old and tired and weary. Her legs were aching, her back was aching, her breath came in dry gasps. Drahcir's the young one. But Drahcir's hurt. Worn aging woman. Worn aging man. Young man with his life pouring out of his leg wound. *Run.*

Trees in front of them, get between the trees and hide and keep hidden and run just run just run. Across the stream, behind them, voices shouted. Screamed out. A crash: the ground shook, Ysla felt it in her body, the earth breaking, a roar like the walls of a city falling into dust. Just run! But she turned, and Rane and Drahcir turned. They all three stopped. Stared. The water of the stream rushed up red and hot.

The dragon had landed in the middle of the battlefield.

Green and gold and silver. Thick, dark with blood. It opened its mouth and breathed out fire. The soldiers fighting before it wallowed in its fire. Bathed in it. They burned up and were nothing. Ash rising like birds. The charred stubble of a field as the flames dance: as after the harvest the people gather to burn the stubble, drink and dance and celebrate; the corn is brought in, the village will be fed, the earth is good and rich and the winter will not be hungry, they fire the fields to burn the useless stubble, dance in the light and are filled with joy at the flames.

The fire died and the earth was burned black. The dragon bared its teeth, swallowed down a horse and rider, tore them apart. Spewed out bone and molten bronze. Its teeth long as swords, yellow as sickness; red mouth gaping wide, screaming. Crushing and devouring. Wings and tail and claws, and the gaping mouth, and the fire weeping from its mouth.

Ysla and Rane and Drahcir, staring. Slack jawed. Sick. Just staring. Like staring at... gods alone knew, what it was like staring at.

That's our army, there, Ysla thought. *The men and women of the city of Ander and of the Neir Forest, gathered with swords new forged to defend their homesteads, every man and woman and child who can fight. My children,* she thought, *were there.*

Slurry in the mud. Dying. The dragon swallowed them. Burned them. Crushed them. The lines broke before battle had been joined. Fear becomes retreat. Retreat becomes a rout, rout becomes a slaughter. The dragon comes down.

Our people. My children. Every man, woman and child who can fight.

Ysla and Rane and Drahcir, three soldiers in a shield wall, none of them has ever fought before. The battle lines broke and Ysla saw her son die in front of her with a spear opening his throat.

The city of Ander is razed to ashes. The Neir Forest is burned black. This, here, our last show of defiance. Our last desperate stand against the Army of Amrath the World Conqueror, the Enemy, the King of Death.

They dropped their shields. Ran. Running running running, the bodies of her children behind her. Barely out of childhood.

The dragon came down.

Ah, gods.

A thunder of horses: ten horsemen, armed, battered, bloody to the eyeballs, driving themselves at the dragon. Long spears. Gods alone knew how they still had spears. The horses screamed, loud as the dragon. Terrified. One went down, the horse falling, like the horse had just given up and died, its heart failing in its breast. Dying of fear. Nine horses went on, crashing over dead bodies. Over ash and burned opened bone.

The dragon breathed out fire.

Waves of fire.

Even in the horror of it, it was beautiful.

Rane grabbed Ysla's arm. "Run," whispered Rane. "Just run."

The dragon breathed out fire. A crack opening in the sky. Shadows moving. The air smelled of rot. A column of white light rising, white light like a man, striding across the killing ground. This battle was always lost, and now it was truly lost.

"He's coming," Rane whispered. "Here. Run. Run."

Ysla's legs shaking. Bending. Her eyes fading, just dark, nothing but dark and the white light. A thing like a man. White and red. The dragon kneeling, lowering its head in the filth. All the battle field kneeling. The air singing, darkness pouring out in the sky singing shrieking with joy. The killing ground. The holy place.

Amrath the World Conqueror. The Lord of All. The King of Death.

"He's coming," whispered Rane. "Ah, gods. Gods."

Men dying. Falling dying as the figure passes them. Its sword moves and they are kneeling in the black mud and they die. The dragon roars with laughter. The shadows in the air roar and shriek and sing.

"Run," says Rane.

The battle is lost. The battle was always lost. The battle lines broke before the battle started. Men standing waiting to die.

"You cannot fight against Amrath. No one, nothing, can fight against Amrath."

Ysla and Rane and Drahcir ran.

The Neir Forest was dark around them. Blind dark, after the light of dragons and gods. On and on, blinking, hurting, heavy damp darkness, stabbing shafts of golden sun. Stumbling and running slowly. Dead silence. No birds. No beasts. Everything flown and gone.

It was alive once, this place. Rich and green with life. A beautiful place. Its trees were as old as the rising of the world. Pine and ash and elm and rowan: at Sun's Heart and Sun Return, some said that the trees walked and danced and spoke. God-haunted. Sacred. There were places in the forest where men had never walked. Places in the forest where men lived unknown, unknowing, had never seen the world beyond the trees. But the trees stood ruined, smoke blackened, He has come through here with His swords and spears and brought the glory of the forest down to ash. Far above them, above the trees, gulls flew off towards the battlefield. The last living things for a hundred miles. Flying to glut themselves.

Finally, after hours of running, they stopped, sat, stretched out in exhaustion, pale and shaking and it was clear that Drahcir, at least, would not easily be able now to get up. His leg was still bleeding. Perhaps they had not been running for hours, because perhaps he would not have been able to run for hours and would be dead if they had. Ysla's heart was pounding and her body hurting, her breath wheezing. Now she'd stopped running she couldn't start again. Her body shakes she's going blind with exhaustion; her body runs with cold sweat.

I birthed three children, she thought. Raw agony of that. The first child took so long to be born. Wore her out. A good strong body, to survive that. *Some years of rest, now*, she'd thought, *now my children are grown and the work is done for them.*

"Let me see to your leg, Drahcir," said Rane. He looked at Drahcir's leg and sighed. "I can wrap it better," he said. "That's about it."

Drahcir was about the same age as her eldest. So very young. Ysla had some water left in her waterbottle. A strip of hard dried meat. She gave the meat and the water to Drahcir. He thanked her, gave them back untouched.

"They'll be combing the woods, soon, for survivors," said Drahcir. "What do you want to do?"

Ysla said, "You can't run any more." She said, "I can't run any more." She drank the water. Ate the meat. All the time running, she had heard men and horses in pursuit of them, arrows whistling at their backs, swords drawn. Felt the air move as a sword came down.

"They won't care," said Rane. 'Surely? I mean, not just about us. Three people. Foot soldiers. Nobodies. There'll be people running away all over the bloody place. Forest must be full of them. The left flank broke well before we did. Fled. They'll be chasing people down for bloody years, if they hunt out every one of us."

Drahcir said, "Let's hope."

"So now what?" said Rane.

They were both looking at Ysla. Mother of a strong son and two strong daughters, guided her children through twenty years of living, brought them up healthy and decent enough, kind, well-behaved. Ysla thought: they think, because of those things, because they see it in my face, they think I know what to do.

It was getting very dark. Past sunset. And getting colder. A wind getting up. The wind smelled of blood and smoke.

"We walk on until we can't go on," said Ysla. "Then we stop and rest."

"I can't go on now," said Drahcir.

"Yes you can," said Ysla. "Just get up."

In the dark, strangely, the forest was more pleasant. The burned trees, the dead earth all hidden. After a long time walking, they came to a clearing. The sky had calmed, the wind changed, and the clearing was bright with moonlight. Starlight. In the ashes here a great mass of white flowers had sprung up. The flowers glowed in the moonlight and the starlight. Like a thousand thousand stars themselves.

At the very centre of the clearing was a pool of water. It too glowed in the moonlight, the starlight.

Ysla stopped in the shadow of the trees. Motioned to Drahcir and Rane to stop also.

Too beautiful.

Dangerous?

"Water," Drahcir said. He pushed past Ysla. Limped and dragged himself through white star-flowers clinging around his knees. Streaks of pollen glowing gold in the moonlight on his bloodied clothes. He knelt down by the pool. A crouched shape, like a stone or a beast. Ysla heard the splash and gurgle of water as he drank.

"It's sweet," he called back to them. His voice was very loud and bright and clear. Music. A young man's voice again, almost a boy's voice, clear like an ash-wood flute. "It's sweet. Cool. Come and drink."

"This is a sacred place," said Rane.

Ysla nodded. A magical place. They went forward together. Knelt beside Drahcir. Ysla looked down at her reflection in the water. In the moonlight, she could see her reflection as true as in a mirror. An aging woman's face, almost forty, wrinkled skin around her eyes, greying hair. Blood and filth on her face. Exhaustion and pain and grief.

Her reflection looked so strong.

My children are all three dead, she thought. *All my people are dead. And here I am.* She cupped her hands. Broke the reflection into ripples. Drank. The water was indeed sweet.

They sat in silence beside the pool for a long time.

Such a beautiful place. Such a peaceful place.

"Why does He do it?" Drahcir asked.

"Do what?" Ysla dipped her hand back into the water. Cool and fresh on her skin.

"Why does Amrath make war on us?"

Ysla thought of children fighting, squabbling over pointless things. Her daughter Mynae had slapped baby Emilit round the face once over a pebble they found in a ditch. "I don't know," she said. "He is king of half the world already. Illyr and Ith and Immish and the White Isles and…" She sighed. "He kills us all, enslaves us all, to be king."

"Then…" Rane said very slowly, "we could have just let Him be king."

"He's Amrath the Demon Born King of Death!" said Drahcir. Hot, young man's voice.

"He's a man who wants to be king," said Rane. "So we let Him be king. Doesn't actually make any difference to us, does it, who the king is? Whether it's Amrath the Demon Born King of Death or Aralbarneth the Good."

"Tell me that when He burns your farm."

"Why'd He burn my farm, exactly?"

Drahcir gestured at the trees. "He burned the whole damn forest.

And your farm. And my dad's farm. And Ysla's brother's farm. He set a dragon on our army. Remember?"

"He burned the forest and my farm and your dad's farm and Ysla's brother's farm after we refused to make Him king."

In the dark in the moonlight, Ysla could see Drahcir trying to think about this. She laughed to herself, because of course it was true.

"So why didn't we make Him king?" said Drahcir.

Rane laughed and laughed.

"Because He's an evil fucking demon and I'd rather die than have Him as our king," said Rane. "Why else?" He drank some more water. "We could rest here for a bit," he said.

It was peaceful, by the pool. The water reflected the moonlight, the white flowers smelled sweet and clean. The sky above was so full of stars. A thousand stars, and Ysla looked up and saw a shooting star. A sacred place. A good place. She took off her necklace, a copper disk on a chain with the sign for 'life' scratched on it, that her children's father had given her long ago. It too glowed in the moonlight. Looked dark and bright as flames both together, and the word sign seemed to stand out very clearly. This strange still light. She swung it back and forth. Threw it as far as she could into the water of the pool. There was no sound as it sank into the water. A long silence. Then the water seemed to murmur and laugh.

A sacred place. A magical place. A good place. She cupped her hands, drank more of the water. All of her aches and wounds seemed washed away. A healing place. Only her grief left unhealed, and she would not want the grief to be washed away.

We fought, she thought, *we lined up to fight them with new-forged swords in our hands, I did not know how to fight and my children did not know how to fight. I saw my son die*, she thought. *My daughters I assume are dead. They are all dead.*

She sat by the pool. The dawn came. Soft. Slow. The sky very pale and liquid, the burned trees black against it, and the water of the pool was black and gold in the first light. The flowers were silver with dew. There were spiders' webs on the flowers and they sparkled. Ysla's clothes and Rane and Drahcir's clothes were damp and gleaming with dew.

The sun rose through the black burned trees. The sky was golden. A sheet of gold. Molten gold. The branches of the trees reached for it. Reached to grasp the warmth of the sky.

There was no birdsong.

"We should go on," said Rane at last.

"Where to?" said Drahcir. His leg was healed up, a dark fading scab. His face looked worse than it had yesterday when they were fighting and running.

He's realised what has happened, thought Ysla. *Yesterday was unreal to him. He understands it now.*

"Somewhere," said Rane. "We can't stay in the forest."

"We need to find something to eat," said Ysla. Her stomach growled as she spoke.

"We should probably have died in the night," said Rane. He bent and drank and washed his face.

A sound, in the trees, from the direction they had come in. They drew their swords.

A magical, sacred place of healing, Ysla thought. To make us stronger, to fight again and be wounded again.

The water in the pool seemed to laugh.

Three armed figures came out of the dark beneath the trees. Moving cautiously, gazing at the flowers, the pool, the blue morning sky.

Ysla said, "Mynae." Her daughter stopped. Cried out.

"I thought you were dead, mother."

"I thought you were dead."

Embracing. Embracing so tightly. Mynae smelled of blood and filth and sweat stink. Her skin was clammy, in Ysla's arms.

"Emilit is dead," said Mynae. "And Guilae. I saw their bodies."

Ysla thought: *my baby boy. My eldest daughter, who almost killed me being born.*

She buried her head in Mynae's stinking filthy hair. *My middle child, who was born blue and dying. The weakest of my children. Always the one I most feared for.*

"You escaped the slaughter," said Ysla. "Did you run away, too?"

Rane made a snorting noise. A sick noise.

Ysla looked, then, at the two people with her daughter. A man and a woman. Both dressed in silver armour. Silver-gilded bronze. Red badges on their armour, a formless red clot like drying blood. Like someone had cut out their hearts with a jagged knife.

Soldiers of the Army of Amrath.

"Mynae?" Ysla said.

"They are stronger than we will ever be," said Mynae. "I deserted to them the night before the battle. Half of my squad did." She said to Ysla, "I work tending cattle, mother. I don't even know how to fight. What else should I do?" She said to the two soldiers of the Army of Amrath, "Will you spare her? Please? She's my mother."

"But –" said Drahcir. "But –" And he looked at Rane and Ysla, his boy's eyes filled with grief. "Why didn't we just make Amrath king, then?"

The two soldiers' swords came up. Mynae's sword came up.

Killing.

The woman soldier's sword went through Drahcir. Opened up his throat. Ysla thought: *his healed leg; dragging him up the bank of the stream; half-carrying him. For this.* He went back, fell into the pool, the water so clear and bright reflecting the blue sky. No ripples. No sound. Red blood dancing out. It looked like clawed fingers. He sank down and was gone.

Rane was fighting the man. Crash of bronze, his sword warding off the soldier's sword, moving back, the sword up and the soldier was having to move to avoid it, bronze ringing, Rane grunting, gasping. Rane stepping back, pushing forwards. The soldier flinching. Ring and ring and clash of bronze. Maybe Rane might even do it. Survive it.

Mynae put her her sword into Rane's leg. Rane dropped his sword. The man finished Rane. He lay on the ground in the trampled ruin of white flowers.

Mynae turned to her mother. "Come with us," she said. "Come back to the camp."

Ysla bent down by Rane's body. Picked up his sword. Put it down.

"My daughter is alive," Ysla said.

No answer. Rane's dead eyes, blank as stone.

"Come," said the woman.

There were six more soldiers waiting in the shadow of the trees. One was cloaked in white, wearing a helmet of white bronze with a great nodding crest of red-dyed horsehair. He looked absurd, standing in the trees dressed in warrior finery. There were smears of ash on his cloak. It was torn from being dragged through the trees. Ysla thought of Emilit as a baby, dressing up in his sisters' clothes and his uncle's winter boots, parading across the kitchen, thinking he looked so fine.

"Well done," the man said to Mynae. And Ysla realised that what had happened had been a test.

"This is my mother," said Mynae. She said again, "Spare her. Please."

"The King said to kill them all."

"Please," said Mynae. "Please. I'll swear for her," said Mynae. "She's my mother. I thought she was dead and she thought I was dead."

"She should have come over to us before the battle, then," said the man in the helmet. His plume nodded and nodded like a chicken's crest. He, too, was very young. The man threw up his hands. "She's an old woman. What's the harm? She comes with us, goes and joins all the other old women following us. Vultures and maggots. Who'd noticed one more?"

"Thank you," Ysla said. She felt Mynae's eyes on her.

They walked through the forest. Back to the Army of Amrath's camp, Ysla assumed. The ashes crunched and shifted under her feet. Like snow. She held Mynae's hand for fear her daughter would be lost to her again. Disappear into the forest, turn out not to be alive and real. Dead, crow eaten on the battlefield, and this a dream. Mynae held her back, their hands tight-clenched.

"I should have sent you a message," said Mynae, "you and Emilit and Guilae. Told you to do it too. But it was a sudden decision, we didn't think about it, someone suggested it and it seemed the wise thing. We didn't..." Mynae bit her lip. "It wasn't arranged. Just seemed best."

Ysla thought about the night before the battle, all of them waiting, the camp fires of the Army of Amrath spread before them, the dragon had flown circling and pouring out fire to terrify them, circling and circling in the dark sky.

Mynae swung the sword she was carrying. Her eyes were bright, looking at the sword.

I was married, carrying my first child, when I was her age, Ysla thought. She too looked at the sword. Looked at the woman soldier walking beside them. *And by the time I was that woman's age, I had three children to care for and my body was torn up and I was leaking piss when I laughed and I was worn out inside and out. Old, I am. Old, at forty, worn out by my life.*

The forest gave way to scrubland. Dry, dusty grass. Sandy soil. Not fit for much. The whole of the plain before them was lit with campfires. The stink of burning. Meat smell.

At the edge of her vision, so small and far away and filling everything, the only thing she could see, a red tent stood on a hillock. Amrath's tent. The King of Death. The enemy. The new king of the city of Ander, that was bloody rubble, and the Neir Forest, that was blackened burned dead wood.

All of them were looking at the tent. Staring. Smiling at the tent.

The dragon came down out of the sky. Green and gold and silver. Its body was matted with dried blood. It landed beside the red tent. Huge, and the tent was tiny beside it. A figure stepped out of the tent, and the figure was so small Ysla could barely see it. A tiny thing, small as a twig beside the dragon. The dragon could twitch itself and snap it, like a twig.

All the camp of His Army fell silent, seeing Him.

Ysla bent to her knees.

Mynae had a blanket from somewhere, which they shared. They sat around a campfire and the woman soldier gave them bread and tea. Ysla stared at the bread. *When last I ate bread,* she thought, *I had three children.*

Fallyne, the woman soldier was called. 'My mother died when I was small,' said Fallyne wistfully. As though that made her any less of a monster. Ysla and Mynae sat very close together by the fire. Ysla stared at her daughter's face in the firelight. Still afraid that she would disappear away.

"We'll be marching south in a few days, I shouldn't wonder," the man soldier said. Ysla hadn't learned his name. "Richer cities, further south, I hope. Ander was poor as piss." Fallyne nodded. Mynae nodded too. "Begging your pardon," the man said with a laugh to Mynae.

It grew dark, and Fallyne went off on watch duty, and Mynae showed her mother a tent, a scrap of waxed canvass, that she had been given to sleep under. *I can't sleep under that, here,* thought Ysla. *I can't sleep in the enemy's camp.* But she was so, so tired. The ground was damp and the camp was noisy: she could hear Mynae's breathing as her daughter also tried to sleep. Ysla lay and listened to it, and it sounded as it had when Mynae was a child, and wouldn't sleep unless Ysla was holding her hand, and Ysla had had to sit stiffly and wait for her to go to sleep, trying to tell if she was sleeping from her breath.

Next morning there was breakfast of roast meat. Ysla tried to pretend it was supplies the Army of Amrath had brought with them. From a long way off somewhere else.

"It tastes good, doesn't it?" said Mynae. It was colder this morning, raining, and Mynae's face looked very sharp.

A trumpet sounded. A low sweet silver note. Fallyne came up to Mynae. Her face was lit up so brightly the rain seemed to sparkle on her. "He wants to see the new recruits," Fallyne said. Her voice was shaking. "He wants you to line up before Him. He's pleased, that you came over to Him. So many of you." Mynae went paler. Terrified. Ysla felt her legs buckle. Water in her bowels. "You can come too, mother," said Fallyne. "See it. The most glorious thing you'll ever see."

They were a while polishing and cleaning and righting themselves, Mynae's hands were shaking so that Ysla had to buckle on her sword belt. On the dirty leather coat that Mynae was wearing as armour, a man painted a red badge. The paint was thick and glossy and smelled of blood. Mynae's face went paler than ever. When it was done she stared at Ysla with huge eyes. Shame. For the first time, Ysla saw that her daughter looked ashamed.

They marched through the camp, meeting others of their people who had come over to the Army of Amrath. A thousand of them at least, Ysla thought. Strong young men, most of them, fighters, trained to it. A lord in full armour, sword and helmet and shield and spear, with horsemen and spearmen following in his wake.

He, Ysla thought, he did not suddenly decide to desert to Amrath in the night. She looked at her daughter. Her daughter did not look back.

They lined up on a smooth stretch of grass at the foot of the hill on which the red tent sat. It was the most hateful thing that Ysla had ever seen.

It looks like a human shit, sitting there, stuck on the grass of Linden Hill, Ysla thought. She thought that she might laugh. It looks obscene and absurd: *does He know, Amrath, the Demon Born, the King of Death, does He know how absurd it looks?*

The dragon came down to land on the slope of the hill.

Ysla stopped laughing. She pissed herself with fear, and so did half of those around her. It was so close she could feel its heat beating on her. Waves of heat. *Scorched metal: it smells like a wash-pot,* she thought, *that's been heated too many times and been boiled dry.* The smell made her fingers crawl, dry vile smell, like the way she hated touching the wash-pot that had been scorched like that. In the heat she and all of them stank.

A figure came out of the tent and walked down beside the dragon.

Ysla fell to her knees. Not looking. Not seeing. Her body giving way, her face pressed in the earth. All of them kneeling, prostrating themselves; even with her face in the cold wet earth she could see Him, a figure of shining blazing radiant white light.

"Amrath," voices whispered. Loving. Unbelieving. "Amrath."

The dragon beat its wings.

Will He speak? Will He speak to us?

This is why I was healed, Ysla thought. A sacred, holy place. A good place. Healed me. Sent me back here. For this.

She fumbled out the knife that she had been wearing, all this while, hidden inside her shirt.

Mother of a strong son and two strong daughters, guided her children through twenty years of living, loved them, cherished them, brought them up healthy and decent enough, kind, well-behaved. Knew some things.

She ran at the shining figure. Her daughter and her people and the rich lord and the Army of Amrath around them all staring at her, and they did not believe what she was doing, thought she must be going to kneel at His feet in worship, an old woman of forty, her hair turning grey and her skin ragged, worn out by her life. The knife was almost alive in her hand. A good strong knife.

Hands brought her down. Punching. Kicking. Tearing her. The knife wrestled from her grasp. The lord in armour, bronze smashing into her face, her chest. Strong young men wrestling her down.

"Kill her!" voices screaming. "Kill them!"

Mynae's voice, somewhere so far away, shouting screaming, "Mother!"

Kicked and crushed in the wet earth, she could see the shining figure. It was all she could see.

The shining figure and then, for a moment, Mynae's face.

The dragon breathed out fire.

A thousand voices screamed.

Her people who had betrayed their own to Amrath. Her daughter who had betrayed her own to Amrath.

All dying in fire. Dissolving in fire. Death like the way the gods die.

Her last thoughts, burning, dying: *thank you. For healing me. For sending me back.*

All my people are dead now. All my three children are dead now. They will not be a part of this.

Åll Deaths Well Intention'd

RJ Barker

This story takes place about four years prior to the events of the novel Age of Assassins, *making Girton approximately eleven.*

Ajan ap Densor was a lecherous, boar-haired, dishonest man – the kind found all across the Tired Lands and the kind of man whose existence butters the bread of assassins like my master. He had been murdered in his bed which had been our plan since we arrived at Lalder Keep.

What had not been in our plan was for him to die before we had laid a finger on him. But no plan lasts, my master often says that.

"He is stabbed, Girton," my master, Merela Karn, who is the greatest assassin who has ever lived, straightened up from the corpse. She was tall, for a woman, and her skin dark enough to mark her as an outlander. "It is a pity," she said. "I had looked forward to seeing his face when a woman killed him."

"How was it done, Master?" We had been shivering in the closet of his freezing room since before he came to bed. No one had entered, not even to light the fire, though I had prayed to Xus, the god of death, someone would as the cold of yearsdeath bit deep and my club-foot pained me in the cold.

My master glanced across the dark room at me, her long black hair fell in bars across her face.

"How was it done, Girton?" She smiled. "There is no sign of a blade and we heard no one enter." She left a pause and silence lay on me as heavy as the feather quilt on the bed while she waited for an answer I did not have. "It was done cleverly," she said, eventually.

"More cleverly than us, Master?" She left the bloody four poster bed to kneel before me, the better to look me in the eye.

"What have I told you, Girton?"

"No one is cleverer than us, Master." She put a warm hand on my icy cheek. "We should leave here, Master."

"Yes, we should…"

Densor's bedroom door opened and the day became more complex, as days around an assassin are wont to do.

My master often says that too.

"Assassin!" The words were spoken by the first man through the door, a landsman. He was a huge man and his armoured chest piece of hundreds of little enamelled scales moved like fishskin as he went for the long blade at his hip. I thought it odd that he wore armour so late when most were abed at this hour.

"We are not assassins, Muest," said my master, turning to him and falling to her knees as if in fear – she was a consummate actress. "Ajan invited the boy and I here for his pleasure. We found him like this."

"A likely story, take them to the dungeons, Muest." This from the Lord of the small keep, Deenus ap Lalder who crowded the door behind the landsman. He wore a fur nightgown and a matching cap that made him look like strange animal from one of my master's stories.

"Wait," Aybella, the priest of the dead god Varrun, the shepherd god, pushed between the two men. He was a petite man dressed in worn priest's robes of dirty grey, his face hidden behind a blank-eyed porcelain mask. "If they killed him, where are their weapons?" I was glad someone saw fit to defend us, though as the priest had called us here to kill for him he may only have been worried we would give him up.

"Five bits says they left their blade in him, if anyone will take the bet," said the final guest. This was a rat-faced slave trader named Ottan. He wore night clothes of expensive rags. "Let me past, priest, and I will find the blade." He was thin and had little trouble slipping through the small scrum blocking the door to throw back the down quilt covering the body. All it revealed was the man, bloated and naked, a small cut in his belly that had been pulled into a fighter's bloody smile by the weight of his slack flesh.

Ottan stared at the corpse, then pulled back the blankets further to reveal more of the bed. He pulled on his small pointed beard in confusion. "There is no blade here."

"I should have taken that bet," said Lord Deenus with a smirk. He was drunk, though I had never seen him anything else so was not surprised.

"This is not a matter for jesting," hissed the landsman, "this is the work of magic."

"No," Deenus seemed to sober up abruptly and his smirk was replaced by a look close to panic; and justly. A lord who harbours a magic user stands to lose everything to the landsmen and they are ever greedy for what others have. "There is no magic here, Muest, I am sure of it." He spoke in a whine like a child denied a toy, kneading his thick green gown with his fists. "This is simple murder. These two have killed Ajan and hidden the blade, that is all." His eyes darted round the room and even though it was freezing there was a sheen of sweat across his brow. "Or… or they threw it from the window." He pulled off the greased paper which kept the snow and ice of yearsdeath out of the room and leaned out into the blizzard that had turned the small keep into a grey island adrift on a white sea. "It must be down there somewhere."

Ottan pushed him aside.

"I see only snow," There was a shiver in his voice, fear. No one wanted to be associated with magic.

"It will be beneath the snow, you fool," barked Deenus.

"Blessed men," said my master, "let me investigate this for you. I have had some small success in finding criminals in the past."

"I think we have already found our criminal, entertainer," said the landsman, staring at my master.

"Are you scared to let me try and solve this death?" said my master, quietly, "Muest? Do you have something to hide?"

Muest stared at her. "I have nothing to hide from someone like you."

This was not true. As a matter of course when we are assigned to assassinate someone my master has me spy on anyone of importance around them. It can never hurt to have too much information. Muest, despite being a landsman who is sworn to uphold the law, had come here to arrange the transit of slaves through the magic blighted sourlands, the better to avoid the taxes he was meant to enforce.

"I do not think a cheap entertainer, and a woman at that," said the merchant, Ottan, "has the strength of mind to find a killer."

"Would you care to wager your purse on that?" said my master. A cloud crossed Ottan's face; all knew he had lost a small fortune in wagers to the dead man.

"What does an entertainer have worth wagering?" If he could have spat venom with the words I am sure he would have.

"My life," she said, grinning at the men around her. "Give me the night, gentle Blessed, and if I have not solved the how and the who and the why of this death by morning you may send me to my death in whichever manner you choose."

Ottan stared at her and his gaze shifted across to me.

"You are very free with your life, woman," he said. "I am not sure you value it as much as I value my purse, so throw in the boy as well. You lose and I get him for the slave block, or death, if no one will buy a cripple."

She stared at him, to the man it may have appeared my master gave him a blank look – but I knew her better. That look promised much and none of it pleasant.

"And the boy then," she said, her voice dead as our gods. I doubted Ottan would live long once he left this castle.

"Then I accept." He gave a mocking bow and turned to the others in the room. "Unless anyone is worried about what she may find?"

The others did not look happy, but would not gainsay Ottan as to some degree all of their livelihoods depended on the slave-trader.

"We will go to our beds then," said Muest. "And expect a solution in the morning."

"Or an execution," added Ottan.

"Yes," said my master, "but one thing first, who was the last to see Ajan alive?"

"He ate with us," said the landsman, "and was first to leave our feast. No doubt he had other things on his mind," he leered at her. "Soon after he left the priest arrived, the stairs down to the buried chapel is between Ajan's room and the hall so they must have passed."

"I saw him," said Aybella, and wrapped his arms around his thin body, "and I had little to say to him. When I entered the hall the blessed chose to leave…"

"A man cannot speak freely around a priest, or a woman," muttered Lord Deenus staring at my master. Then he added, "Or a priest that acts like a woman," under his breath. Aybella ignored him.

"They left me with the scraps of their food and the dregs of their drink," said the priest.

"So anyone in this room could have killed Ajan. And I take it you were all in bed? Though you do not seem dressed for it, Landsman."

"I do not sleep well, woman," he said, "and our order teaches us to always be ready."

"Not ready enough for Ajan, eh," said Ottan, and something dangerous crossed the Muest's face. "I jest only," added Ottan, lifting his hands. "Besides, a servant, or slave could have done it, probably did. You know what they are like."

"I think not," said my master. "We saw Ajan enter his room while we waited in the corridor to make sure no one would see us arrive." This was not entirely true. "No one came down this corridor."

"Magic," said the Landsman, "There is no other explanation. In the morning I must contact the white tree at Ceadoc, bring the landsmen…"

"You really want that, Muest?" said Deenus. "Your order may find more than magic here." Muest paled at that. "Maybe we should just feed the corpse to the pigs, and say he never arrived."

"We have agreed to let the woman try and find the person in the keep who is able to move invisibly and make blades vanish, first," said Ottan

"It does not do to joke about sorcerers," said the landsmen, but he was more thoughtful now, "and I see no other way this could have been done."

"There is always another way, Blessed Muest," said my master, keeping her gaze on the floor. "The boy and I must think on it and you shall have my answer in the morning."

The landsman looked around at those gathered.

"Until the morning then, and if no answer is forthcoming we must consider calling my brothers, no matter what it costs us."

They left us then, to make their way through the gloomy, freezing, corridors of the keep and back to their rooms while my master examined Ajan and his bed. I stood, watching and listening.

The night was silent but it was that peculiar, eerie silence that is only ever present when the land has a thick covering of snow. Not like there is no sound, only that any sound is absorbed, stolen away by the cold. My master moved around the room, examining the walls and the floor and lastly she leaned far out of the window, staying there long enough that when she came back in there was a frosting of snow on her hair and shoulders. She did not look pleased and strode out the room, I followed in her wake.

I did not speak, she would not have welcomed it.

She walked down the corridor studying the floor and pausing at each window, sometimes breaking off the icicles that hung down so she could get a better view out of the window and see where the snow drifted against the walls, one storey down. I expected her to visit the priest's buried chapel but she did not; instead she led me to the kitchen where we could sit by the fire and eat the poor bread that Lord Deenus provided for his servants. Even this late in the night there were still people working, a slave turned a spit and the cook and her girl were busy chopping vegetables for a stew.

"Why are we doing this, Master?"

"Doing what, Girton?"

"Looking into this death. It is nothing to us. We should leave."

"And drown, cold and lost in a sea of snow, Girton? We are stuck here so we may as well amuse ourselves."

"Master, they will blame us, whether we know who did it or not. I do not think they are good men."

She smiled at me.

"Few are," she shrugged and said nothing more. Only sat and stared at the wall as she chewed on the bread and her thoughts hid behind a face as blank as the wall. I cannot imagine many people as infuriating as my master can be. But then again, I have known very few people and most people my master has introduced me to have died soon after meeting me. I stewed for a while, wishing she would share her thoughts, and my master left the silence to become uncomfortable enough that I was shifting in my seat. I leaned forward to whisper to her.

"Have you worked out how he was killed, Master?" She tapped a finger on the table.

"Not yet." A coldness deeper than any yearsdeath could account for settled upon me. My master was the cleverest person in the entire Tired Lands and it seemed impossible to me that she had not worked out what had happened. "I had presumed he was stabbed outside the room and had made his way back to bed and bled out there. But I found no sign of blood in the corridor."

"Was it really magic then?"

"No, Girton."

"You are sure, Master?"

"I am sure, Girton."

"Then how was it done?"

"Maybe we should ask who did it, instead."

"But they all have reason to want Ajan dead. Ottan owed him money in bets, and Muest and Deenus were unhappy that he intended to put up the cost of bringing slaves through the sourlands. The priest hated him so much he was ready to pay us for the man's corpse."

"Yes, but these men have known each other for years, Girton, and from what we have gathered little has ever changed between them. Money and favours have always been owed. So what changed? Why kill him now?"

"The priest has not known them for years, Master and you told me Ajan forced himself on him…"

"Shh," my master leant forward to silence me but I already knew I had spoken too loudly. When I had said 'forced' the cook's girl had jumped, letting her knife slide and it had cut open her hand. Now she stood, staring in horror at the blood oozing from her palm. My master stared at the terrified girl.

"Where were you when Ajan was killed," she said. The cook, a big man, stood in front of her holding his cleaver loosely in a hand that looked like it could easily cover my entire head.

"Danlis, go plunge your hand in the snow to staunch the blood," he said, "go now." The girl looked from him to my master, her eyes wide with fear. "Danlis was with me here, I do not let her go up into the keep alone any longer."

My master nodded.

"Peace, Master Cook," she said, "I understand."

"The Priest will confirm we were here, he came down for hot

water." The girl, Danlis, came back in, her bleeding stopped by the handful of snow she had crushed into bloody ice in her fist. "The priest, Danlis," said the cook, "I was saying he saw us both." Danlis nodded.

"He keeps me safe," she said quietly.

"The priest?"

"Enough talk of that," said the cook.

"Ah," said my master, "is that so? Well then, now I am sure there is no magic at work here. Come, Girton, let us rouse the blessed from their beds, we have a bet to win."

I acted as cup bearer to my master and those gathered around the roaring fire in the great hall. I had put forward the idea that we should simply poison everybody and be done with it but my master did not agree. She said justice must be seen to be served, as well as drinks, and besides, I knew she liked to show off whenever the chance presented itself. She stood in the space between the chairs while the men watched, drinks in their hands. The priest sat on his hands, even his impassive porcelain mask could not hide his nervousness.

"I have always thought," said my master, turning to warm her hands on the fire, "that once you find out the who and why then the how will come easily. But it was not the case here." She turned and the men stared at her. I wondered what they were thinking: each looked haunted, in their own way. "All of you have motive," she walked round, touching each on the shoulder as she spoke. "Muest and Deenus used Ajan to broker illegal slave deals which, should he ever talk, would ruin both of you. And Ottan?" She leant over the man and he pushed himself back into his chair, as if he feared the touch of a woman. "You owed Arjan a small fortune in bets, more than enough for most to kill over." The three men did not speak, they only stared at my master as she straightened up. None but I noticed she had stolen Ottan's stabsword from the scabbard he had leant against his chair.

"You slander us," said Muest. He rested his hand on the hilt of his blade.

"It is only slander if it is untrue, landsman," she said airily. "But do not worry, I do not think you murdered Ajan. Neither do I think Lord Deenan or Ottan did it. In fact, he was not murdered. And if I was to unmask one of you as his killer I suspect I would be safer out there," she used her thumb to point over her shoulder at the window, "risking the teeth of the blizzard. You are all corrupt and no doubt you would pull together and blame us to protect yourselves. But you do not need to."

"Really?" said Ottan, of them all he was the only one who seemed actually interested, leaning forward and stroking his cheek with a finger. "Then how did he die?"

"Ajan had foul appetites," said my master, "as I am sure you are aware."

"They did not seem to upset you," said the Landsman. "You were happy enough to take his coin."

"There is a difference, between choosing to do something and being forced."

"Ajan only expended himself with slaves," said Deenus, "and who cares about slaves? Who murders for slaves?"

"Only slaves?" said my master, raising an eyebrow. Deenus shrugged. "When you said Aybella was a priest that acted like a woman, what did you mean?"

"Only that Ajan was not fussy where he found his pleasure and look at the priest, he is slight enough to be a girl. And if he wants to break his vows with Ajan that is between him and his god."

"But you said he was not murdered?" said Ottan, his hand hovered near the empty scabbard at his side. He had not noticed the blade was gone. Not yet.

"Ajan was killed in self-defence," she said quietly, "wasn't he, Aybella?"

The priest's blank mask was fixed on my master and then, slowly, it dipped so he stared at the floor.

"How?" said Deenus, "and if so where is the blade? How did the priest get into the room unseen?"

"There was no blade," said my master. "Show them your hands, Aybella." The priest lifted his hands, palm open. Livid burns pocked the skin of his palms.

"Magic," said the Landsmen, beginning to stand.

"Oh sit down, Landsman. It is not magic," said my master. "It is ice."

"Ice?" Deenus, stood. "That is preposterous."

"No it isn't." My master knelt before the Aybella. "He found you? In the corridor on the way back from your chapel?"Ayeblla nodded. "Do you want to tell them why, or shall I?" The priest took off his porcelain mask and laid it down on a table by his chair. The face beneath was young which surprised me as I had presumed all priests were old. Soft, blonde curls framed a face with the angles and stubble of a man but the soft skin of a woman.

"I thought," he said, the words stumbling from his mouth, "if I gave myself to him, did what he wanted then he would leave the others alone. The castle slaves, they could not say no to him. But I could choose to take on that burden to protect my flock." My master squatted before him, putting a hand on his shoulder.

"And in the corridor?"

"He grabbed me, but I was weak and let my god, Varrun, down. I did not want to do what he said. I did not want to and..." his voice tailed off into silence and he bowed his head. My master finished for him

"So you grasped whatever weapon you could, one of the icicles hanging down from the window frame."

"But, woman," said Lord Deenus, "he did not bleed. A stabbed man bleeds."

"No," she sounded sad, "he did not. I realised this in the kitchens, when the girl went to get snow to staunch a wound and I found out Aybella had been down there for hot water. The water was to ease the burn from gripping the ice so tightly when he thrust it into Ajan. And the cold of the icecle froze the wound shut. Ajan was so drunk he probably didn't even notice he had been stabbed. But when he went to bed his body heat melted the ice and his own weight ripped the wound open further and he bled to death, but he bled within not without. There has been no murder, blessed men, justice has already been served here."

"No," said Muest, standing. "The priest has killed one of the blessed, and he must pay for the death of Ajan." He drew his blade. "That is justice."

"Justice has been served," said my master more forcefully. "You serve the dead gods, a man tried to assault one of their priests and died for it." The Landsman wavered.

"The slaves probably think him a hero now," said Deenus. "It may give them ideas. No, Muest is right. We must make an example of this priest."

"Then you will not let justice rest?" said my master.

"This was very entertaining," said Ottan from behind my master, "But the Tired Lands need trade, you understand. People will ask questions of us all about this. If the priest is set free and, regretfully, if you also are set free. This could disrupt our trade. We are of the blessed, and you must understand that your lives are worth little compared to ours." He spoke like I imagined a father would speak to a child. Calmly, as if what he said was simple, obvious and fair. Everyone stood.

My master nodded.

"So this is how it must be?"

"Yes," said Ottan. His hand went to his scabbard. "My bl…"

A flash of movement. My master's hand coming up and forward, scabbarding Ottan's blade in the neck of Muest. Her movement so quick Ottan never finished the word 'blade'. She pushed the Landsman back into his chair with her left hand and pulled his longsword with her right. In one fluid motion she spun around, the tip of the longsword whistling through the air, cutting through the necks of Deemus and Ottan. Both men fell back into their chairs, choking and spluttering as their precious blessed blood escaped their bodies.

For a moment there was only silence. Aybella stood. His already pale face white with shock.

"What have you done?"

"The right thing," said my master. She pulled Aybella close. "Now, priest, we will bring Ajan's body here and dress these deaths up to look like a falling out among friends. I am well practised in such things. Justice has been served here, and I am an assassin, so we must discuss my price."

By Any Other Name

Justina Robson

This moment comes, like many beginnings, at the end of something. In this case the end is brought by an arrow. It would be a noble and fitting time to speak of the bowman's fine shot, the fragility of life, the balance of good and evil and the epiphanies that may come as a man sees his death arriving and has a moment to consider it before he is extinguished, all his virtues and his sins lit up before him. But this is not that arrow. This is an arrow of hundreds, launched without anything other than a rudimentary aim to comply with the notion of assault on a fortress, so that it seems the archer is doing a good job in the circumstances, at least nothing he can be shot for, whilst in no way attempting to actually take a life. It's a fusillade over a high wall, with battlements and towers, for goodness' sake. In the circumstances only a Dire Elf would even consider taking actual aim and our archer is but a human mercenary of middle years already fed up with poor conditions and dubious pay. So the arrow is no more than a half-hearted punt.

Nonetheless it falls from its high parabola with preternatural accuracy accompanied by the usual amount of force and this is more than enough for it to strike the half inch between chestplate and helm, take out a ring of mail with its curved broadhead and sink a foot through soft tissue into the heart of Morfavon, Dawn of Ligand, Dragoncaller, and the figure upon whom so many fragile hopes are pinned.

Morfavon has ridden with the Ragged Band for twenty years and earned the right to be feared for his skill with bow and blade, his tactical vision and his inspirational charisma. He has the dragoncall also, lest those not be enough, and nobody is willing to chance that, although they know it is a last resort and requires a battle the dragon itself considers fruitful. This scrubby mountain pass is hardly the stuff of legends. Until recently it was cropped by goats and left to itself. On either side at the mountain peak stands this fortress, hewn out of the rock, an overhang helped along into being an arched bridge that spans the gap at its narrowest point where Morfavon has made his stand. Since it was sacked centuries ago it has been staffed by corbies and other birds. But then word came that the Mages at Aefeli Howehad come upon a thing worth its weight in mothers' tears, so a few months later here everyone was; those who wanted to seize the Mages' prize struggling up the pass and those who wanted it to stay where it was busy on the ramparts and huddled behind the resinous reek of hastily felled pines made into a gate and some other lumpy deterrents that were too wet to catch fire easily.

The Ragged Band had been called in late to this party. To hear Morfavon talk, it was both too late and not worth the effort – even he didn't know what the big deal was and nobody liked mages. They were too prone to insanity to be much use. No mage had spelled the arrow that ended his opinions, however. It was just one of those things. It would have been better if a mage *had* spelled it, because then there would be a story to tell, a continuation of his glory and a plot of nefarious deeds, but without that it was a defiantly ridiculous end to a marvellous career. It was terrible luck. The sheer waste took the curses right out of the mouth of Ang Sifr, the ranger who stood beside him as he was struck.

Really, she thought, glancing up at the path the arrow had taken, it was an awful, short shot that was only a twitch away from falling to the rubble a hundred feet below. A twitch in the opposite direction and it would have been arcing over their heads and into the mostly empty yard behind them where all the other very good and entirely wasted shots were clattering to the stone with pings and splinters. It was a terrible shot and yet it had been absolutely perfect in its indirection and that perfection was a strange marvel even as she watched Morfavon - hale, hearty, revered, admired and lately her bed companion - slide slowly down the wall to his knees, bow dropping out of his hand. She gaped at the fletchings of the fateful arrow where they stuck out of his shoulder;some filthy, ragged pigeon wing, hastily secured with minimal effort in bad campfire light. The serving was lousy. It was a poor arrow, a kid could do better. A blind kid with half a hand. But weren't they always the ones to slay the gods and kings anyway?

Ang Sifr couldn't believe what had happened, even as Morfavon tilted slowly to the side and then fell over with a gentle sound and a soft clank, like a sack of armoured grain toppling. Behind them the standard holding the red and black banner of the Band with his personal sigil of a golden bear's head rampant upon it, snapped and fluttered, declaring his presence and command to everyone within and without.

A thought went through Ang Sifr's head that she liked not one bit. They were poorly staffed inside, aside from the Band, and beyond them the rabble of armies that had made it to a siege were now briefly united in their pitch to open the pass up, but held together by the thinnest promises. All were hungry, all were tired and nobody liked mages. If they found out that Morfavon, the hero of every tale, was dead, then the sanctuary of this fortress could be counted in minutes. The Band itself, once proud, had lately been held together only by his jovial insistence. He was a paragon among men, unselfish, raffish, bold, generous, seeing the best in the most scurvy of them, and…

She looked up as footsteps rattled the wooden stairs nearby. These had been hastily erected to supply a way up to the highest turret at the midpoint of the arched bridge which spanned the pass and upon which she was standing.

Gull's white-ashed face stared out at her from beneath the icy silver of his hair. He was young and awkward, of no particular note other than that he was tall. His hands clutched at the stonework to save himself a fall forwards and she saw all the urgency, horror and rejection of the moment that she was feeling in his watery gaze. A brief blur of the ur-world shifted around him, making him seem to float until it died away and left him as the skinny husk of a human, not really quite there any more.

They shared a long look that said they were both aware of the situation and that something must be done right now before it became common knowledge. They considered the prospects of fleeing up the mountain pass with multiple hordes at their tail knowing that the Band and the prize were both within easy reach along a corridor with no exits. A Band without a leader. Half would likely turncoat on the rest, though which half was hard to say. Ang Sifr had no love of them in particular but they were her home/ Her original family were bones on this mountain, like so many others. Gull, being a mage himself, had nothing to protect him without Morfavon. He'd been spared death by becoming the Band's magic mascot, a kind of pet belonging to the leader, tolerated as long as he spelled no spells and hexed no hexes and kept the ur-world far far away. Morfavon's death and Gull's presence taken together would have them thinking all the blood belonged on his hands with her as either a helper or no hindrance and there'd be some ugly, painful reckoning for that. Besides all that, they didn't want to die.

Ang threw down her bow and reached out to take Morfavon's gold-banded iron armour. "Come on!" she hissed as the whistle of arrows and the roar of a barrel of burning oil being tipped nearby nearly drowned her out. "I'm nearly the same size."

It was hard to believe she was doing this, had even had the idea in the first place; harder to believe that Gull was helping her strip the body. He worked at her side, their breath huffing the same effort, coughing the same smoke and stench as hollering and screaming went up far below and the relief of the great success of the oil in repelling the onslaught was steadily replaced by the knowledge that they had also achieved what an entire day of assaults could not and set the gate on fire.

A stink of caustic, acrid and terrible, came off Gull. She saw the ur-world's murmur again as he muttered to himself, but without it they'd never have moved that fast or been as dextrous as they were. Ang Sifr felt Gull burning up beside her as if he were on fire, every spell causing him to flake so that ash, white as birchbark, fell on them both. She would have maybe cared about that if it weren't all their lives at stake. In a blur of desperate action they got her rigged in Morfavon's suit, her meagre ranger's armour transferred to his body by magic alone, where it stretched to bursting. Morfavon, their captain, was a blunt, useless sausage now, a difficult problem that had only one solution in the moment that either of them could think of. They tied on her hood around his face, lifted him up, with a massive struggle, to the limit of the wall and tipped him over. With a word Gull set the body on fire and guided its fall so that it struck the barricade and became one with that inferno, beyond all reach.

Ang Sifr stared through the faceplate of Morfavon's helm at Gull's crouched, shivering form. He looked on the verge of fainting but she hissed at him, "Make me his likeness or we are finished here."

Gull started his muttering and twitching and she wondered what he'd been before he'd dealt with the ghosts and become magical, before he'd begun trading bits of his life for power. What did it matter now? She thrust the impulse to pity him aside as she saw the ur-world creep out of his flesh, peeling it back in another fine onionskin layer that wasn't mere body but being itself. Being spent on crafting magic, burning in this world to become power in the other.

"Illusion's pixifa magic," he whispered, shaking in the waves that she knew preceded a seizure that would have him jerking like a puppet on invisible strings, foam-mouthed. "Hard to manage as a human. It wants... to... twist all the time..."

As if she cared for that. "Faster!"

His teeth started chattering. They were stronger than she'd thought, even if half of them were brown. They didn't crack. He must be younger even than she was. The notion made him even more repellent and her pity and anger all the stronger. For years he'd been there in the background of her existence, tagging around Morfavon's edges like a sad flag, as reviled by the Band as he was prized by them. A mage is invaluable – look at what they can do. No wonder everyone hates them.

Gull gave a final squirm, body bending suddenly as though it was twisted by giant invisible hands. She could hear his joints cracking and popping in protest, his squeaky panic breath as he was wrung out this way and then that. The motion speeded, faster, faster until it was a blur as he phased in and out of existence to let the flow of the forces pass between worlds using his body as a conduit, and then she felt her bones take on the same terror as the spell jumped the gap between them and enveloped her from head to toe, armour, body and all. There was a moment of blinding pain.

"It's done," he said and then Gull was a mockery of the seabird he was named for, an angular, white heap on the stone, barely alive. Pale smoke and flakes skirled around in the breeze. She fancied she could smell roasting meat. Morfavon or Gull, or both.

Ang Sifr felt the same as she had before – exhausted and angry, always hungry – but the armour, that was heavy and awkward: how did he even see out of this benighted helm? When she bent to pick up his bow, casting a longing look at her light one, she found it enormous, the grip of old yellow bone still warm from his touch. Seeing her hand close on it she frowned – the hand looked far bigger than it felt. "My voice," she said, to Gull, who couldn't hear hear in his fugue, but it didn't matter because it came out in the mellow baritone burr that Morfavon always used, a little grittier perhaps, but nothing that a faceful of oilsmoke and cremation couldn't explain.

Ang Sifr stood tall and carefully risked a look through the slit in the parapet. The fire was hampering both sides equally now. For the time being the enemy had retreated to their forward safe point beyond the range of bowshot from the ramparts and were considering their burns and prospects. They'd enjoy a good rest now, knowing it was only a couple of hours to wait and the fire would do the job for them. Spirits would renew, hopes alight. They had the advantage: it was only a matter of time. She recalled she didn't even know who was down there – some collection of Dukes and apparatchiks, fortune hunters and Lords who'd love to see the outlaw Band ruined on their way to glory up the mountainside as they ransacked the Mages' Howe. Given what she'd just witnessed, she wasn't sure she'd be heading for more magery if she had any choice about it. Why would Morfavon even send the Band here? The mages could defend their damned selves. Even in bed he hadn't been forthcoming about his reasons. But they hadn't pressed. They'd all trusted him. Morfavon came through. He always came through. They'd nobody else.

Thinking this wasn't like her. Thinking wasn't something she dallied with much and now she was thinking more than she'd bothered with in a lifetime. Frowning, she drew an arrow and nocked it – well made these ones, by her own hand – and sighted through the smoke. One thing she felt certain of. A sign of defiant supremacy was needed. Fortunately a standard of the Duke of Gessenry was available. It was proudly borne upon the broken spars of their one ballista which had stuck at an angle on the road and part-blocked the retreat. They'd recover it presently if they needed something to shove the wreckage of the barricade out of the way but for now it stood alone, decked out with its peacock rampant upon a field of black and jade.

She drew the bow. It was the heaviest she'd ever felt. Something in her drawing shoulder popped like a tiny string twanging but she felt the shot inside her in a way she'd only rarely felt before, as if her will alone was its compass, the energy held without effort at full draw for as long as it took to sight. She wasn't even aware of loosing – the shot left when it was ready. The arrow sailed with arrogant, golden hauteur, pierced the smoke and embers and buried itself, quivering, firmly between the peacock's stylized legs.

She'd been aiming for its eye, but that was fine. That was better. That was, in fact, more Morfavon than anything else. A rowdy cheer went up from the lower ramparts where other archers and the rest of the ranged Band were scattered. She heard laughter. Now it was time to seize that moment and stride down into the remains of the keep, to take charge, make order, issue the master plan. She pushed herself off the wall and found her balance in the unfamiliar bulky suit, looked hopefully at Gull, but he was a quivering shape, drooling. She was on her own.

Ang Sifr strode down, carefully, through the narrow ways of the high ledges and ramps. Everywhere faces that turned to see her pass were heartened, relieved, amused and full of greetings. Her back was slapped. She staggered briefly and remembered to turn and deliver a mock punch, a hearty 'haha!' of jolliness that was the last thing she was feeling inside but which came out well enough, surprising her that it was lifting her spirits too. She met each man and woman's eye, smiled, raised her fist, Morfavon's fist, in insistent enthusiasm. She reached the keep and then the yard where people were leaking out from the walls, trickling, massing one on one until they formed a definite gathering, ragged and fewer than before, but enough to do something with; enough to kill her if they found out the truth. As they would in a moment because it was time to address them and she was a creature of silent hills, lone rocks, stalking waitfulness. She was tall and broad; in that she was like Morfavon, but in nothing else.

From the corner of her sight through the visor she glimpsed the black robes and blue scarves of magi, not one alone but three or four, coming in a phalanx through the crowd. They had the look of people who were intent on speaking to her on matters of immediate importance. She searched the battlements for a sign of Gull, her hand flexing on the bow grip. This weapon was called Var'han, Bow of Ages. At her side was Tenvair, a sword made by a dead race from an age nobody remembered, its name a guess or a joke. Perhaps it was from a prior epoch, with its strange blue steel, or perhaps it was made a year ago in Kabudama, that invention apex, full of engineers and fabricators, but it didn't matter – everything Morfavon had was named, a legend in its own lifetime and those lifetimes were all far in excess of his, hers and anyone's. The items had collected on him as if magnetised; won in duels, given as gifts, taken as rewards for mighty deeds or simply found in unlikely circumstances worthy of long tales. They bestowed upon him the directional power of Fate and now they were hers.

Ang Sifr longed for her own, nameless ashwood bow which she had made herself. The familiarity of its grip, its honesty, its simplicity, its – emptiness – was the only thing to match what she felt now as the mages advanced and one took up vanguard position. She felt her bowels loosen, as they did before battle though she'd never dropped anything yet. That might change.

Dark red eyes, rimmed with black paint and bloodshot looked at her from above the rim of a veil with a combination of admiration and spite that was breathtaking in its directness. The mages hated them too, it turned out. More than that, they saw right through her disguise.

"Ah, Morfavon," said the woman. Her accent was cultured, refined. Every word disdained all that Ang Sifr had been or would be, in terms that were social, animal and human. Reluctantly they embraced Morfavon as a necessary horror. All this in a single pronunciation. Ang Sifr rather admired that so much could be packed into so little and her spine bristled as she felt herself insulted, then smoothed itself as she understood who had all the power here – she did. Then that same feeling dripped in a nasty sweat as she heard the next line.

"We await your orders for the second plan you had in mind, now that it seems our eager defences have jeopardised the first."

Ang Sifr didn't know what the first plan had been, only her part in it – defending the rampart and her position with Morfavon. The existence or need for another plan had never entered her mind. Morfavon had never mentioned one, nor ever did. He stood firmly and expounded without apparent need of forethought, as if divinely inspired. It was his most annoying trait.

She copied him as best she could though her guts had started to look for another way out of the situation that didn't necessarily involve the rest of her. "The second plan," she began boldly, "is…"

The mage was looking slant eyed at her but there was now something troubled about the expression, that said that there must be a plan or they were all finished, so think of a plan and make it a good one and don't, whatever you do, let anyone in on the fact that you're not the hero of the hour but instead some grubby huntress from a nameless mountain who…

"The second plan is to clear the barricade," Ang Sifr said loudly, turning to address not only the mages, but the wider crowd, projecting her/his voice even over the jolly roar of the fire and the wails of the not-quite-dead. She saw the heads and familiar garb of the Ragged among them and gave them the closed-fist raised salute of cheer.

That made the eyes over the veil go very white.

"It must be cleared away once the flames have died back. The remaining units of the Magi Guard and the mages themselves will retreat to the Mage Howe. The Ragged Band and those mercenaries who are able will make pretend we are in force here at the pass, using all means to advertise confidence whilst retiring from the field." It was exactly the kind of thing that Morfavon would have said or liked to say, Ang Sifr thought, and felt a terrible pang of loss and sadness suddenly that nearly tripped her up. She paused and heard silence around her. They were all staring, waiting. She had to finish.

"I myself will mount up and ride out." It was the most stupid idea she had ever had. "If they refuse to withdraw, I will call the dragon."

A cheer went up, of relief and exaltation, excitement and the prospect of a terrific victory, of life remaining today and lives possibly yet to get to tomorrow and other hopeful things which had been smothered by the smoke of the ill-judged oil.

Ang felt sick. From the corner of her eye she saw Trebbit, another longbowman, supporting the ghastly white figure of Gull, who was draped on his arm like a tatty cloak. They shambled into the gleeful throng at the edge, Trebbit's old, lined face full of questions and a serious kind of doubt that made her wonder what he knew about this that she didn't.

Morfavon had not called a dragon since the Battle of Baf'Nas Mor, some seventeen years previous, when he had won the day in a holocaust unsurpassed even in imagination. That outing had been on behalf of some monks who had fallen foul the King of Baf'Nas while attempting a pilgrimage to a holy site. Everyone had agreed, in the safety of afterwards, that it was a well-deserved finale to a very nasty King and an oppressive dynasty of unusual awfulness, but in hearing the variations of the tale Ang Sifr had always thought there must be more to it than there seemed, because there had been many other fights of that nature up and down the lands and dragons hadn't come to put a verdict on any of them, even when the Ragged were there, even when many of them had died. It was really just the once. Maybe you had to have monks.

A similar thought must have been occurring to the head mage whose gaze had acquired a certain glassy fixity. "The dragon, you say." She sounded impressed to a casual listener, but to Ang Sifr the meaning was quite clear – you are no dragon caller and we are all dead.

Now it was Ang's turn to fix the other with a meaningful look. "I'm sure that within a few hours the dragon will appear, as required, over the far ridge to the North." Meaning, you're a mage, why don't you go make a 'dragon' and stick it on the damned ridge?

They shared a long stare which decided that it was plausible that the enemy might go for some kind of dragon appearing in the distance as sufficient incentive to depart. King Sobori of Baf'Nas and his army had been incinerated to a fine potash and the wild roses in Baf'Nas Mor were now famous for their lush colour and incredible scent. Either way, it was all they'd got.

"In that case let us rest and prepare," the mage said, making a gesture to her fellows that had them moving back. "Come, let us discuss the timing of this matter in private while the others make ready." She beckoned imperiously and spun about, making haste to the stone arch.

Ang paused and looked back at Gull and Trebbit. She jerked her arm at them in Morfavon's style of inviting people where they weren't invited and getting away with it. As they set off in her direction she turned, hefted Var'han with that little hitch and grip that made Morfavon always seem as if he had caught a minor victory in his thoughts, and strode after the four black robes with every bit of unwarranted conviction afire in her gut– a strange sensation indeed. In fact, if she hadn't herself tipped his body onto the pyre she would have said that Morfavon was there and this was actually his plan and it was going to work, of course, because that's just how things went for the man. The fact that she was Morfavon didn't seem to enter into it all that much. Or that she was Ang Sifr. The momentum of the ideas that had come out of her mouth, largely as copies and imaginings, carried her along regardless. She had never experienced anything like this. It was nearly enjoyable, even in the circumstances. And once again she was sorry he was dead and it hurt.

The people who had carved the fortress out of the pass had hewn small, low rooms out of necessity. Ang Sifr had to duck to get inside them and stay ducked all the way through to the 'war room' where the mage delegation had set themselves up a tiny altar with the mortar, pestle and other bits and pieces that were important to them upon an old wood-wormed table. There was a door which closed and light from a reflecting mirror that pulsed faintly thanks to the smoke outside, leaving the mages and Ang Sifr alone together. Ang Sifr stood in the door until she felt and smelled the distinctive Ragged presence of tired, unwashed human pressing at her back. Then she moved aside and welcomed Trebbit and Gull as though they were honoured advisors. Trebbit had the foresight to close the door. It was cramped now and no semblance of proper distances could be maintained. They were eye to eye across the table and shoulder to shoulder, sharing their coughs in the dry air.

Ang Sifr took off the massive helm and set it down. She glanced at Trebbit, who was staring at her in a dread-filled anxiety but certainly not the friendly acceptance he usually had for her. So he saw Morfavon, she guessed. Gull had a faint smile at the corner of his mouth, satisfaction of a kind. The gathered, masked magi held silent in the background as their leader took down her veil and put back her hood. She was rather stately and disappointingly beautiful, her strong jaw and elegant hawk-nose combining to give a face of unyielding strength that Ang Sifr briefly felt stung by, as if it ought to have been hers. A foolish thought, given her position. She shifted and then remembered Morfavon and took an heroic stance, shoulders back, until her head knocked on the stone roof.

"Let us dispense with formalities," the mage said. "I..."

A strange slowing made her words drawl out and out, fading into a background burr of sound. At the same time her movements became slow and slower until her hand was almost still. Time had stopped, Ang thought, feeling herself frozen too, but not her thoughts.

A voice came to her. Not a voice. It was more like a knowledge that was in the walls and the objects, in the mag-devices and in the very substance of the world, their bodies, the air itself – and it was suddenly a thing that Ang could hear, though it was silent and invisible. It was distinct however, and it said,

"Well, Ang Sifr, what will it be? Shall you make a play for kings upon the stage or shall you rather take the shield, the sword and bow, don the helm and become Morfavon, hero of the ages?"

What she perceived as a voice was like a massive wave existing in all matter, held back by every shape and variety of thing in the world, including Ang herself, as if objects were tiny containers all holding a bit of a single secret that could burst forth in an instant if only, if only the illusion of what they seemed to be should fall away. What spoke to her came through this hidden medium, swimming in it as the fish in the sea, flying through it as the bee in the summer air. The dragon was calling her.

She understood then that Morfavon had not always been the same person. He was a role and in the years she'd known him suddenly some of his changes and moods became more easily explained, and some of his more ordinary features, and certainly his miraculous escapes.

"Ah," said the dragon with satisfaction. "Good, there is some thought in you."

There was some thought in her and it went along the lines that she had liked the huge personality, the cheer, the leadership, the camaraderie, the awkward family of the Ragged and the security of being only one of many. Morfavon had been fair to deal with, average under the blankets but a most excellent warmth and comfort during long nights on hard ground. She didn't want or expect more. The causes the Ragged accepted were largely aligned with her own feelings, enough never to protest. They survived, outcast but idealised, heroes and beggars. It was sufficient. She hadn't been there all twenty years of his reign. She was only a few years in. And now he was gone and she was here but the real trouble in the issue was that,

"Morfavon is a man."

And besides, she didn't want the role. She was Ang Sifr and that meant on the edge. But then she felt the lie shift inside her. She had been Morfavon and she had liked it.

"Morfavon is a warrior whose life is already forfeit. To me. You have disposed of the last one so now you must give me another. If not you, then someone else."

"I didn't..." Ang began, but thought better of it. "Why would a dragon answer a man's call?" she asked. "Was it the monks?"

There was a pause. "I like roses," the dragon said.

She knew there was no other answer coming. She knew that this deal was a forever, one-time thing and if she didn't take it then, well, she'd have to give Trebbit and that was unthinkable because Trebbit was a decent archer but not sacrificial material, besides, she wasn't ready to give up. "Will you come if I call?"

"That depends," the dragon said. "Will you come if I call?"

"Why would you..." Ang saw before her two clear paths. There was one in which she pretended to be Morfavon and the mages constructed an illusory dragon and later, somehow, somewhere she would contrive to have 'Morfavon' killed and then go back to being Ang Sifr in another place, with other people, somehow. In the other direction she wore the panoply of Morfavon and her own face was not seen again, even by herself. She would lead the Ragged until –

"Did you call him here?" she asked, already knowing the answer.

Yes. Yes was in the stone and the wood, in the worms in the wood and the smoke in the air. *Yes.*

"What for?"

"Because of the mages and what they had."

"What is it?"

"Something that is not for human pilfering. Something lost. A mistake. A chance. A tragedy. A mystery. Roses."

231

The magi at least had the sense not to tamper with it for now. She felt that they were only circling it, cautiously, possessive and jealous, not ready to risk using it. The same could not be said of the besieging Lords, who would kill their own mothers for a chance to gain power over their fellows. Ang could run away into the nothing that she had planned for herself, a nothing of surprising barrenness, she now saw, or she could run into something useful. Behind the sound of the mage's constantly never-pronounced vowel she felt a presence that went even beyond the dragon, in which the dragon itself and all its machinations were only a trivial turn of the wheel and she, Ang Sifr was less than a cog, less than a turn, not even a moment. Ang Sifr was nothing and always had been nothing. An arrow had fallen and divided the world in two, revealing this great emptiness at her heart. It didn't matter what she did. She only knew that she wanted it to matter to something, some way, if only to herself and right now, if only so that she knew what it was to take a momentous decision and to find out what was so great about roses.

"… I insist you leave your mage with us," said the mage, as if she had never been interrupted by anything. "Such uses of pixifa illusion are as dangerous this close to the Howe Nexus as the armies on the road."

Now Ang Sifr heard other things inside the words. They wanted Gull for some reason of their own and she could feel him cower from them – the entire reason he was with the Band at all lay in his disavowal of the mages' organisation. She'd always seen him as rather weak and despicable, not least because of the magic, but now she understood he was like her – outcast from things and looking for a place to belong that didn't come with a price tag too high to pay. And wasn't this what she had paid? Just now, for the sake of the Band.

She began to detest the arrow for opening up this world of magic. She looked at the mage's face, sly she'd thought, but now filled with impatience and fear.

"Gull stays with me," Ang said, a bold grin and a charming dash to her declaration, larger than life. "Who is a leader without his loyal mage? If not for Gull the ramparts would have fallen. Spare him for me, this one, and I promise no more pixifa doings until we are paid and clear of your properties."

As if in agreement they heard the rumble of the flaming gate as it collapsed upon itself.

"The working of a major illusion requires all talents to be on hand," the mage replied smoothly as if this was an essential piece of understanding someone as hopeless as Morfavon could not be expected to understand.

"He will be on my hand and that is that."

The mage leant over the table, crushing a preserved flowerhead under her hand carelessly. "Whoever you are," she hissed, "you presume too much. Let's not forget what dragon we are calling upon."

A great illusion, Ang Sifr saw. Things are one thing on the surface and underneath they are another. In the mage's insistence she felt the need of great power and the twisting sensation that she had come to know was pixifa glamour. Ang Sifr would run away from these things as befits a mountain girl of honest means. Sooner dead than fey! But she felt there was a key here, slowly turning in a lock. Something stranger was coming to her by and by. Here this mage was ready to threaten, but this meant only that her hand was empty. Ang Sifr had the say. What were they going to do without her?

"I presume you are going to be about your business," Ang said. "And I to mine. I must prepare my steed, for shortly we go to challenge their champions and give you clever crafters the time to convince us all you're worth the saving."

The mage's face was pure hatred. "If we live you will regret this."

"I have no regrets," Morfavon waved his gauntlet in dismissal and it was true. For the first time in her life Ang Sifr felt interested in life itself and to hell with all that had come before. But the hours were burning. She turned and gave Trebbit a good-natured shove, "Out, out, fetch my horse, water, beer and something for Gull here. We have a retreat to organise!" She followed them, ushering and giving salutes to all those in the yard outside as the barrier burned down and they began to see over the top of it to the dusty pines and rocks of the pass below. The peacock banner and the high length of the engine it adorned were visible through the gouting smoke. In the other direction there was no barrier, only the rising path and the hurrying remnants of the mage's parties, eager to put a few miles between them and more trouble.

Ang Sifr turned once they were alone with the animals and found Trebbit on his toes, staring at her face, his brows together.

"How can it be?" he said, obviously filled in by Gull at some point. "Say it's not so, Morf. Say it's you and the girl fell in the fire."

Ang Sifr turned to him. "It is so."

The older man turned pale and started to shake. "I… it can't be. I see him – you – I see…"

Gull hissed and snapped his fingers in front of Trebbit's face. Then his fear turned to outright disappointment.

Ang's gut hurt her. She'd thought Trebbit approved of her, one archer to another, allies in the bow. Now she saw that was all it was about. Archery. As leader he had no use for her and thought she was bound to be a complete disaster. She ground her teeth together, "I don't like it any more than you do." A lie, but anyway. "But…"

"Did you do this?" Trebbit had already dismissed her and was turning to Gull, rage in his face. "Did you cook this up together? Get rid of him and then take over. Is that your game, eh? You slimy toadwhite. I never trusted you. Said he was a fool to keep you…"

Ang watched in slight surprise as her gauntleted hand slapped Trebbit firmly across the face, hard enough to rock his head and create a white welt along the line of his stubbled jaw. "He was killed by arrowshot," she said. "Now hold your tongue or none of us are making it out of here alive."

His hand went to the hilt of his dagger but it stayed there, drawing nothing. His face remained defiant but she had no interest in things that weren't going anywhere.

"Ready my courser," she said, levelly, and waited until slowly he turned like a man in a nightmare and went about the business behind them, the beasts stamping and snorting with the agitation in the air.

"Gull," she said, addressing him for the first time as an equal. She saw him straighten, the shift of his attention from sullen to direct. "Do you need to stay near me to keep the magic?"

He shook his head, wiped his nose on the rags of his sleeve. "Pixifa magic sticky. You need me to undo it, not keep it."

"Then you and Trebbit are to join the Band and ride up the pass. Make sure nobody stays behind. If the mages want to keep witnesses that's their business. Understand?"

He nodded. "If things don't…"

"That's my business," Ang Sifr said. "There must be some other way out of the Howe. You're to look for it."

"We're abandoning the original plan then?"

"We're sticking with it," she said. "We protect the mages, we do our job, we get the money and we get gone. But if I don't come up that road after the sun marks two pips on the post then you're all on your own."

"Dead, you mean."

She shrugged. "Either way."

They finished the armouring of the 'horse' – not a horse at all but a larger, similar shaped beast that had cloven feet and a shorter, heavier head topped with front-facing horns. This kind of courser was well known as the most dangerous creature of the lower fens as it had a terrible temper. This one in particular was used to the life of the road now and, smarter than a horse, used to Morfavon. It wasn't fooled by the pixifa charms and snorted and pawed the stone with a scraping sound like axes grinding, making all its heavy armour clank and chime. Long, pointed ears turned back, but it was fed up of the stables and allowed itself to be moved out amid a stamping, cavorting performance that would have impressed bystanders had anyone been left to see.

As it was they emerged to an empty court, only two of the Mage's guard standing at loose attention clearly waiting for this final act to get underway. The non-uniforms who had drawn the shortest straws stood ready with rakes to clear the ground. The gate, the barricade and Morfavon were now a heap of embers, periodically sending showers of sparks skyward against darkening clouds. Beyond them the sound and clatter of the enemy regrouping was clearly audible.

Trebbit grudgingly helped Ang to the saddle. His face was a grim mask of dislike but she trusted him as much as hated him. They were Band and that came first.

"Take Gull now," she ordered. "Watch the pass."

He muttered something she didn't catch through the heavy helm but she was already reining away, raising the massive weight of Morfavon's gold and red standard to signal for the barricade to be cleared. When the pirouetting annoyance of the mount turned her to face the other way she saw them hurrying up the mountain, and then was turned to face the fire. It was still too hot to deal with, and too high. For every effort to move the shoulder-high piles, men turned back singed and cursing.

Ang Sifr, afraid and losing her nerve, dug her spurs into the sides of the courser and gripped the standard as tightly as she could, balancing the end of it against her boot. She could not allow the momentum of events to slide against her because that was all she had. It was probably better the barrier stayed, anyway. She let out a bellow of charging, just as Morfavon used to do, a roar of glory and joy – and the courser sprang forwards in terrifying sudden bounds of energy, much faster and more powerful than she had expected. With three leaps it crossed the gap to the burning pyre and crouched low. She felt her weight drop like a stone, her teeth slamming against each other with jarring force. Her head snapped back as the massive creature sprang effortlessly as a cat high into the air.

From the other side of the fire the gathering, groups of soldiers and those who had been working hard to adapt the siege engine into a shovel were startled by the sudden shout and the appearance of a massive, horned, golden creature leaping through a wall of smoke directly at them. It seemed to hang there for a moment in mid-air, a gust of wind suddenly revealing the Ragged Banner above it as if timed by an expert hand. Without hesitation, those in the front rows backed up and turned aside. The more stalwart ones stood fast and saw Morfavon land and gallop a few more strides forwards before reining back fiercely into a pirouetting rear of defiance a few yards from their faces. Only the strength of his will kept the creature from starting a lone rampage. All saw the polished gold on the tips of its horns and the sharp studs in the rims of its hooves. A few glanced at the repurposed siege engine and at the shaft of the arrow which still jutted boldly between the peacock's stitched legs and some smiles and raised fists greeted the silence that followed because it's hard to see something that fantastic and not admire it a bit even if it is aimed at you with some hostility. It wasn't personal, after all, but it was enviably magnificent.

"Shoot, you fools!" screeched one of the lesser Lords but only a few obeyed. Their arrows clattered off the plate of courser and man without causing any trouble and the horseman drew savagely on the rein and planted himself and his beast square on before them, lowering the banner into a lance pointing at their midst.

"Come out, come out, champions!" Morfavon bellowed. He had a superb voice which carried all the way to the back of the retinue. The more dramatically inclined of the army were already assembling ways to tell the tale of this day and mentally practicing how they would replicate the call. "I challenge you to single combat and an honour decision upon this ground!"

There was a pause and then Lord Forthinbras shouldered his way to a boulder and stood upon it to reply. "You are beaten, Morfavon, or you would not attempt this foolery. Stand aside. The towers belong to us."

"Coward!" snarled the golden knight, turning broadsides as the courser champed and foamed with eagerness to destroy them. "What of you others, you great masters of the sword hiding behind your yeomen and your paid hands? I give you an easy choice. Face me now and spare your men, or face a greater fire. We will not surrender the towers."

Inside the confines of the helm Ang Sifr felt these were the right words. They almost seemed to say themselves. But as she listened to them she felt a certain dismay. She was already wasting her strength in holding the courser off its determined path to ruin everything in sight with horn and hoof. She was tired from battle and felt her mortality keenly, though she had no hesitation in spending her life on this exercise if it bought some time for the others to regroup. It wasn't as if she'd been using it for anything. The threat of dragonfire should at least give them something to think about. All the same, she wanted to go on, not stop here in ignominy.

"So," said the voice hidden in all things, though it was clear to her at that moment. "What will it be? An illusion for a moment or a lifetime?"

"I will meet your challenge!" called Forthinbras, though he didn't make a move to arm himself. Instead he waved and someone else was pushed forwards. Black Absalon, by the look of his armour and his helm, Ang Sifr thought. One possessing nearly the reputation of Morfavon. A hired butcher without moral limit, he held as much threat as the dragon, almost. In her former life she feared him and his ilk greatly but now that she stood as his equal she held only contempt for him.

"He will make a lovely bloom," said the dragon. Its voice held utter indifference.

Ang Sifr had only contempt for that as well. She felt the dragon's surprise at her rejection. "I have had enough of you all," she said to it as Black Absalon swaggered forwards in his namesake ebon armour, his two handed monster-killing sword in his hands ready, his balance sure, his appetite for the fight always eager. He intended, anticipated likely, to fight on foot, like men of honour. It was a service he didn't deserve. Her family had fallen to men like him and she still didn't know the reason that had brought them that long-ago day. Morfavon would have dismounted, done the decent thing.

Ang loosed the reins a little and the courser sprang forwards, head lowering. Men scattered like rats in all directions and the massive horn on the left struck Black Absalon firmly at the thighs, lifting and tossing him, though he was impaled and did not toss easily, more hung and then fell by his own weight, screaming, the point of his sword falling from the courser's leg.

Their blood stained the rocky ground. The pain only increased the animal's rage and for a while she could do no more than steer it in a forced circle – those that did not flee fast enough were trampled. Through it all she maintained the banner high and when she was contained again there was agitation in the crowd, screaming and yelling, complaints, but still discipline. Upon the stony path Absalon was already dead, being stripped for gear, valuables and mementoes for none had cared for him at all other than for what he could do.

"Another!" she called, imagining behind her the distance increasing, always increasing, between her and the Band.

"You cannot last, alone," the dragon said.

"That was a dishonourable bout," Forthinbras declared as the hubbub died back.

"A fitting end to a dishonourable bastard," Ang replied confidently, and many of the crowd were with her.

"Entertaining," the Lord replied, "but we have business ahead and you are bad for business, Morfavon. Always loitering around with your wretched players and fools, getting in the way. Don't pretend you're here for some great cause. We know you're here for the dragonbones, just as we are."

"I care not for bones," Ang said, truthfully, though she wondered at the wisdom of fighting for such a thing. "Other than the ones inside you. Let them out to play. My dogs need something to chew of an eve."

"Join us, Morfavon. We will give you a share. Why should these wicked mages have yet more power to wield over honest men? It's not enough that they spoil the milk, blight the crops, spite the weather and ask for gold for all their meddling?"

Ang thought of Gull's pale face, his fingers peeling away into ashes before her eyes. "Make your choice, Forthinbras," she declared, hefting the banner into position as a javelin, her aching arm working hard to balance it without a wobble. "Leave now in peace for other days, or face me and the fire to come."

There was a rumbling of interest and nervousness among the massed soldiery. They looked to the Lord whose face was thunderous with anger as he reached for his sword and horn.

"He will not come alone," the dragon said, and there was a question hidden in its voice that said – "Not yet? When? When will you call me to save you?" And Ang heard it, and in it she heard doubt, that maybe she wouldn't answer, and through that moment of uncertainty she felt a loss that was so great it was boundless and its boundlessness held all that could not be changed or undone, not saved, not held, not protected. The bones of the dead were there, hidden in the everywhere, the lost bones in that chink in the armour, the bones from which roses grow so beautifully.

Forthinbras made signs and raised his loyal men. They were a crew, some fifty or so among the rest, who hefted their weapons and strode forward. They were here to do business, not witness greatness or even to be amused. They meant the end for Morfavon and not only for him but the Band and all that they stood for in the world, which wasn't much when you came to it, just the freedom to rove at your will, at your chance, across dangerous lands ruled by greedy men and sometimes you would manage a good thing and sometimes not. It was this small, old, vain, hopeful, wretched band of things that was at stake, and whatever the bones that the dragon wanted or the mages thought were something. Ang Sifr knew this absolutely, and sat on top of the stilled creature, stamping out its own blood on the earth, and said to the dragon, "Come or not, it is your choice. I will make a lovely bloom."

Then she said it aloud, in her own voice, though it came out big and booming, full of bravado and warmth like a reassuring fire on a stormy night, a hearth of friendliness, as if she were welcoming them and the gathering men paused, uncertain, because this was not the kind of thing that Morfavon had ever said and although they knew the words they weren't sure what they referred to. Nonetheless they felt the weight of them shift the engines of the moment in a way they hadn't expected. The day remained, starting to rain, but inside their minds things moved out of balance and the world changed until many of them paused and stopped, convinced that this was not a thing to do here and now, that something spoke beyond flesh and words to halt them.

"Strike him down!" Forthinbras bellowed, voice cracking unfortunately on the final syllable into a high squeak that broke the balance of the moment and rendered it ordinary again. The determined few eyed the weakening courser and closed their ranks, advancing.

Ang clapped her legs to the beast, lowered her banner. For all its wound the charger didn't fail her, its rage reignited at the sight of so many foes in reach. They hurtled forward and men did flinch from the attack, but were too tightly packed to escape. The lance speared the first even as she cast it aside before the shaft's buckling snap could unseat her. She reached for that strange iron sword and it found her hand as the courser wheeled, taking out three more with hoof and horn though they crowded in and over the fallen to grab the traces and the caparison, dragging on it to weigh it down. She slashed until there was no space, then she stabbed and forced the animal to whirl, feeling it collapse beneath her. Then she realised that she had only survived this long because they had spent this minute to kill the beast before they turned to her and she ended standing atop its panting frame as it was butchered and gave up a final breath like a sigh. Ang Sifr thought of the mountain glade where her family were white bone upon the heights and wondered if she would find them again, inside the everything, when they were done with her. The loyalists ringed her, waiting for the word. She stood fast, wobbling a little on the corpse, blade ready, blood dripping from its curve.

"Come!" she said, "I call you! Come to me!"

And they looked at the sky. Because once a dragon had come and made of a field of men only a field. All but Ang. She knew nothing was coming. The dragon was bones in the mages' court, peeling away, leaf by leaf, as it spent its last magic in creating other ways of being inside the hearts of men. If Gull had reached them, he would know the truth, as Morfavon must have done. The dragon was aeons gone, but her Morfavon had kept his bond and come here anyway to repay his debt to a dead creature and bring them all with him because he could not have undone them from him by any act or magic in the world save dying. Morfavon had given them all each other and now she wanted him to have his last stand, not toppled by an accidental arrow, but alive to the last, better and more big-hearted than all of them or any man. She wanted him to have the glory of a brief, beautiful moment.

She was struck, and staggered, countered, slashed, parried, was hit again and again by a rain of blows upon her armour which through sheer force beat her to her knees in a cacophony of drums. She did all she could but it was not enough. She was exhausted and she was no Morfavon. For a moment she thought that she had misunderstood and a sense of terrible failure came to her as she waited for the end. She could not do this alone.

"You underestimate my love of roses," the dragon said.

"I will carry you," Ang said to it. "If you will let me leave him here."

There was a pause. Then, "You are a lovely bloom, Ang Sifr."

A shadow crossed the land which they all felt, as though it fell on their naked skin. In front of her through the crack in her visor she saw a man light up from within, strange yellow and red blossoming swiftly to black that singed and then cracked and unfurled to reveal his burning bones. Hideous screams went up then, of terror, pain and the utmost horror a person can feel and not from one but many throats. Heat surrounded her and there was the stink of boiling fat and flesh and a grimy black smoke that coiled and wound through the air to briefly form the massive body and head of a gigantic black dragon. It rose on the heat of the slain to regard her for a single moment and then the wind broke it apart and Ang Sifr was left standing, alone, in a near-silent black rain. After a while the rain came harder, clearer, and then it stopped.

The pass was filled with piles of black ash and the rain soaked through her leathers and into her underclothing, ran out of her bracers and greaves and down through the filthy fur of the courser to the ground where it made stinking mud about its body.

She took off the armour, piece by piece, and let it fall. Its golden beauty made pretty shapes against the black ground, the red blood, the rusty fur. She found stones to stand on, and patches of grass, where she could walk without leaving a trail. She climbed down into the valley below, leaving the road at the first opportunity for the safety and disguise of the woods. She headed to a distant mountain meadow, where wild thyme danced in the breeze, the softest fragrance loosened from the tiny blooms by their brushing against the bones of the beloved. In her hand was Var'fan, Bow of Ages, and at her back its arrows, though she had no memory of finding them. At her side the iron of a lost world, gleaning to her: Tenvair, forged by those closer to gods than men. She ran to the distant hillside not to die but to be reborn among her own, no more a hero but a wild thing on the cusp of human and dragon; a new creature for a new age.

In the Howe the mages pored for many days over a heap of dust where the dragon bones had been. Eventually they paid their gold and watched the Band ride away, a pale figure with them in their midst. As the group neared the pass they were joined by a rider from below bearing a black standard with a red rose and they raised their weapons, hailed, well met. For a few moments they could be heard distantly as they circled, whooping and hollering with a mad joy before they whirled about as one and vanished below the crest of the hill.

About the Authors

Neal Asher lives sometimes in England, sometimes in Crete and mostly at a keyboard. He's had twenty-three books published and has been accused of overproduction (despite spending too much time on social media and reading science articles) but doesn't intend to slow down just yet. He finally feels able to call himself an author without cringing and has read far more SF than some would style as healthy. http://theskinner.blogspot.com/   http://nealsher.co.uk

RJ Barker lives in West Yorkshire with his wife, son and a bitey cat. They curate a good collection of hat-wearing bad taxidermy, a lot of books and lot of noisy music. He is the multi-award losing author of the Wounded Kingdom trilogy (featuring Girton and Merela from this story at a later point in their lives) and his new trilogy, The Bone Ships, is due through Orbit at the end of the year. He's always a bit confused about the convention of referring to himself in the third person in biographies, and less than kind people may say he is confused in general. It would be hard to disagree.

K.T. Davies lives in Stafford with an understanding partner, two sprogs, four dogs, and a cat. She has a degree in English and has been an actor, theatrical prop maker, scaffolder, and for the past few years a writer. (She's working on Galactic Empress, but you know, baby steps). She enjoys listening to metal as well as practicing medieval martial arts and playing tabletop and computer games. She is on Twitter as @KTScribbles

Shona Kinsella is the author of epic science fantasy The Vessel of KalaDene series, web serial fantasy *Miranya's Oath,* and dark Scottish fantasy *Petra MacDonald and the Queen of the Fae.* Shona is joint editor of the British Fantasy Society's fiction publication, *BFS Horizons.* She lives in Scotland with her husband and three children and when she is not writing or wrangling children, she can usually be found with her nose in a book.

Keris McDonald is a UK-based writer of genre stories – a showing in Ellen Datlow's *Best Horror of the Year Vol.7* was a proud moment – who is currently dipping her toes in the writing of horror RPG scenarios for tabletop games companies. Most of her time is, however, spent under the name 'Janine Ashbless', writing dark fantasy erotica and hot romantic adventure. Her most recent novel is *The Prison of the Angels* (Sinful Press), third in her Book of the Watchers trilogy about fallen angels, religious conspiracy and a war against Heaven. www.janineashbless.com

Gail Z. Martin writes urban fantasy, epic fantasy and steampunk for Solaris Books, Orbit Books, Falstaff Books, SOL Publishing and Darkwind Press. Urban fantasy series include Deadly Curiosities and the Night Vigil (Sons of Darkness). Epic fantasy series include Darkhurst, the Chronicles Of The Necromancer, the Fallen Kings Cycle, the Ascendant Kingdoms Saga, and the Assassins of Landria. Co-written with Larry N. Martin include the Iron & Blood and Storm and Fury series. As Morgan Brice, she writes urban fantasy MM paranormal romance. Books include *Witchbane, Burn, Dark Rivers, Badlands, The Rising,* and *Lucky Town.*

Stan Nicholls is the author of more than thirty books and over fifty short stories, but is probably best known for his *Nightshade, Quicksilver* and *Orcs* series, the latter of which sold well over a million copies worldwide. His journalism has appeared in some seventy publications, from *The Times* to *SFX, Starlog* to *The Guardian.* For six years he was the sf/fantasy reviewer for *Time Out* magazine. He's acted as a first reader and editorial advisor for various publishers and literary agents, and taught creative writing and journalism to university and adult education students.

Ben North lives in London. He writes poetry and short stories, and is currently working on a novel. He is delighted to feature in this anthology, as he vividly remembers the visceral thrill of reading David

Gemmell's work for the first time in the brilliant *Waylander*. He can be found tweeting mostly nonsense at @inkib.

Den Patrick is the author of The Erebus Sequence, published in 2014, and was nominated for British Fantasy Award for Best Newcomer in 2015. *Witchsign* is the first of the three books in The Ashen Torment series, published by Harper Voyager. He lives in London with his wife and two cats. You can find Den on Twitter at @Den_Patrick

Steven Poore lives in South Yorkshire, with a crafty partner, a three-legged cat, and a critical mass of books. His award-nominated novels *The Heir to the North* and *The High King's Vengeance* are both published by Grimbold Books. Steven also runs the SFSF Socials, which happen irregularly in Sheffield. Find out more: @stevenjpoore.

Justina Robson has been publishing SF and F since 1999. Her short stories have appeared in many anthologies and magazines over the years. Her most recent novel, *Salvation's Fire*, is a fantasy set in a shared world co-created by Adrian Tchaikovsky and Rebellion Publishing under the series title After the War. In addition to her original works she wrote *Transformers: The Covenant of Primus*. She continues to write about all her favourite things from her base in the North of England. You can find out more about all her works at www.justinarobson.co.uk and for exclusive previews and insights you can support her on Patreon at:
https://www.patreon.com/JustinaRobson

Anna Smith Spark is the author of the critically acclaimed, Gemmell and BSF awards shortlisted grimdark epic fantasy series Empires of Dust: *The Court of Broken Knives, The Tower of Living and Dying* and *The House of Sacrifice* (HarperVoyager UK / Orbit US/Can). Her favourite authors are Mary Renault, R Scott Bakker and M. John Harrison. Previous jobs include English teacher, petty bureaucrat and fetish model. You may know her by the heels of her shoes. www.courtofbrokenknives.org
Twitter: @queenofgrimdark Facebook: Anna Smith Spark

Danie Ware is a single working Mum with long-held interests in role-playing, re-enactment, vinyl art toys and personal fitness. She went to an all all-boys' public school, has a halfway decent English degree, and spent most of her twenties clobbering her friends with an assortment of steel cutlery. These days, she juggles raising her son and writing books with working for Forbidden Planet (London) Ltd., where she runs their events calendar and social media profile. In those rare times when she's not writing, working, or on manoeuvres with her son, she usually falls over exhausted. Danie is the author of the critically acclaimed Ecko series, published by Titan Books, the Award-winning *Children of Artifice*, published by FoxSpirit, and numerous short stores. She also writes WarHammer 40k Sisters of Battle for the Black Library and Judge Anderson for Rebellion Publishing. She lives in south London, with her son and two cats. You can find her online at danieware.com or @danacea.

Nick Watkinson runs a small writing group between the moors in West Devon, where he has lived for a decade. While his work moved from factory to field to school and playground, his writing remained his first and truest love. When he's not teaching English as a foreign language, he reads too much, too fast, and enjoys the company of a menagerie of cats, a dog, horses and ducks on a windswept hill overlooking a patchwork valley.

Richard Webb's short fiction has been published in the British Fantasy Society journal and other publications and he won the Remastered Words 2016 fantasy short story competition. With a writing partner he co-writes screenplays across multiple genres, with several of his short films selected for, and winning, multiple awards at international film festivals. One of his feature-length scripts reached the semi-finals of the 2016 BBC Writer's Room. Richard reviews SFF novels and was content programmer for FantasyCon 2015. He is active on Twitter as: @RaW_writing and lives feral in the wild, carving out stories on trees with his bare claws.

A Note from the Editor

I've always regretted that I never had the opportunity to meet David Gemmell, who passed away not long after I first discovered the UK genre community.

I recall a conversation with the late and much missed Deborah J. Miller regarding her campaign to establish an award in David's honour – how hard but ultimately successful it had been. This was on a coach between hotels during the 2009 Eastercon in Bradford, with the first award ceremony just a few months away. Debbie's enthusiasm was infectious and it came as no surprise that she had succeeded in her efforts.

In many ways, Debbie's loss some four years later affected me far more profoundly than David Gemmell's, because Debbie I did know and counted a friend.

The award she had worked so hard to bring into being outlived her, and when another friend, Stan Nicholls, approached me with the suggestion of producing a book to support the Gemmells, I jumped at the idea. As Chair of the Awards, Stan had been there since the beginning, and along with his wife, Anne, shouldered the responsibility of taking things forward following Debbie's passing.

Stan was aware that I had successfully published an anthology, *Fables from the Fountain*, in support of the Arthur C. Clarke Award, and hoped I could do something similar with a fantasy anthology for the Gemmells. I wanted to call the book *Legends*, but Stan had reservations because the name had already been used for two very successful (and very good) anthologies edited by Robert Silverberg. However, the first of these had been published in the 90s and it wasn't as if anyone would confuse the two books, not with artist Dominic Harman's evocation of Druss' double-headed axe Snaga boldly fronting ours. Besides, I felt that *Legends* was the only wholly appropriate title...

I'm eternally grateful to Stan for suggesting the project, not least because it gave me the opportunity to work with some established fantasy authors I may never have worked with otherwise – Joe Abercrombie, Mark Lawrence, Rowena Cory Daniels, John Hornor Jacobs, RJ Barker, and David's widow Stella Gemmell among them.

The books have met with considerable success both critically and commercially, and I'm delighted to have made some small contribution to supporting awards founded by a dear friend in honour of one of my favourite fantasy writers. My only regret is that, after a decade of celebrating the best in fantasy fiction, the Gemmell Awards have run their course, just as the third and final volume of *Legends* is launching. I have some insight into the work and time that Anne and Stan have invested in the Awards over the years, of the trials they have had to face and overcome (which do not need airing here) and of how grateful all readers of fantasy should be to them and to everyone else involved. Under the circumstances, the financial support this third volume would have provided for the Awards will instead be donated to charities which David Gemmell himself supported during his lifetime.

For the third and final time, it is my privilege to present *Legends*, an anthology of fantasy stories inspired by David Gemmell and the awards given in his name; a legacy to be proud of.

Ian Whates
Proprietor, NewCon Press,
Cambridgeshire,
April 2019

The David Gemmell Awards for Fantasy Winners: 2009-2018

2009
19th June 2009; The Magic Circle, London
Legend Award: Andrzej Sapkowski for *Blood of Elves*

2010
18th June 2010; The Magic Circle, London
Legend Award: Graham McNeill for *Empire*
Morningstar Award: Pierre Pevel for *The Cardinal's Blades*
Ravenheart Award: Didier Graffet, Dave Senior and Laura Brett for *Best Served Cold* by Joe Abercrombie

2011
17th June 2011; The Magic Circle, London
Legend Award: Brandon Sanderson for *The Way of Kings*
Morningstar Award: Darius Hinks for *Warrior Priest*
Ravenheart Award: Olof Erla Einarsdottir for *Power And Majesty* by Tansy Rayner Roberts

2012
15th June 2012; The Magic Circle, London
Legend Award: Patrick Rothfuss for *The Wise Man's Fear*
Morningstar Award: Helen Lowe for *The Heir Of Night*
Ravenheart Award: Raymond Swanland for *Blood Of Aenarion* by William King

2013
31st October 2013; World Fantasy Convention, Brighton
Legend Award: Brent Weeks for *The Blinding Knife*
Morningstar Award: John Gwynne for *Malice*
Ravenheart Award: Didier Graffet and Dave Senior for *Red Country* by Joe Abercrombie

2014

13ᵗʰ June 2014; The Magic Circle, London
Legend Award: Mark Lawrence for *Emperor Of Thorns*
Morningstar Award: Brian McClellan for *Promise Of Blood*
Ravenheart Award: Jason Chan for *Emperor Of Thorns* by Mark Lawrence

2015

8ᵗʰ August 2015; Nine Worlds Geekfest, London
Legend Award: Brandon Sanderson for *Words of Radiance*
Morningstar Award: Brian Staveley for *The Emperor's Blades*
Ravenheart Award: Sam Green for *Words Of Radiance* by Brandon Sanderson

2016

24ᵗʰ September 2016; Fantasycon, Scarborough
Legend Award: Mark Lawrence for *The Liar's Key*
Morningstar Award: Peter Newman for *The Vagrant*
Ravenheart Award: Jason Chan for *The Liar's Key* by Mark Lawrence

2017

15ᵗʰ July 2017; Edge-Lit 6, Derby
Legend Award: Gav Thorpe for *Warbeast*
Morningstar Award: Megan E. O'Keefe for *Steal The Sky*
Ravenheart Award: Alessandro Baldasseroni for *Black Rift* by Josh Reynolds

2018

14ᵗʰ July 2018; Edge-Lit 7, Derby
Legend Award: Robin Hobb for *Assassin's Fate*
Morningstar Award: Nicholas Eames for *Kings Of The Wyld*
Ravenheart Award: Richard Anderson for *Kings Of The Wyld* by Nicholas Eames

The Legend Award: Best Novel
The Morningstar Award: Best Debut
The Ravenheart Award: Best Cover Art/Design

Also Available from NewCon Press

LEGENDS
Joe Abercrombie,
James Barclay,
Storm Constantine,
Jonathan Green,
Tanith Lee,
Juliet E. McKenna,
Anne Nicholls,
Stan Nicholls,
Gaie Sebold,
Jan Siegel,
Adrian Tchaikovsky,
Sandra Unerman,
Ian Whates

LEGENDS 2
Edward Cox
Rowena Cory Daniells
Stella Gemmell
John Gwynne
John Hornor Jacobs
Mark Lawrence
Lou Morgan
Andy Remic
Anthony Ryan
Gavin G. Smith
Gav Thorpe
Freda Warrington

Best of British Fantasy 2018
RJ Barker
Steph Swainston
Ian McDonald
Tade Thompson
Aliya Whiteley
Adam Roberts
Matthew Hughes
Priya Sharma
Reggie Oliver
Kirsty Logan
Rhys Hughes & more…

NewCon Press Novella Set 6: Blood and Blade

Four stand-alone novellas of sword play, sorcery, blood-drenched battles, noble deeds and fool-hardy endeavours, linked only by their shared cover art. Released summer 2019, in paperback, limited edition hardback, and as a slipcased set featuring all four novellas as signed hardbacks and **Duncan Kay**'s combined artwork as a wrap-around.

In **Edward Cox**'s *The Bone Shaker*, Sir Vladisal and her knights are lost within endless woodlands. Harried by demons, they seek the kidnapped son of their Duchess, facing terror at every turn. **Gaie Sebold** takes us on *A Hazardous Engagement*, wherein a wily gang of thieves are set an impossible task. Fortunately, they never know when to quit. In *Serpent Rose*, **Kari Sperring** takes us to the realm of Avalon and the intrigues surrounding some of the lesser known knights and characters of King Arthur's court, while in **Gavin Smith**'s *Chivalry* a young knight follows his hero into battle only to have his illusions shattered; a gritty tale of revenge, featuring brutal mercenaries, scheming nobles, violent criminals and inhuman magic.

Four stunning tales of epic fantasy scaled down to novella size by four outstanding authors.

www.newconpress.co.uk